C000175008

LOST LUGGAGE

SAMANTHA TONGE

Boldwood

First published in Great Britain in 2022 by Boldwood Books Ltd.

Copyright © Samantha Tonge, 2022

Cover Design by Head Design Ltd

Cover Photography: Shutterstock

A CIP catalogue record for this book is available from the British Library.

Paperback ISBN 978-1-80415-417-5

Large Print ISBN 978-1-80415-418-2

Hardback ISBN 978-1-80415-416-8

Ebook ISBN 978-1-80415-419-9

Kindle ISBN 978-1-80415-420-5

Audio CD ISBN 978-1-80415-411-3

MP3 CD ISBN 978-1-80415-412-0

Digital audio download ISBN 978-1-80415-415-1

Boldwood Books Ltd
23 Bowerdean Street
London SW6 3TN
www.boldwoodbooks.com

For everyone who can relate to Dolly and Phoebe, coming outside to face the world again after a difficult period. Things may not go back to exactly how they were before, but that doesn't mean there's no happy future in the new normal.

1

The shop's doors swung open and a crowd jostled Dolly Bell into the small auction house and away from the scents of Manchester's Christmas market. She stuffed a half-eaten white chocolate bar into her rucksack. She'd finish it on the train back to Knutsmere, a village thirty minutes away from the city centre.

The lost luggage auction took place on the tenth of every month. People were given an hour to inspect the locked cases going under the hammer. Every December Dolly and Greta attended and the two cases they went home with were gifts for each other, not to be opened until Christmas Day.

Unused to people after the last year, Dolly folded her arms and held her sides as if to stop herself falling apart. Regulars Ben and Joan made their way over to say hello. Joan's charity store always needed clothes and eagle-eyed eBay seller Ben would bid high for the rarer designer luggage. Neither of them mentioned the obvious: how this time last year Dolly hadn't been able to talk for tears because she'd visited the auction just ten days after one fateful afternoon – after five brief, tragic minutes that transformed her life for ever. Not even one of Joan's toffees had been able to plug the flow as sobs had convulsed her body.

A sense of anticipation rose through Dolly's chest and she loosened her scarf. On Christmas Day Greta would rub her hands together and circle the cases as if she and her sister were vultures. Dolly preferred to think of them as kinder birds who offered their nest to orphaned belongings. She hadn't been sure about attending the auction this year and had asked her sister, who was better than her at making decisions. Living together for nigh on fifty years meant you could read each other's faces, and just one look at Greta this morning had given Dolly her answer.

The airport held on to lost cases for six months or so before passing them on. Dolly inspected this December's selection, laid out on white tables: a practical canvas one, a plastic pull-along covered with stickers, and on from that a bulging polyester holdall. One case decorated with a pink and pine botanical pattern caught her eye, with its smooth, plastic outer shell. The legs of the stool in front of her small dressing table had been coming loose for months. This pretty case, upturned, would provide the perfect replacement chair. Dolly and Greta always upcycled the cases where possible and had become experts at removing wheels and handles. Yet a bright yellow ribbon caught her attention, tied to a tan steamer trunk that was scratched, with a flat top and studded sides. She touched its strong leather straps. Its treasure chest vibe made her think of adventures and the stories behind those scratches. Yet its botanical neighbour was so pretty. Dolly examined both; she couldn't decide.

Dolly found seats in the front row of the auction room – the best position for seventy-one-year-old eyes – and sat waiting, her hand on her purse, her open rucksack on her lap, turquoise tea flask in one of the side pockets. Underneath her seat lay detachable suitcase wheels. The two sisters always came well prepared.

She murmured to Greta that she reckoned luck might be on her side today, although her stomach fluttered as it always did until it was the turn of the lot she was interested in. Bids started at eight pounds unless it was a designer suitcase. Ben had just snagged a Louis Vuitton for a hundred and ten. As the auctioneer brought forward one of the cases she'd shortlisted, Dolly accepted one of Joan's toffees, struggling to unwrap it with fingers impatient to start bidding. Quickly the bids increased. Eight pounds. Fifteen. Twenty. Thirty. Sucking harder on the sweet, Dolly studied the other bidder, a woman with a short red bob and scarlet glasses.

Dolly's eyes narrowed. Call your rival's bluff. Stick to your budget. Quit now. 'Forty pounds,' she blurted out.

The other woman hesitated for a moment and then slouched back in her seat as the hammer sounded.

'Isn't it handsome, Greta?' said Dolly, back in their bungalow, and she tilted her head, straining her ears, with a sense that the trunk had something to say. But she wouldn't discover its secrets until she opened it. Dolly sat down on the sagging rose-pink sofa opposite the front window, a fresh cup of tea on the small table to her right. She'd changed into her favourite jogging bottoms, soft and creased, with fraying hems. Close to her chest she hugged a hot-water bottle – Greta only approved of turning up the thermostat if the temperature dropped below sixteen degrees. The leather trunk posed in the middle of the room, revelling in its air of mystery. Greta was now settled on the armchair to the left, underneath the shelving that housed her books and decorative Royal Family plates. She wore her usual no-nonsense expression, with her set hair, pleated skirt and string of pearls. 'The yellow ribbon cinched it,' Dolly said to her.

'I can't wait to find out what's inside it at Christmas. Only fifteen days to wait.'

She let go of the hot-water bottle and dabbed her eyes. Stepping through discarded newspapers and sweet wrappers, she went over to the armchair. Dolly picked up the framed photo, smeared with white chocolate, and stared Greta straight in the face.

2

Avoiding the two identical circles of beige turkey, and tiny rock-hard peas, Dolly cautiously prodded a perfect sphere of stuffing. She hadn't cooked much since Greta passed and missed the flavours of previous Christmases: spiced mince pies, smelly cheeses, packets of Rennies. Dolly sat in front of the television with the meal on her lap, still in its plastic container. Greta would have tutted. Whilst the Queen spoke of family and community, Dolly gazed at cards on the windowsill, from well-meaning villagers, and a handmade one of a female Santa wearing a super-hero mask from little Flo next door. Most had fallen over now.

Unable to wait until Her Majesty stopped talking, the usual cue for present-opening, she laid her dinner on the floor and hoicked the steamer trunk case over. For many years she'd longed for laminate flooring, to get rid of the outdated patterned carpet, but it was only right that Greta had the last say, being more than a decade older than Dolly.

'What do you think is in it this year, Maurice?' He'd watched them open every single case since he'd moved in, in 2011.

Maurice carried on eating his peas. Greta had always thought

him a moody bugger, as if a goldfish should provide smiles and
conversation. Dolly stood up, turned off the television and went
over to a black suitcase upturned and wedged into the front-right
corner of the room; it made an excellent stand for the record
player. A mahogany cabinet stood next to it for extra support,
against the wall. Dolly moved a couple of dirty mugs off the
record player, before lifting its lid, and opened the door of the
cabinet. Grunting, she bent over and searched through her
collection of old vinyls, until she came across the greatest hits of
the Bee Gees. Appropriately, she lowered the needle on to 'Saturday Night Fever'.

Through the wall of the tank she caught Maurice swaying in
time to the beat. Unable to remember the last time she'd danced,
Dolly ran a hand over the trunk's studs before laying it on its side.
The auction house removed electrical items and toiletries, selling
them off to make extra money, and they shredded personal documents, before repacking the cases that people bid for. Every year
she'd fantasise about the case's contents. Perhaps they'd discover
a really exciting object, like an exquisite antique, a pouch of
diamonds or an unused coffee shop voucher. Yet the reality never
disappointed, even when it was just well-worn items only suitable
for doing DIY or gardening, or children's and men's wear they
could pass on to neighbours Flo and Leroy. At best they'd find
brand new clothes, in their own sizes, that the cases' owners had
bought for a holiday. Ben had taught Dolly and Greta that it was
worth looking up coats and shoes online – designer items sold for
a fortune second-hand.

She and Greta would try and guess what the owners were like
before opening the cases. Dolly stared at the leather straps. This
trunk looked masculine, as if it belonged to a traveller who had
arms strong enough to carry it a distance when full; a person
used to the way the world worked before expandable zippers and

spinner wheels. Understated, functional – yet the studding and straps had been forged with style.

It felt like an old friend. She didn't know why.

With fumbling hands, she undid the buckles. Heart thudding quicker than the LP's disco beat, she lifted up the lid and gasped. Dolly had misinterpreted the outside of the case. How unusual. How luxurious. She lifted up the down-filled, quilted nylon material, a dusty-pink gilet with a maroon collar and hood – a lightweight coat. That made sense, seeing as this case would have been packed earlier in the year. The gilet had pockets and discreet, matching buttons down the front, along with a logo in the shape of a letter Z. Untidily, she draped it over the sofa's arm, not noticing it fall on to the carpet. Her eyes darted to a small octopus plushie, bright orange with a smile on its face. The case's owner might have a child. She turned the plushie inside out to a blue side that wore a sad frown, left it that way and turned her attention to a sports sweat top, with a hood, in a lovely shade of mint green. A graphic of a cat's face poked out of a small pocket on the front. Dolly paused before tugging the top over her head. It clung to her body as if grateful to have a new home. Dolly ran a hand over the soft material, unused to the smell of clean laundry.

Next, she took out a pair of white trainers with shiny rose-gold heel caps. She held them in the air, marvelling as they shone, lending the lounge an unfamiliar sense of glamour. Like Cinderella, Dolly kicked off her holey slippers and pushed her feet into them. Up and down she paced, in time to the music's beat, like eighteen-year-old Dolly who'd lived for nights out in town, dancing and stealing flowers from Piccadilly Gardens because the ones in her hair had wilted.

The remaining clothes were all sporty, like a pair of drawstring trousers tapered at the bottom. As decades had passed since the first auction they'd visited in 1985, it had become more difficult to guess the age of owners; gone were the days when people dressed their age. Dolly had never looked anything like her mum when she was young, but nowadays relatives from different generations could have shared the same fashionable wardrobe.

Dolly packed everything back into the case, apart from the sweat top and reversible octopus. She placed the plushie on top of the record player's dusty glass top. Maurice might appreciate it. She kept the sweat top on and reached for a plain white notebook she'd fetched from her sister's bedroom; tattered now with curled edges, it looked a little brown. In it, over the years, Greta had recorded the contents of every single case they'd brought home. It was time now for Dolly to pick up the mantle – or, at least, her biro. After scrawling the last item, she took her uneaten Christmas lunch into the kitchen and came back with a thick cheese sandwich and a tube of Pringles.

Greta loved notebooks and never threw them out. In her room they were stacked neatly in a corner. Around ten full of book reviews – she'd read at least four novels a month – others full of recipes, and a pile recording everything the two of them had done together on their holiday trips in the UK. Dolly didn't pry, but Greta seemed happy to share the latter. They weren't diaries of their breaks, as such, just lists of the restaurants or places of interest they'd seen.

'What about "Jive Talkin'"?' she asked Maurice, who was looking less perky now that he'd finished the peas, his favourite treat. She went to the record player, moved the plushie, dusted crisp crumbs from her fingers and lifted up the lid again to turn over the record. Then she knelt down and stared into Maurice's eyes, as black as a mermaid's purse, smiling as his tangerine dorsal fin shot back up at the sight of her face. His tank was to the right as you walked into the lounge, away from the window, the radiator; not too near the telly or next to the record player – she'd done her research when she'd agreed to take him off a colleague at work who was moving abroad. Greta would wrinkle her nose and say goldfish only had three seconds of memory, but Dolly had never needed Google to tell her this wasn't true.

She went to close the trunk but couldn't resist trying on the gilet, even though it was too small. In the hallway, she stood in front of the mirror. Dolly wiped the glass with the sleeve of the green sports hoodie. The dusty-pink colour softened the pinched look of her face, the maroon collar lifting her pasty cheeks. Over the last year, outside, buds had unfurled into green leaves that were outshone by flowers, until trees blazed with their autumn hues, the elements showing off their vibrancy. However, indoors, everything had become as grey as February rain, including Dolly's reflection, the hair now more salt than pepper at the roots, the shadows under her eyes deeper.

The gilet's buttons wouldn't do up. She dug her hand into the pockets and turned from side to side.

Oh.

A sheet of paper.

Dolly pulled it out of the pocket. A map of the Paris underground? A deep-rooted ache rippled through her. She closed her eyes, forcing away the memory of a trip to that city that was never to be.

The owner must have been going to France – or perhaps they'd just flown home from there, or maybe Manchester was a stopover. Dolly squinted at the names of stations, Château Rouge sounded like wine, Victor Hugo so romantic, and as for the Champs-Elysées, she'd always wanted to shop along that avenue. Perhaps a Frenchman with a silky accent would treat her to champagne; they'd wander around art galleries. The bubbles inside her produced by opening the case burst into nothing as she thought of all the countries she'd never seen. Greta said Mother Nature would have given people wings and trees that grew pound notes if she'd wanted them to travel to another country. She always spoke such sense, so the two sisters instead enjoyed getaways to all the corners of the UK, Greta happy to fall in with Dolly's choices. Whilst other people wasted money on expensive trips abroad, Greta preferred sensible spending – like on an upgraded burglar alarm. Dolly carefully folded the map up again and slid it back into the pocket.

Legs heavy, she plodded back into the lounge and took off the gilet. She dropped it back into the trunk, on top of the other items, and tried to close it. However, the lid resisted and an urge overwhelmed her. She'd once known someone who owned a similar trunk and it had a hidden compartment. He'd stash his most loved objects in there, including her love letters. Pushing those memories back into the mental box she rarely opened, Dolly ran a finger around the edge of the felt lining and... She jerked her hand back as her finger found a small tab. She touched it again and gently tugged. It came away.

A well-worn white T-shirt was visible first. She unfolded it and held it in the air, trying to make sense of the symbol printed on the front, made up of a long curved line on the right and a shorter one on the left. The latter curled in so that, overall, both lines formed a heart that was decorated with small blue flowers and green leaves. Dolly folded it up again, and reached for a small round leather case. Hidden personal items? Dolly unzipped the case. Inside lay a yellow crystal bracelet and a silver necklace with a ring hanging from it, that had a pearl in the middle of a diamond circle. Dolly held it up in the air, mesmerised by the beautiful workmanship. She couldn't resist taking the ring off the chain and sliding it on to her finger but it wouldn't fit over any knuckle. Finally, right at the bottom, a rectangular item caught her eye. It shimmered as light from the tall lamp at the end of the sofa hit it.

A notebook? Greta would have clapped her hands. It was floral, with colours that could have come straight from Monet's water lily paintings, lacquered with a metallic effect. After hesitating, Dolly put on her glasses and opened it. Handwritten in italic were the words:

Phoebe Goodbody's Year of Firsts.

3

Boxing Day morning, Dolly wriggled into a pair of jeans, the first thing she spotted in her wardrobe, and kept on the hoodie that she'd slept in. Without looking in the mirror, Dolly dragged a brush through her hair, giving up because of the knots; at least a week had passed since she'd last washed it. After sticking her feet into slip-on boots, not bothering with socks, she took down a voluminous, brown anorak from the rack in the hall. Despite being a little tighter these days, it acted like an invisibility cloak, especially with the hood that hid her face. Dolly never used to wear it due to a tear under the arm, but with peplum trim around the cuffs and bottom, it was too stylish to throw out. It was the only item she'd kept from her... yes, the 2015 lost luggage case that had been deep, and wide, and made an especially good storage box in the loft.

Out of curiosity she'd searched for the gilet online. It was so different to anything Dolly had ever seen. By the collar, on the left, she'd found a size label with the word Zadorin on it. A site popped up and she'd scrolled until she'd found it, in dusty pink and maroon.

'Good grief, Maurice,' she'd stuttered. 'It's worth eight hundred pounds.'

Maurice had stopped dead and a pea had popped out of his mouth.

She pushed her flask into one of the deep pockets. Dolly had to get outside, had to get away from the temptation of reading the floral notebook that she'd put in the bedside drawer in Greta's room. She hadn't looked further than the title page and her conscience told her it must stay that way. Its contents were private and none of her business.

Despite the big hood, she caught Leroy's eye. They exchanged a short wave before he returned to fitting fairy lights to a crab-apple tree. She kept her head down as she reached the main road and Mr and Mrs Burns from the church approached. Briskly, she passed the mini supermarket and turned a sharp right, earbuds in despite no music playing. They'd provided an effective defence this last year, deflecting attention and upsetting questions.

The park had transformed into a Christmas card, as if the night had sponge-painted it with frost, but its beauty couldn't prevent her thoughts from returning to the notebook. She went to sit on one of the benches but spotted her hairdresser walking her dog, so instead, eyes to the ground, she carried on.

'Dolly. How are you, chickie? I've seen you pass the salon a few times. I'm so sorry about—'

Dolly needed bigger earbuds. Abruptly she turned away from the woman who was trying to intrude on her solitude.

There's absolutely no way I'm reading lost private musings, Dolly firmly told herself, as she opened her front door. Only the worst sort of person would delve further into the notebook, and thus earn a terrible punishment, like no Earl Grey for eternity. However, having changed back into her jogging bottoms, she walked past her sister's room. Since losing Greta, Dolly had

thought differently about the possessions that had come their
way over the years, and how much they might be missed. What if
some had sentimental value and were a gift from a lover or a
hand-me-down from a deceased relative? Items like the vintage
ring could never be replaced. Could she really hold on to the
case's personal items, whilst *she'd* kept all of Greta's, even the
clothes that still hung in her old wardrobe? Now and then, Dolly
took out a cardigan and put it on; the smell of her sister's perfume
lingered and made her think of all the fun times they'd shared.
Like eating their favourite biscuits in front of the telly – oat for
Greta, chocolate for Dolly; competitive Greta's face when Dolly
secretly let her solve the last crossword clue; and enjoying one of
their good-humoured political arguments – Dolly's views leaning
to the left, Greta's to the right.

Dolly placed a cup of tea on the little table next to the sofa
and sat down. The yellow crystal bracelet from the steamer trunk
dropped forward to the end of her wrist. On her lap, Monet
colours flirted with sunlight streaming through the window. Like
a matador waving his cape, Maurice gave a disgusted swish of his
fantail and turned away his egg-shaped body as Dolly ran a hand
over the notebook's cover.

'If you must know, I have an honourable motive,' she said in
an important voice. 'To look for clues that will help me find the
case's owner. Aside from returning this notebook, I must give
back the personal items: that pearl and diamond ring, this
bracelet... and that expensive gilet.'

She and Greta had once bagged a pair of Jimmy Choo shoes,
but they were too worn to be worth much. It was almost as if
Greta had sent down lucky vibes, a reward for being brave and
going to the auction. A lump rose in Dolly's throat. If only her
sister was here. She'd have insisted they lunch at a garden centre
to celebrate, with a small sherry at home afterwards.

Once before, Dolly had wanted to track down a case's owner. The 1992 case had contained an antique teddy. It had been kept despite missing one eye; it must have meant a lot to somebody. But Greta believed people reconciled themselves to loss, said that going back in time would only bring back hurt and anger. She'd scoffed at Dolly's suggestion to return the teddy, yet her laugh had sounded forced. Dolly shivered and picked up the notebook again, its purple and green metallic front shimmering. Maurice stared her way without breaking his gaze. Not that he could blink anyway – goldfish slept with their eyes open. Respecting each other's privacy was one reason Dolly and Greta had lived so easily together. They'd never opened each other's post, nor snooped in each other's bedrooms. It was one of the reasons Dolly found it hard to clear out Greta's things, fearful of stumbling across a secret, even though she knew that as sisters they'd shared everything important. Did she owe a stranger the same respect?

She flicked to the title page, as far as she'd gone before, and then slowly turned on to the first full page of writing.

I, Phoebe Goodbody, need CHANGE. The past twelve months I've not lived. Oh, I've done the essentials – breathed, drunk water, binged Bridgerton – but I've hardly gone out, not spoken to anyone but my grandfather, Susan and Maisie. The world has felt dark and hopeless, as if there's been a permanent solar eclipse. However, now I'm ready to step outside again, to chat about the weather with passers-by as rain splats on my cheeks. But more than that, I need to set challenges in order to stop old habits pulling me back indoors, and into myself once more. So every month I'm going to HAVE AN ADVENTURE, do something I've never done before.

Some might think the challenges in this notebook are everyday and easy. Others might agree with me that they are positively scary. With the help of a friend I've chosen ones that will push me to my limit. I don't know how I'm going to do them all. But what's the point of a year of firsts if it doesn't mean stepping outside of your comfort zone? And several will need planning and booking in advance – that should stop me from chickening out.

I owe it to Granddad. Even at my age I know he still worries about me, and he's not as strong as he used to be. I owe it to those friends who aren't lucky enough to still be around. I owe it to the woman I want to be, who's been lurking in the shadows for too many years now, who's hit her rock bottom, had no lower to go, and is now, finally, ready to emerge.

A Phoebe rising from the ashes.

So Phoebe was the author. It was her story. Dolly tapped fish flakes into Maurice's tank before leaving the lounge. She walked down to the right and turned left past the kitchen, and into the dining room. Furnished in mahogany, it was the tidiest spot in the bungalow; she'd hardly used it this last year. Unlike her younger sister, Greta preferred the dark wood, due to its durability. Dolly headed to the end and into the much brighter conservatory. She'd decked it out by herself as a surprise for Greta, a place to uplift her when her sister's joints hurt most. Dolly had put a three-tiered plant stand in the left corner but instead of using it for flowerpots, put on scented candles and a small stack of books, along with an ornamental duck in an anorak, holding an umbrella. Greta's face, when she first saw it, suggested she liked the little room almost as much as Flo next door did. It was just big enough for two people, with two wicker chairs upholstered in yellow. On top of a leaf-patterned rug, a polished basil green case lay sideways, a perfect table, from the 2009 auction. The case had contained nothing but dirty laundry. Pushing a couple of used plates aside, Dolly put the floral purple and green notebook on top of it, along with Greta's white one listing lost luggage contents. The glass windows, all around, provided a clear spyhole to life in the orderly garden, or had done when Greta was alive – grime was smeared across them now. Outside, moss lay deeply entrenched in the lawn, the soil in the borders was hidden by weeds, and an aluminium suitcase from the late 1980s, upcycled into a flowerpot, belched out straggly dead plants. She studied the oak loveseat, encrusted with pigeon droppings now, where she and Greta often enjoyed sandwiches.

Poor Phoebe. Imagine believing you'd not realised your potential. An uncomfortable twinge flicked against the inside of her stomach.

It was difficult to guess Phoebe's age. If some friends of hers had already passed, she could be middle-aged with a grandfather as old as Greta, who was eighty-six when the worst happened. Phoebe sounded brave and caring; perhaps the reason she'd hardly gone out in the twelve months before the notebook was written was that he needed looking after. Greta had certainly needed more help with day-to-day life after hitting her eighties, not that she'd ever admitted that she couldn't manage. Dolly's sister had always fought hard for her health, insisting they cook from scratch, and she didn't like to over-indulge with alcohol. Greta had also jokingly hidden a silver cigarette lighter Dolly had used in her twenties. So Dolly gave up smoking. She still enjoyed takeout, but just as a treat, and only occasionally got a little tipsy. As the years passed, Dolly felt grateful to Greta for encouraging her to follow her sister's lead and look after herself. However, when Greta died, Dolly found no appeal in clean living for one. She'd had to stay strong and healthy to look after her sister but all alone, now, that pressure was off.

She picked up the white notebook and updated the list in

terms of what she'd do with the contents. Greta used to be ruthless about throwing away impractical items straight away and Dolly did her best to channel that sentiment now. She could have kept everything from the trunk to hopefully return one day, but the truth was, she might never find the case's owner.

Leather Steamer Trunk with hidden compartment – not sure yet how to upcycle.

Vintage ring necklace – return as a priority, sentimental value.

Bracelet – return, might be missed too.

Pink and maroon Zadorin gilet, the price of a week in Margate – return to owner.

Old T-shirt – the intriguing symbol is too pretty to throw it away, keep.

Baggy sports hoodie with peekaboo cat – feels like a second skin.

Temperamental octopus – the perfect friend for Maurice.

Mix of baggy casual wear – charity shop.

Rose gold and white trainers – KEEPING.

Underwear – bin.

Dolly placed the white notebook back on the green case and drummed her fingers. She moved it on to the top of Phoebe's, but the edge of that one's metallic-effect cover still temptingly glinted. Crossing her legs, she stared through a smear of dirt and spotted a blackbird outside listening for worms. Tea tonight – she should think about that... but she never planned these days. Freezer food was her staple.

The information in the notebook's introduction wouldn't be enough to trace Phoebe. She needed to read more, just a little bit. Anyone could justify that. Maurice need never know. Dolly flexed her hands.

May.

My Year of Firsts starts now. You know what they say, 'Go big or go home,' so I'm kicking off with a trip to Paris. There, I've said it. Me going to France is really going to happen. I've wanted to visit my whole life but haven't considered myself sophisticated enough in case all French women looked like Coco Chanel. Well bugger that, as my grandfather would say. City of Lights prepare to meet one down-to-earth, born and bred Man City fan. Granddad would also say, 'Well done, Phoebs! Fighting talk, lass.' By the time I come home I hope to have visited all the obvious attractions – the Eiffel Tower, Louvre, Sacré-Cœur, the inside-out Pompidou Centre. I'll have eaten croissants and snails, drunk wine and bought a beret, and sat for my caricature to be drawn in Montmartre, dreaming of Gene Kelly in the movie An American in Paris.

All in one week.

Only joking.

For my first trip there, I really want to visit Père Lachaise Cemetery where so many literary greats are buried, and go into Les Deux Magots café that used to be frequented by Sartre, Hemingway and de Beauvoir.

Makes me sound pretentious? I'm not. It'll just help me reconcile myself with flunking my French degree. It's a lifetime ago I dropped out after the second year. This trip might diminish that sense that I've wasted what I learnt. That's one reason I've really got to see this challenge through, even though going to Paris, for me, feels like visiting Timbuktu. Maisie suggested this would be the perfect first challenge for an avid reader like me. She's been to the French capital and knows first-hand how fantastic it is for literary spots and fans of independent bookshops. My grandfather's insisting on paying for this trip. He believed me when I said I'd found a half-price room right by the Seine.

Well, it wouldn't be an adventure, would it, if I knew exactly where I'd be sleeping?

A trip to Paris. The glamour, the style, the magic and romance... Dolly pushed away that rippling ache and re-read the page, relieved to think about someone else for a change. This Phoebe sounded approachable, funny, and was no youngster if she knew of Gene Kelly. The year of firsts began last May? Unless the notebook referred to an earlier year and she'd already completed it. However, that seemed unlikely, given the map of the Paris underground in the gilet pocket and how new the notebook looked. She would have met half her challenges by now, if she'd continued without these notes. Dolly shivered, a familiar chill she always felt in the days after opening a lost case, a niggling sense that something might have happened to the owner and that was why they'd never claimed their luggage. She read the page again. Manchester airport served many customers local to the North West, and being a Man City fan too, Phoebe might well live in Manchester – she did say 'born and bred'. What a great clue! Dolly's quest to find her might really succeed. Odd that out of all the worries a trip abroad could raise, this Phoebe had been most concerned about looking chic enough, instead of losing her passport or phone or missing a flight – or not having any accommodation booked. Dolly thought croissants and the Eiffel Tower sounded about as exciting as life got. Whereas Phoebe was clearly an intellectual and nothing like Dolly. She deserved to have the notebook back and that would mean reading just a little more. Her hand went to turn the page when a frantic knocking at the door made her jump. Dolly snapped the notebook shut and shoved it behind the ornamental duck, hiding it from herself.

4

No one had ever rapped on the door like that. They didn't dare when Greta was alive, not even when the new burglar alarm had kept going off. As Dolly was about to investigate, through the lounge window a voice she recognised rang out. Dolly went into the hallway and opened the door.

Leroy wrung his hands, as if trying to squeeze words out.

Dolly sighed. 'I... suppose you'd better come in.'

He followed her into the lounge. Only six people had been allowed in this last year – Leroy, Flo and her parents, the doctor and the gasman. As Leroy did now, they always looked around for a few moments. Dolly didn't know why. Junk mail, empty tissue boxes, squashed fizzy drink cans, used crockery; it was all so boring. Despite that, now and again, Leroy insisted on tidying. His place was vibrant, interesting – like him, his clothes always looked as if they were hoping for a night on the razz. The dark slacks fitted well around his bottom and complimented the candy-red shirt, and lemon cravat just above a patch of tantalising curls visible on his chest. Dolly never thought she'd notice such things once she'd retired. Certainly not on a sixty-six-year-old pensioner, not that she'd ever call Leroy the P word out loud. After a glass of something strong, they used to laugh together, say if things had been different they might have made the perfect couple.

'What is it?' she asked.

'There's the biggest spider on my kitchen wall.' He lifted the palms of his hands in the air. 'I won't sleep tonight if I know it's in the house. I thought about killing it with hairspray but I'm not sure that would have worked. You're the only person I can ask, Dolly. Anyone else would laugh. Sorry for the ruckus but we'll have to hurry before it disappears.'

Laughs had been few and far between this last year, and now she finally found something funny she felt duty bound not to show it.

'Please, Dolly. I'll sign you a blank cheque, do anything. Just get rid of it!'

Dolly hesitated, an ingrained habit, waiting for Greta to tell her what to do. Her older sister never thought twice about squashing spiders. Picturing the poor creature stuck to the wall with hairspray, Dolly hurried outside, grabbing her brown anorak from the rack on the wall. She followed Leroy to his place. It felt good to be needed. They lived in Pingate Loop, a small circle of three bungalows off Pingate Road: Dolly in the middle, Flo and her parents to the left and Leroy to the right. This last year she'd appreciated the privacy, away from the eyes of the village.

It wasn't like Leroy to panic and with him at six feet tall, the spider would have been far more frightened. She made it to the kitchen that seemed more spacious than hers without the lace doilies Greta loved, the collection of ceramic teapots and fruit-themed wallpaper. Yet Leroy's had a collection of novelty corkscrews on the windowsill and photos on the walls from his birthday parties over the years. The main difference was his clean worktops, the empty washing-up bowl and a bin that didn't over-flow with used drink cans and food cartons.

She craned her neck to search for the spider, but Leroy led her out of the kitchen. His bungalow was the same L-shaped layout as hers, with two bedrooms and a good-sized bathroom at the far end. She walked into the dining room. What a welcoming committee: bowls of sprouts, carrots and roast potatoes, next to a glistening turkey, along with giant Yorkshire puddings and slices of nutty stuffing. Steam rose out of the gravy jug and her stomach rumbled. Leroy had set two plates, each with a Christmas cracker. Festive pop songs played in the background.

'I've been pulling your wheelie bins out all year, Dolly. I knew you wouldn't cook for yourself and it's no fun eating on my own.'

He must have gone to so much effort, even if he had worked as a restaurant manager for over thirty years and picked up cooking tips. Leroy had a cheeky glint in his eye and, come to think of it, he'd even chase bluebottles outside rather than hurting them. It was one of the things he and Dolly had in common. Greta would have seen straight through this ruse.

'But don't you usually go to a party in town on Boxing Day?'

'That's where I met Tony, last year.' His voice wavered. 'I wanted to go, to see if he was there but then... he's probably with his latest young stallion.' He glanced sideways. 'I know. Hypocriti-cal. But he's well into his forties and going by his Facebook page his latest squeeze could be my grandson.'

Dolly eyed the sumptuous spread once more. She looked down at her worn slippers and joggers bearing a ketchup stain, but this was Leroy – he'd not seen her dressed any other way this last year. That hadn't stopped dapper him forcing his way in, every week, to check she was still eating, even if her diet consisted of biscuits, crisps and anything the microwave could spit out in a less than five minutes. Dolly took off her anorak and held it out in the air, unable to stop staring at the mouth-watering dishes before her. Leroy took it from her, his attention wrapping her up in a hug of nostalgia from when Greta would make her chicken broth for a bad cold, or fill her a hot-water bottle at that time of the month, when she was younger.

Dolly settled in a chair, picked up a cracker and shook it from side to side. They pulled them both at the same time and duly donned paper hats. Savouring each mouthful, Dolly cleared her plate and declared Tony would never find anyone who made such moreish Yorkshire pudding.

Leroy topped up her wine glass and fetched himself another beer. He took off his hat and smoothed out the creases, as if the paper bore a speech. 'I hoped this meal would whet your appetite for cooking from scratch again, gal, because... I'm not going to be around to drop meals off.'

Dolly flinched. Perhaps he was ill. She studied his face and the eyes that had looked more tired these days.

'I'm flying out to Jamaica on New Year's Day.'

Leroy visiting the other side of the world? Out of the blue? On his own? Suspicions confirmed – he needed to see a doctor immediately.

'I'll be gone for a while.'

'But why go so far?' Dolly had never even owned a passport, Greta was so against flying and travelling abroad. Dolly hadn't minded, not really; she and her sister always enjoyed comprehensive coach tours around Great Britain. They'd ridden trains in the Scottish Highlands and sailed the Norfolk Broads, visited the home of Cheddar cheese and learnt about Vikings in York.

'A second cousin I didn't know about has tracked me down and reached out via Facebook.'

Reached out. Greta used to roll her eyes at modern word usages like *moving forwards* or *sorry not sorry*.

'Winston has invited me over. He lives in Negril on the far western tip of the island. I can stay there for up to ninety days without a visa.'

'But you're British through and through, born here like your mum, why would you want to—?'

'It's still family, Dolly, still part of my roots. A break. Sunshine.'

'But there's Southport or Blackpool for that, they've got sunny beaches.'

'At this time of year? Anyway...' Leroy placed his hand on her fingers. 'I'm not going there to top up my tan.'

She clamped her other hand over his, a realisation flooding her chest of just how much it had meant this last year knowing Leroy was next door. Mark and Kaz, Flo's parents, had also been very good, bringing around baked gifts, and little Flo would stop for a while. Dolly's young neighbour often used to come over when Greta was around and made it quite plain that there was no reason that shouldn't continue. Her singing and school chat added a different dimension to a day stuck indoors. But Leroy was the only adult who treated her like the old Dolly, helping out in little ways, inviting her out even though she never said yes.

Then there was the time, three months ago, when he came around, eyes swollen, voice scratchy. It was the nearest thing she'd had to a night out since Greta died, Leroy sitting in her garden, them sharing a family-sized packet of roasted peanuts, digesting the news that, after nine months together, Tony had dumped him.

'But it's so... brave,' she whispered, 'flying all that way to a strange country, to stay with strange people. Aren't you a little afraid?'

'Honestly? I can't wait. My life needs a shake-up. Sometimes I ask myself where that man went who interrailed around Europe and danced on top of tables whenever Diana Ross played. I broke one in half on my fortieth birthday, you know. But now I've become stuck in a rut. I imagine you aren't the same person as you were years ago, either. What's happened to us, Dolly? Here we are trapped in the groove of suburbia as if it's an LP stuck on repeat. I didn't really think about it until Tony moved out.'

The thing was... she was still *exactly* the same person she'd been, in her late twenties at least. Life hadn't changed one jot since Greta had saved her from a terrible mistake and they'd moved in together almost five decades ago, when Dolly was twenty-five. What with this Phoebe challenging herself to a year of adventures, and Leroy's imminent thousand-mile trip, a familiar sense of being left behind made Dolly feel hollow, despite the Christmas feast.

'Me retiring in the summer triggered our break-up, as if Tony saw that as an end to really living.'

'The problem with chasing young stallions is that you can't ever tame them.' She gave him a beady look.

Leroy swigged his beer. She knew he'd always wanted to visit somewhere like Jamaica, with its rhythmic reggae vibes, often humming Eddy Grant's 'Living on the Frontline', one of his favourites from the 1970s, dreaming of chilling on white sands. And, of course, there was his family connection.

'Come around New Year's Eve?' he said, a couple of hours later, after coffee and mints and Dolly beating him at Cluedo. 'I've bought a bottle of rum to get me in the mood for my trip.'

Dolly gave a tentative nod and pulled on her anorak. Going to Jamaica would help him forget Tony.

She waved her hand and opened the front door, calling to him without looking back. 'That blank cheque you promised, if I dealt with the spider, make sure you write it out to Dorothy, not Dolly.'

5

Dolly walked past the still life oil painting in Leroy's hallway, past a large black suitcase, and dumped two shopping bags in his kitchen, trying to guess the contents of his case and what exciting thing a bidder at the auction might find in it. Soul music boogied out of the lounge. If a place called Motown actually existed, the two of them would move there in an instant. Changing out of her joggers and fleece required too much effort but she'd half-heartedly applied a slash of lipstick. Whilst Leroy checked his flight time again, Dolly heaved one of the shopping bags on to the kitchen table and took out her flask.

Leroy's lips twitched upwards. 'My tea still not good enough for you, gal?'

'You know I'm very fussy when it comes to a cuppa.' At least that's what Greta used to say about Dolly, insisting tea tasted the same whether the milk went in first or last, but Dolly could always tell. 'What's happened to your metallic case with the rainbow stickers?' she asked.

'In Jamaica I just have to be a bit... careful.'

Dolly went to protest about him going.

'I'll be fine,' he added firmly.

She pulled out a packet of sausage rolls, tipping them uncere-moniously into a bowl. A ready-made, pale-looking quiche followed, and two packets of sandwiches that she opened up and broke into smaller halves using her fingers. Next, crisps and a tub of brownies, biscuits too.

When she stopped, Leroy was watching her.

'Told you I'd provide the food,' she said and licked her fingers after turning a Swiss roll on to a plate.

'You will look after yourself, won't you Dolly?'

'I've been out to the shop, haven't I?' The increasingly snug fit of her wardrobe proved she wasn't wasting away; Leroy was just fussing. Her eyes pricked. Fussing she'd miss. But it wouldn't do to be sad on his last night in Knutsmere. She raised her glass as he slid the rum over. Each then stacked a plate with beige and headed into the lounge, chatting about the soaps and how she'd have to message Leroy the latest plotlines. Another rum later, he took their empty plates into the kitchen and strutted back as a song about blaming the moonlight came on. The burgundy leather sofa bounced up and down as he collapsed next to her.

'I blame moonlight. When I first met Tony on Canal Street, after that Boxing Day party, he stood staring at the moon's reflec-tion, dancing on the water, looking damn sad – and damn fit. I asked if he was all right just before he threw up on to a patch of daisies. Some of it splashed on to my shoes.'

'How romantic.'

Leroy went to the wooden drinks' cabinet, poured two more rums and came back. Tony had insisted on swapping numbers. As an apology he'd taken Leroy out to dinner the following week and was waiting outside the restaurant with a bunch of large daisies. Leroy swirled his tumbler and explained how he'd hoped

Tony might have texted or rung him today, even dropped by, to wish him a Happy New Year.

'I still miss seeing his shaver next to mine, or the funny Italian accent he'd put on if I made lasagne, how he'd put his arm around me if we watched a movie. I miss the way people stared at him, the admiring glances, the fact that he'd chosen me. It was the best birthday present ever, last April, when he moved in.' His voice broke. 'I hadn't been so happy since Charlie...'

Dolly squeezed his hand. Charlie was a chef with dual citizenship and an infectious sense of humour. Born in America but with a British mother, he'd grown up in Miami but moved over here in his twenties. Leroy had met him at work and fallen hard. They'd dated for over a year. Charlie had organised a disco-themed party for Leroy's sixtieth and baked him a red velvet loaf cake with a jam heart running through the middle. Leroy couldn't take enough photos. But then Charlie decided he had to move back to the States – his brother had fallen seriously ill and he wanted to be there for his family. This only made Leroy love him more.

Tony had reignited a romantic spark in Leroy, and like him, loved fireworks. They'd let some off in his garden the night Tony brought his stuff over, and when it was the sixth-month anniversary of them meeting, in June – and for Tony's July birthday. Leroy had stayed in for Bonfire Night last month, on the off-chance that Tony would call by. She understood. All these months later, Dolly still expected Greta to walk through the front door, calling to her to put the kettle on, as if the worst hadn't happened after all. Leroy may have only been with Tony nine months but wounds that have got infected don't heal – infected with phrases such as *what if, if only, why me?* The wound doesn't scab over so there's nothing to protect it.

He gave her a sideways glance. 'I know there was... you had...

What would you blame it on?'

Her eyebrows knotted together.

'You know... that time you fell in love.'

'It's a long time ago, I was barely out of my teens,' she said briskly. A nagging pain jabbed her stomach, no doubt due to eating too quickly. Leroy nudged her with his elbow and she exhaled. 'I blame his silliness, I suppose. The world was a less serious place with him around. He brought out my lighter side.' None of the other men she'd dated over the years had ever managed that. 'But enough about that. Before you go, I... need your help.' She disappeared into the kitchen and came back. Dolly hovered in the lounge doorway, one hand holding the tub of brownies, the other behind her back.

Leroy looked over. 'Now I'm intrigued.'

She put the brownies on the coffee table, and the notebook fell to the floor. As the pages fanned open she couldn't help catching sight of several words. Her eyes widened. *Frankenstein's monster*? *Eating jellyfish*? Swiftly she closed the notebook and showed it to Leroy. Explained about this year's lost luggage.

'I don't suppose it would harm, you looking at the bits I already have,' she said. However, Greta would have called it nosiness. Once, when Dolly was little, her big sister had caught her rummaging through her bedside cabinet. Dolly had been looking for make-up to play with. How her ears had hurt after Greta shouted, saying you should *never*, *ever*, pry into people's belongings.

Leroy read the two pages at the beginning, allowed by Dolly. 'This Ms Goodbody from Manchester, she's as bright as a button and... I kind of like the sound of her. She's had a hard year and is trying to move on.'

Leroy and Dolly looked at each other.

'Is she on Facebook?' he asked.

'No. I had a quick look once I'd unearthed my password. And I put her name into Google.'

'You're a whizz at Cluedo; this is a chance to polish up those detective skills. Her surname is quite unusual.' Dolly would need to look on Twitter, Instagram and TikTok, then there was LinkedIn.

'But if she's not on any of them, I can't read the whole note-book, Leroy, it wouldn't be right. I should shred it myself. The pages are full of her most private thoughts.'

'For that reason she'd want it back.' He stared at the cover. 'Of course, there is an obvious answer to your dilemma if social media's no help.'

'What?'

'Do the list of firsts yourself. Go to the places she's planning to go to. That way, you stand a good chance of finding her.'

'Leroy! Please. This is serious. Anyway, I think I'm more than six months behind.'

'Forget about the ones you've missed, then, and start with the upcoming January challenge. You might meet her in person, and be able to give the notebook back without reading the whole thing. Month by month more clues might surface, so if you haven't found her by the end of January, then try the February "first", and so on.'

'I can't do that!' Dolly exclaimed, despite her insides fluttering just like they did every December when she bid on a suitcase. 'In any case, she said the challenges might be scary. What if they are dangerous, like doing a bungee jump or skydiving?' Or meeting a monster created by a scientist? Or eating jellyfish?

'Or flying to Jamaica,' Leroy said and took her hands. He pulled Dolly to her feet as a favourite track played. He twirled her in a circle, before slipping an arm around her waist. 'It's time we both moved to the beat of the drums again, baby.'

As her body bounced up and down, as her feet followed his, an unfamiliar effervescence inside, warm and fizzing, kept her moving. The only challenge Dolly had faced this last year was crawling out of bed before the sun set. They sang 'Auld Lang Syne' and drank more rum as distant fireworks burst into glittering bouquets.

'No more moping, then,' he said, slurring a little. Dolly hoped he wouldn't be sick on the plane. 'We both need to get back on track.' He cocked his head. 'Did you get the results back from those tests the doctor ran last month?'

Dolly had slipped on an empty pizza takeout box and sprained her ankle. Leroy had persuaded her to get it checked out. Whilst at the surgery, the doctor had suggested checking her vitals, weight, blood pressure, cholesterol levels... Dolly had a moan to Leroy about it when she came out. If only she'd kept her mouth shut.

'She rang me. We discussed everything.' Back on the sofa again, Dolly prised the lid off the tub of brownies.

'And?'

She pushed the moist dough into her mouth. Her blood pressure was high. So was her cholesterol. The doctor had worked out a ratio that said she was at risk of a heart attack. What a fuss over a bunch of statistics. She had her appetite and her mum always said that was the most important thing. Not that Dolly remembered much about her mother, who was always at work, often too tired for a hug or a natter. It was Greta who took Dolly to school, who wiped away tears, who provided her with a home when, Dolly aged ten, Greta got her first flat and their mother lost her job. Everyone said it made sense. Mum always seemed closer to Greta who, being older, had more in common with her. She'd named her after the sophisticated actress Greta Garbo, famous for playing strong-willed heroines, whereas Dorothy must have been inspired by a girl with sparkly red shoes and pigtails who got lost.

'So what if I eat too much cake and pizza? I've got my eyes and ears and can walk from A to B.'

'What exactly did the doctor say?'

'Leroy, don't ruin things. You're the one person who doesn't think I need fixing. You haven't tried to jolly me along with sentences starting with *at least...*' Yes, Dolly had a decent pension, a nice home and Maurice, but none of that would bring back Greta. 'You've just been there for me. Please don't change now.'

He folded his arms.

It spilled out, how the doctor thought she was at risk of heart problems if she didn't change her ways; that she needed to revamp her diet, and exercise. The doctor wanted to put Dolly on tablets.

'Ridiculous. I'm as fit as a fiddle.' As for the doctor offering to visit, to discuss her situation, 'I said no, of course, I'm sure she has far more ill patients to concern herself with. Don't worry about me, Leroy. We'd joke Greta had scones with her butter, and not the other way around, and look how long she lived for.'

Leroy looked her straight in the eye. 'Yes, and look what happened...' He bit his lip. 'This notebook could be a sign from the universe. You can't carry on as you are, gal.'

She took his hand in hers, lifted it up and gave it a kiss, before they relaxed back into the sofa and their heads leant against each other.

* * *

Dolly stumbled home after waving him off in a taxi. Hadn't she spent tonight dancing, up until all hours? She wouldn't be able to do that if she was on the verge of snuffing it. She'd just felt a bit out of sorts this last year. No one, not the doctor, not Leroy, needed to know she had occasional chest pains. Everyone knew indigestion was more common as you got older. Shaking her head, she went inside, took off her anorak and headed into the lounge.

Oh, bugger. She'd left the lid off the fish tank. The hole to drop Maurice's flakes through had become bunged up and Dolly had lifted the lid off to push a finger through, but, running late, she'd placed the lid on the floor, her mind on the buffet bits she'd needed to take to Leroy's.

Squinting, she bobbed down by the tank, about to put the lid back on. Wrinkling her nose at the smell of weed, she peered closer to see if Maurice was hiding under his bridge. The lights might have woken him up. Where was he?

A shudder spread across her shoulders and Dolly studied the carpet around the bottom of the tank. A shiny object caught her eye and stole the breath from her body. No. It couldn't be. Poor Maurice gasped for his life, flipping his gold body from side to side. He still looked wet; he couldn't have been there long. Carefully Dolly scooped him up, terrified of damaging his scales as she eased him into the water. He gulped and twitched and after a few minutes she took her hands away. Maurice sank to the gravel, his top fin flat.

'Come on little chap,' she said, gravel in her voice. 'Don't leave me. I'll make it up to you. I promise.'

She hurried into the kitchen and pulled out a handful of peas to thaw, his favourites. She brought a hard-backed chair in and positioned it as close to the tank as possible. For minutes, hours, she kept watch, until her head lolled and jerked. Just before nodding off, she caught sight of the sad, blue octopus face, on top of the record player.

6

Rubbing her back, Dolly sat up, regretting rowing on the orange carpet with Leroy last night to 'Oops Upside Your Head'. Orange. Carpet. Maurice. He was still at the bottom of the tank.

'"Stayin' Alive", that'll help, won't it?' she croaked and put on the vinyl, ignoring the pull to play the Bee Gees' hit 'Tragedy' instead. Dolly put the kettle on before heading to the bathroom. After splashing her face with cold water, she pulled on a limp woollen dressing gown, made a cup of tea and padded back into the lounge. 'Happy New Year, my darling boy,' she whispered. She tapped flakes into the tank, hoping he'd swim up to the surface. He didn't. Dolly sat on the sofa, picked up her phone and tried to find out why he'd jumped out. Her eyes scanned the screen, and her tea went cold as she read about poor water quality. Dolly stole a look at the tank's sides. There were only a few small patches of green. The one thing she'd managed this year was to clean out Maurice's tank regularly, with Leroy picking up fresh weed when she asked. She maybe didn't check the pH as often as she should, but the water looked clear and his ornamental bridge was clean.

Yet she'd left the lid off and Maurice had almost died because of her... She surveyed the lounge, the strewn newspapers, the empty, soiled mugs. Dolly took her glasses off and held her head in her hands. Over the last year her approach to life had become more scatter-brained. Slowly she opened her eyes and a metallic shimmer from the left caught her attention.

She picked up Phoebe's notebook that she'd left on the sofa last night.

It's time we both moved to the beat of the drums again, baby.

For a long time she stood in the conservatory, staring out at the garden. After fetching a generous chunk of Swiss roll, she sat down and checked out what Leroy called socials. Phoebe Good-body was not to be found on any platform, which was unusual these days. Even Greta liked Instagram for following accounts that offered the essentials – local crime updates, book recommen-dations and dissections of royal fallouts. She picked up the note-book, skipping the entries from June to December, and turned the page like a criminal as she left behind chocolate fingerprints.

January

For this one I need to be really brave as it means standing up and speaking in front of people. My legs feel unsteady just thinking about it. I'm going to take part in a balloon debate. Maisie came up with the idea after seeing a poster; she reckons I'll smash it. There's one that runs every month in the New Chapter Café on Deansgate. Susan says balloon debates are popular in her granddaughter's class. If a ten-year-old can take part, why not me? The café puts a list on their website on the first of each month, five literary characters, you choose one to represent. One of the five must be thrown out of the fictional balloon as it is too heavy and sinking. You have to give a talk, setting out the argument for why the character you've chosen should remain safe. Mid-month they hold the debate after closing hours, randomly picking five volunteers from the audience. This month's takes place on Tuesday 18th. As soon as Maisie knew about the bookish theme, she insisted I had to do it. We talked about who the characters might be. Maisie laughed and suggested Frankenstein's monster. Well, I've always felt sorry for him, so that would be an easier one.

I know I'll blush harder than a Christmas cranberry but I need to put myself out there after this last year of hiding away. I might stumble over words, even freeze in the middle of my speech, but I've got to give it a go.

It's time to let myself be seen.

Dolly re-read it, not once but twice, glad she wasn't expected to meet a monster in real life. Tuesday the eighteenth fitted the dates for the upcoming January, so the firsts in the notebook were definitely not for a different year. She went on to the internet again and found the café. If picked, Dolly would have to speak to the crowd for two minutes. Over the last year she'd barely spoken more than one sentence to anyone apart from Leroy – and Flo, who didn't ask how she was, didn't ask about Greta. Instead she wanted to know interesting facts about Maurice such as did the water bubble when he farted. At least at the balloon debate no one would know who she was. But she wasn't a reader like Greta. A lot of research would be required for this challenge. After another large bite of Swiss roll, Dolly found the list of characters.

Bella Swan, Sherlock Holmes, Scarlett O'Hara, Mr Darcy, Matilda.

She knew Sherlock Holmes from the telly, he seemed too smug for his own good; Scarlett O'Hara was vain and spoiled in the film of *Gone with the Wind*. Reader or no reader, everyone knew Mr Darcy played too hard to get. Greta had read the

Twilight series and spoken about Bella Swan's naivety. As for Matilda... wasn't she the naughtiest girl on the planet?

Dolly might do this January 'first'. She might not. A trip to the library would help her decide. On the morning of Tuesday the fourth, after the Monday bank holiday, she actually set her alarm – she hadn't done that for so long, without Greta's porridge to prepare, or her appointments to get ready for. Today marked, possibly, the beginning of a quest that might make the dawn chorus sound less like a hymn at Greta's funeral service. Knutsmere library would be empty when its doors opened at nine. Stiff morning hands allowing, that was Greta's preferred time to go. Same for Stockport library – Greta went there at least once a fortnight on a Wednesday as the book choice was wider, insisting she could manage alone as it was near the train station. It was her favourite place but as her arthritis had got worse she'd made do with the one in Knutsmere more often. It couldn't compare with the grandeur of Stockport's, though, and she often talked about the baroque building with its glazed dome, the rich green carpet and stained-glass windows.

Dolly wrestled a jumper on and dragged jeans over hips that had become wider this last year. The stain down the front looked like baked beans that were easy to eat straight out of the tin. All good intentions to have a shower disappeared at the prospect of running late and crossing paths with nosy well-wishers. Hood up, earbuds in, she walked down her short drive, past her Skoda that probably wouldn't run well now, past her overgrown lawn and empty birdbath. She stopped at Leroy's crab-apple tree. He'd messaged her from Jamaica last night, sending a photo of chips made out of bananas.

Despite her fear of bumping into villagers, first off Dolly called into Knutsmere's small pet shop. New Year's Day she'd changed Maurice's water, even though it didn't need it, and rinsed the gravel; she'd scrubbed the glass sides and the bridge, just to make sure she removed all germs. His dorsal fin still lay flat, a couple of scales looked discoloured, but the gasping and twitching had abated. Fresh bunches of weed and a mermaid ornament might cheer him up.

The librarian smiled when Dolly finally walked in but she ducked her head, lips firmly closed – it was a library, after all. She headed for the fiction section and M for Mitchell. *Gone with the Wind*, a hefty novel, was easy to spot. Greta already had the Twilight series and a copy of *Pride and Prejudice*. Dolly found one of Arthur Conan Doyle's Sherlock Holmes books. That only left *Matilda*, and Dolly went over to the children's corner, with its plastic chairs and embroidered cushions. Her fingers ran across the books under D for Dahl. Cheeks sweating under the warmth of her anorak, she checked out her books. Dolly had never used her card before, having only registered at the library to please her sister.

Just as well it wasn't raining. Her head had been so full of Maurice this morning, she'd forgotten to bring her rucksack. With the novels under one arm and the pet shop bag grasped in the other hand, Dolly hurried back along Pingate Road and into Pingate Loop. As she neared home, a sense of relief washed over her, only to evaporate when Flo came out of nowhere. Dolly lurched to one side and the books tumbled to the ground as brakes screeched.

'Sorry, Dolly, are you all right?'

'It's okay. I... I didn't see you.'

'Look at the new bike I got for Christmas! Isn't the basket on the front the best? It'll be great when I go to the park and collect' – she lowered her voice – 'you know what.'

Dolly never had a bicycle as a child and would have loved this

one, with its silver frame and shiny bell. Carefully, Flo laid it on
its side and picked up the three books. Her face lit up.

'I love Matilda.' Sprigs of ginger hair stuck out from under her
luminous cycling helmet. 'Her dad is horrible and she glued his
hat to his head. Mum prefers books about people kissing each
other.' She grimaced. 'I try to get her to read my favourites like
The Wonderful Life of Worms and *Secrets of Our Smallest Creatures*
but she just flicks through them quickly.'

'Greta liked romance but considered it important to read
widely, to broaden the mind,' said Dolly, cursing herself immediately for bringing up her sister.

'Heaven is lucky to have her,' said Flo and looked thoughtful.
'Imagine how tidy its library will look now.'

Since she'd seen it on a blogger's Instagram feed, Greta had
colour coordinated the novels on their lounge shelves. A sudden
longing almost blew Dolly over, to watch her sister on the step
stool, humming to herself as she sorted through them.

'If you like *Matilda* I've got other books by the same author,'
said Flo. 'I could bring them over. *Charlie and the Chocolate Factory*
is my favourite and—'

'No. No, thanks. I'm not actually reading it for pleasure...'

Flo leaned closer. 'Why not?'

Dolly broke eye contact.

'It's okay. I don't often like Mum and Dad's questions – some
are too hard to answer 'cos there's too many answers. Like why I
hate art. The paint we use stinks, Billy thinks it's funny to colour
my hair and I don't see the point of drawing when taking photos
is so much easier.' She handed the books back. 'I especially don't
like those questions where they already know the answer. I'm
never going to finish my homework before tea and I don't see the
point in cleaning my teeth for a whole two minutes.'

Dolly stared at the book cover of a girl in a blue dress

standing on piles of books. All those sentences inside. All those words.

Flo cocked her head. 'We could read together, if you want. Dad's busy this afternoon.'

'Do you like Swiss roll?'

'Chocolate flavour?' asked Flo.

'Come around after lunch and tell me exactly why *Matilda* is so brilliant and... I'll tell you why I might need to know.'

Flo clapped her hands. 'Mum's at work, I'm sure Dad will say yes. Now don't tell me, not straight off, I'm very good at guessing.' Flo blew out her cheeks. 'Got it! You're going to become a teacher... no, wait, a children's author! Or, of course, it's obvious, you want to know how to glue a hat to someone's head.'

Greta always used to say it was no surprise that Dolly and Flo got on.

7

Chocolate crumbs tumbled down Flo's chin. She'd just shown off the jam jar inside her backpack, home to ants walking over leaves, feeding on lumps of fruit. Her parents would never see them.

'It's called compromising,' she'd told Dolly and had puffed out her chest, not long before Greta died. She wasn't allowed pets so she secretly collected her own. Worms. Beetles. Once a butterfly. Flo had kept that just long enough to show Dolly. Her young neighbour understood that wild pets were only on loan.

They sat in the conservatory; Flo had insisted. When she was little she'd come over and Greta would read her books, with juice and biscuits, under a stream of sunshine. Flo's parents, school sweethearts Mark and Kaz, both worked hard running their own cleaning business. Kaz was more hands-on with the staff and customers; she was far more of a people person than her husband. Mark enjoyed working with figures and spent most of his time in the office or working remotely at home when Flo needed him. It was a hectic life and the two sisters liked to help out. Flo always called into the lounge first to visit the one pet she'd been made an honorary co-owner of. Flo insisted she and Maurice had a special bond as they were exactly the same age: eleven.

'I said hello but Maurice didn't swim up to the side like he usually does. That sad octopus might be scaring him, so I turned it to the orange side.'

Dolly blinked away threatening tears that wouldn't do, not in front of Flo. Growing up, she'd often thought her big sister looked sad but Greta had never opened up when Dolly was little, even those mornings when she'd ask why Greta's eyes were red and puffy.

'I like the mermaid,' continued Flo.

'Might become a girlfriend,' said Dolly and she forced a smile.

'Don't be silly – even if she were real, a mermaid's only half-fish. In any case, he might prefer a merman like Leroy.'

How quickly Flo had grown up. Would she still want to go around to Dolly's for juice once she started high school, next year? What if Leroy got hurt in Jamaica? And if Maurice never recovered...

Flo stopped eating whilst Dolly told her about the café in Deansgate. She didn't mention the notebook or year of firsts.

'Amazing! Balloon debates are so fun. We did one at school and we had to choose someone we thought was a hero. I got it down to David Attenborough and my Auntie Fran. He saves plants and animals and she saves old people. Well, kind of. She works in a care home.' Flo shrugged. 'I chose Auntie in the end 'cos he's nearly one hundred and one day she might end up looking after him. Heroes who save other heroes are extra special.' Crumbs flew through the air as she rubbed her hands together. 'Which character will you choose? If it's Matilda, I could help. Of course, you'll have to read the book first.'

Dolly stared at the vinyl flooring – pine-coloured, warm, and covered in dust. 'What's the point if I might not even get picked?'

'I was scared, too.'

'I'm not,' said Dolly quickly.

Flo explained that was what she'd told her mum, but to her annoyance, Kaz saw through it. She gave her daughter a tip, said to make her speech funny. So she told them about Auntie Fran when she was little, how once she fell down the toilet backwards and got stuck for an hour. The whole class giggled. Her aunt never forgot how stupid and afraid she'd felt, and how she loved caring for old people and making them feel safe.

'Didn't stop her getting thrown out of the balloon. Auntie Fran couldn't compete with Beyoncé.'

The knots in Dolly's shoulders eased and now she wanted to know why Matilda was so naughty. The story took her back to primary school where she was picked on for not having a dad. Years later, she'd found out that the worst bully was beaten by her own father and had been jealous of Dolly for not having one around.

'Dolly!' Flo patted her arm. 'I was asking, so why are you thinking about doing this balloon debate?' She crossed her heart. 'I'm really good at keeping secrets.'

Dolly fetched the notebook from the lounge and explained about the lost luggage auction, the gilet and beautiful ring, the bracelet, how she wanted to find Phoebe, how doing the challenges might be the answer. By the time she finished Flo was on her feet, doing a little jig.

'This is so exciting!'

It was?

'The best thing to happen in Pingate Loop since that flash flood. Can I take a look? I won't read it.' Dolly hesitated before handing the notebook over. Flo ran a finger over the shiny flowers on the front. She walked to and fro, holding it out as if carrying the Crown Jewels. 'It must have been hard to get her list of firsts down to twelve 'cos there are loads of amazing ones I'd want to do, like sail around the world, meet Ariana Grande, beat Dad to the last custard cream.' She stopped pacing. 'How about you?'

Dolly hadn't felt like doing any since Greta died. Doing lasts had been more appealing, bit by bit letting go of her old life, the invites from former colleagues, the trips to the swimming pool, cinema outings with Leroy. She tried to think of a first she'd always fancied doing but that kept taking her back to the past and how it was all too late now.

'I can't think of one.'

'Then this notebook is perfect – Phoebe Goodbody has done all the thinking for you.' She put it down and grabbed Dolly's hands. 'You've got to stand up.' Flo's eyes shone as Dolly got to her feet and she swung their arms from side to side, the little girl's ginger ponytail moving in time. 'It's a thing I do with... I mean, *used* to always do with Teddy,' she added hastily, 'whenever there's good news like no homework, or pizza for tea.'

'I really don't think—'

Flo gave her a sharp look. 'I wish the notebook was mine. You can always start doing the firsts but stop if you don't like it much. This time next month you could be flying on a trapeze in a circus tent. Imagine that!'

Dolly would rather not. Nor regarding any other of Flo's other suggestions such as trekking through a rainforest, taking singing lessons, or piercing her nose. As their arms continued to swing, a heaviness infused Dolly's until they fell to her sides. She sank into her wicker chair.

Flo put the notebook down. 'Sorry, I shouldn't push. I hate it when Mum and Dad do that. Other people don't always know what's best for us.' She sighed. 'We had another big argument last night.'

Dolly shot her a curious look.

Flo blotted the crumbs on her plate with a wet finger and licked them off. 'Tell me a lorry story,' she said, and sat down.

Dolly leant back. From leaving school at sixteen, until she retired, she had been employed by the same trucker company, Hackshaw Haulage. Greta had worked there as a receptionist and loved it, especially the stories the drivers used to bring back from the continent. Strange really, as Greta had no inclination to travel herself, and stranger still that Greta left to work in a car showroom shortly after... that event... in Dolly's twenties. Teenage Dolly had thought the work sounded so boring, but grew to love it. Over the years her job title changed from secretary to personal assistant; the paperwork about insurance, mileage, routes and billing all got transferred to a computer database; and transportation law became more complex. She was grateful to have retired before Brexit. Yet some things never changed, like the Christmas and birthday gifts from Mr Hackshaw, and the banter of her colleagues. After so many years the company had become her wider family.

Harry was one of Dolly's favourite drivers; they had the same sense of humour. If he went overseas he always brought her back a different chocolate bar. One summer night he pulled over by a field in the north of France. It was dark, it was humid, he was tired and after a quick wash he turned the lights in his cabin off. He lay there for a while, tossing and turning, and was very nearly asleep, only half-conscious, when he thought the passenger door slid open, a pungent aroma wafted in, like strong cheese, along with a chilly breeze. The next morning he decided he must have dreamed it, as the passenger door was still locked.

Flo nodded her head vigorously.

'But when Harry climbed out to stretch his legs, before driving off again, he saw a bunch of flowers tied to a nearby lamp-post with a newspaper article attached. He had enough French to work out that a man had recently been killed at that exact spot by a speeding lorry. The man was a well-known local cheesemaker.'

Flo gasped. 'That's the only reason I'd join Guides, the Investigating Badge sounds really cool.' Silence fell and she folded her arms. 'Not that it's going to happen. No way.'

Dolly sipped her drink. 'I was a girl guide, in the sixties. I didn't want to go either, none of my friends went and Mum didn't seem bothered. But Greta offered to volunteer. She thought it would be good for me.'

'She was the best older sister. Wish I had one.'

Dolly tried to imagine her past life without Greta. It was easy to forget not everyone was lucky enough to have had a sister. She closed her eyes for a minute.

Flo unfolded her arms. 'The uniform I'd have to wear looks stupid. It'll make me look like a Domino's Pizza worker.'

'We wore brown dresses and berets, a bit dull but I liked it. Money was tight at home, there was never much for fashion, but at Guides I looked like everyone else.' Dolly's voice softened. 'Is this what you've been arguing about?'

'Why do my parents worry about me not having enough friends? I'm happy with my phone games, my drawing pencils, and my books about insects. And I'm never alone in the playground – Mrs Jones who supervises is really nice. Sometimes I play tag with Callum from over the road.' She sighed. 'Mum and Dad both say I'm going to need to make more of an effort to be sociable at high school.'

Mark had told Dolly once how building the business took so much time and energy and this meant he and Kaz hadn't been able to be playground parents, easing the way for Flo to join friendship groups. Perhaps it was lucky Dolly had never been a parent. The ones she knew always blamed themselves for things she considered out of their control.

Dolly reached out and gently took Flo's hand. 'A very wise little girl once told me "You can always start but stop if you don't like it much."'

Her bottom lip jutted out. 'That's different. A year of firsts sounds exciting and you won't be under pressure to make new friends.'

'Guides is exactly the same – challenges, trying things you haven't done before, and doing the firsts would mean I'd have to meet new people as well.'

Flo lifted her chin defiantly. 'But if you're too scared to go for it, why should I bother?'

Dolly gazed at Flo and the years fell away. Instead she saw her as the four-year-old who'd cried when Greta had poured gravy from the weekend roast on to her ice cream, thinking it was the chocolate sauce Dolly had made for the pudding. Then the seven-year-old who'd broken her arm falling off a climbing frame; she'd rushed around for the two sisters to sign the plaster, upset forgotten with all the attention. Flo's parents sharing their daughter had made up, a tiny bit, for Dolly losing the life she thought she might lead before everything went wrong and she'd moved in with Greta. It was time to reward their generosity, to stop the family arguing, to help lovely Flo make new friends. Dolly had never made many, hadn't put in the effort. Life without her sister now might have been easier if she had a well-thumbed address book.

But could Dolly really face standing in an imaginary balloon and talking in front of strangers? She glanced at Flo's downturned features and held out her little finger.

'Let's do it, flower.'

'Pinky promise? You do the challenges in the notebook and I join Guides?'

Dolly nodded.

Flo thought for a moment and then wrapped her little finger around Dolly's. 'Right, let me tell you all I know about Matilda. There's no going back now. A deal's a deal.'

8

Tuesday the eighteenth arrived sooner than Dolly would have liked. At just before seven, Deansgate was quiet. Most shoppers and commuters had hurried away to avoid rain that spat its warning of an imminent cascade. She blinked through the darkness at New Chapter Café across the road, along to the left from the small Tesco. Dodging headlamps, she left the bottom of Market Street and crossed over. Her rucksack contained the belongings she felt compelled to return to Phoebe. Dolly stopped outside the café, admiring the illustrations on the front glass, in white and green, of books and pens and quills.

Setting out on an adventure should have lifted her spirits. But then, Dolly didn't do 'shoulds' any more.

She pulled her hood down further and pushed open the glass door, twitching under the fluorescent light like a disorientated moth. She'd expected a cosy, olde worlde atmosphere but the bookish café looked more like an American diner with glossy tables and chairs, chrome bookshelves that matched the coffee machine, and black-and-white floor tiles. Anime sketches such as one of Ebenezer Scrooge and another of Hogwarts brought life to the walls. Warmth, laughter, the aroma of coffee, all did their best to welcome Dolly, but she'd become used to the dim light of her living room with only Maurice and the continuity announcer for company.

Throat tightening, she spun around. What had she been thinking? Dolly charged into a woman with a shock of purple hair and eyes that wrinkled in a kindly manner.

'First time?' she asked. 'We don't bite. At least not until you become a regular.' She winked and walked on.

Dolly continued towards the door. There was no shame in leaving. She had every right to keep the contents of the steamer trunk.

But what about Flo?

Tonight coincided with her first trip to Guides. Over the last two weeks Flo had read *Matilda* with Dolly, listening whilst she practised her speech, and Dolly had helped her research Guides online so she knew what to expect. Despite her confidence with people she knew, Flo had always been shy with anyone new – like with Tony; she'd not been her usual talkative self if he and Leroy popped in to Dolly's whilst she was there. Not until the time he brought a bag of doughnuts and they played Monopoly all together.

Flo had been told by her dad, Mark, not to bother Dolly quite so much, but Dolly didn't mind; it wasn't as if she were ill. A disagreeable sensation gnawed at the pit of her stomach. She tugged off her hood, leaving her hair standing on end. With a sigh she sat at the back, feeling crumpled and out of place. She only had to talk about Matilda for two minutes. Greta used to tease her sister about her non-stop chat. Funny that, seeing as it must have been Greta's fault because since she'd died Dolly hardly spoke. She studied the other customers, a group of students and people of every age including a man who looked older than the Scrooge sketched on the wall. A few fitted her idea of how Phoebe must look.

A barista walked past, glanced at her rucksack and shot her a dirty look. Dolly looked down at her turquoise flask. After a moment's thought, she got up and ordered herself a pot of tea. As she carried it back to her table, the woman with the purple hair stood at the front and took hold of a mike. She introduced herself as Trish.

'Welcome, everyone. Thanks for attending. Great to see a couple of new faces. We'll kick off in ten minutes, to give you all time to grab another drink or snack. New Chapter Café doesn't charge us for having this room, so let's give back.'

Dolly found herself with no appetite, so bought a giant cookie to take home to Flo. She counted the size of the audience – forty-five people, not including the compère.

'Right, folks, here we go,' said Trish. 'Let's pick our five to go into the balloon.' She waved her hand across the floor space next to her, in front of a wall bearing a sketch of an attic surrounded by petals. Years ago, Greta had thought *Flowers in the Attic* sounded like a lovely, cosy read but stopped a few chapters in and wouldn't let Dolly try it.

'First off, Bella Swan.'

Three students raised their hands. Several people volunteered for Sherlock Holmes and two were middle-aged women – one of them could be Phoebe, although one had feet too small for the rose-gold-heeled trainers and the other sounded Romanian. Scarlett O'Hara proved popular and the volunteer picked was in her late forties and wore a sweatshirt and loose jeans. Dolly would try to catch her afterwards for a chat. The elderly man was chosen to represent Mr Darcy and suddenly it was the turn of Matilda and...

Only one hand went up. Somehow Dolly got out of her seat

and headed to the front, banging into a table as she did. She could have simply spectated – not everyone had put themselves forward. Two, four, six, eight minutes passed as the others gave their speeches. The young woman defending Bella went first and talked about how fearless it was to fall in love with a vampire. A young man spoke up for Sherlock Holmes. Stickers of book images littered his wheelchair's handles. He declared Holmes was the best character because his unappealing personality traits made him relatable; despite his admirable intelligence he was only human. Dolly forgot her nerves briefly when it was the turn of Scarlett O'Hara and the middle-aged woman took the floor. She sounded like a university-educated person who might go to Paris, well-spoken and measured as she outlined how Scarlett was brave to go against the era's conventions of how the female sex should behave.

Next, Trish introduced Mr Darcy but Dolly didn't hear a word, practising her own speech in her head, fighting an urge to fetch that giant cookie and shovel it down. The out-of-date cake she'd eaten for breakfast was less dry than her mouth as Trish turned to her and passed the mike. Dolly wavered from foot to foot, like she had at Greta's funeral, up by the pulpit. How could you sum up a life in a few sentences? How could you express the loss of a person who was your whole family? Yet she'd got through it for Greta's sake, done her homework on public speaking. She'd made herself pause, made herself slow down, suppressed the tears. Dolly had sworn, at the end, she'd never go through that again.

However, Matilda was a fictional character. There were no emotional binds.

'Um, hello. For those of you who don't know the story of Matilda...'

'We do,' called an impatient voice.

'Down, John,' said Trish, 'we all remember our virgin balloon debate.'

Heat crept up Dolly's neck. She longed to be sitting on her sofa, immersed in the soaps and eating toast. But then she thought of Flo again, who'd called in after school yesterday, not meeting her in the eye, suggesting it wasn't too late for either of them to drop out, saying she'd had tummy ache all day.

'You may think you know her story, you may write Matilda off as a naughty schoolgirl. But really...'

'Speak up, love,' another voice called.

Perspiration prickled in between Dolly's breasts.

'This book is about a young girl blessed with as big a power as any Marvel hero. I'm not talking about her telekinesis, although I wish I could move objects with my mind, it would make turning pages whilst eating far easier.' Flo had found that line really funny. Dolly should have practised on an older audience. 'Although I'm sure my copy of Joanne Harris's *Chocolat* didn't mind the smudges of my crème egg.'

One smile. She'd take it.

'No, there is more to Matilda than being able to move objects as, more importantly, she's able to move young readers who can relate to feeling like an underdog.' Come on, keep going. 'Despite her small size she has masses of courage and not only calls out, but punishes the behaviour of her criminal father and bullying headmistress. She's a strong, female role model for today's readers...'

A bulky man in a trilby hat yawned loudly.

'She teaches us that the underdog doesn't have to kowtow.' Dolly's voice got louder. 'That even though people are bigger than her, even though they have authority, she shouldn't surrender to their toxicity...' Her old self glared at the yawner, before going on to quote from the book and explain how Matilda was empowering in other ways. 'Finally, of course, there's an excellent reason for not throwing this child out of the balloon.' Dolly folded her arms. 'Scientifically, it wouldn't make sense. She's the lightest by far.'

The group of students laughed. *You can't ask for more than that,* said a voice in her head. That had been one of Greta's favourite phrases. It was very important to be satisfied with your lot. The two sisters had each other, food on the table and an excellent burglar alarm.

'Thanks to the five participants.' Trish took out a small jotter pad. 'Without further ado, let's take a vote for the character you'd like to see thrown out.' Ten people voted for Bella Swan. Only six for Sherlock Holmes. Seven for Scarlett O'Hara. Dolly bit her thumb nail. What if classic, handsome Mr Darcy only got a couple of votes, leaving the rest for Matilda? 'Mr Darcy... that's nine,' said Trish. 'Matilda... eight.' She scanned the figures. 'Bye, bye Bella.' The students booed but Dolly hardly heard, heading back to her table in a daze. John, the impatient man who'd shouted at the beginning of her turn, came over.

'Fair dos,' he said. 'I always test newbies out with a little heckle and you passed with flying colours.'

For the first time in months a sense of achievement washed over her and oddly, she couldn't wait to tell Phoebe. She'd really done it. Seen the challenge through. Leroy wouldn't believe it. He was video-calling tomorrow to see how she got on. That was his official line, anyway. Dolly knew he had another agenda.

But this was no good. People were leaving, she hadn't found out any names yet. Dolly got up with a start and went over to the woman who'd defended Scarlett O'Hara.

'Um, well done,' she said and held out her hand. 'My name's Dolly.'

'Sarah. Pleased to meet you. Matilda's a great character.'

Dolly scoured the room and introduced herself to the other women who might have possibly fitted the bill but no. She screwed up her balloon debate notes and threw them in the bin. Phoebe wasn't here. Flo's dad had said there was a bug going around Manchester; she could be ill. The walk back to Piccadilly station dragged out further than the inward journey earlier. On the train back, rain trickled down the carriage window that Dolly leant against. The whole evening, all the practice, not being able to sleep last night, it had been for nothing.

As the train pulled into Knutsmere station, Dolly's phone buzzed. A message from Mark? She read the text and took a sharp intake of breath. She dashed up the carriage aisle to the train's doors, her rucksack bashing a dozing reveller in the face.

9

Dolly strode into Pingate Loop, splashes from disturbed puddles drenching her shoes. She rapped on Flo's family's front door. Mark yanked the door open. His shoulders sank.

She clutched her phone tighter. 'Still no sign of her?'

He shook his head. 'We had a late job on, but Kaz left our staff right away and has just got back from the church hall. I waited here in case. The pack leader can't understand it. She spotted Flo ten minutes before the meeting ended at nine. We've finished searching the house together, from top to bottom. Kaz is on the phone to the police.' His voice trembled. 'We knew she didn't want to go to Guides.'

'If it's anyone's fault, it's mine. Flo and I made a deal. I'm so sorry.'

'The lost notebook? She's been so excited, imagining what all the firsts are going to be. Don't blame yourself. We're grateful it finally gave her the incentive to try out Guiding. But I wish we'd listened to her more. We've been pushing for months, because Kaz used to love Guides and I enjoyed Scouts.' He kept looking at his phone, panic rolling his words together. 'Kaz and I were drawn to each other at school, you see, as two shy pupils who were never part of a big friendship group, and activities away from the classroom gave us confidence. We want that for our daughter.' He gave a big sigh. 'It's tricky to talk about. Shyness is always seen as a flaw, and whilst it makes life more difficult, we don't want Flo to think there's anything wrong with her.'

'Have you told her all this?'

He frowned and shook his head. 'We don't want to make a big deal of it.' He glanced down the road. 'Why aren't the police here yet?'

'Where have you looked?'

'In all the wardrobes, under the beds, even in the loft.'

'What about the garden?'

He shrugged. 'You know what it looks like. Nothing but lawn and a few low-growing shrubs. There's nowhere to hide. She must be in the village. Or the park, but you'd think that would be frightening at night on her own. Unless...' A look crossed his face. She recognised it from when she'd caught a glimpse of her own reflection in Greta's dressing-table mirror, right after finding her sister on the floor, not breathing. 'If anything happens to her, Dolly, I'll never forgive—'

'Now stop that this minute. Your Flo's a sensible little girl. Very independent.' Fearless too. 'Let me check something out. Two minutes.' Dolly hurried towards her bungalow. She let herself in, dropped her rucksack, and went straight into the kitchen and unlocked the back door. There was a small chance... it was worth checking... She stood on the lawn, heartened by the oak tree's branches waving at her through the darkness, drawing her attention to... yes, it really was, a flash of lilac amongst the twigs. She pressed a hand over her heart and texted Mark, before approaching the trunk.

'Flo, chickie. Come on down, you'll catch a chill.' The lilac froze. 'You're not in trouble, sweetheart. Your mum and dad just want to know you are safe.'

'How did you know I'd be here?' came back a sulky voice.

'If you come down, I'll tell you.'

'I hate Guides and I hate Mum and Dad. I'm not speaking to them.'

'You won't have to. Not for the moment. Come on darling... I've got you a present.'

Nothing. Then rustling. Dolly gave Mark a quick call, suggested he and Kaz let Dolly dry Flo off and give her a drink, that they give Flo a bit of time. He could hardly speak, such had been his relief on receiving Dolly's text. Feet thumped on to the ground and Flo appeared, arms folded, lilac anorak grubby, ponytail half undone and soaking.

'I think we could both do with a hot chocolate,' said Dolly, staring at the blotchy cheeks.

Flo traipsed inside. Dolly hung up both of their anoraks and fetched two towels, one of which she draped around Flo's small shoulders. She washed up two mugs with the last squirt of the Fairy Liquid. The cocoa was only a month out of date. Dolly smelt the milk. She'd used worse. They went into the conservatory and Dolly switched on the light. Flo sat down on one of the wicker chairs, wiped her eyes and put her elbows on the green case, resting her chin on her hands, next to her drink. Dolly passed her a half-empty tube of biscuits.

'Are Mum and Dad mad?'

'Mad with worry,' said Dolly. 'They love you to bits.'

She sat up. 'Yeah, right, that's why they've kept on and on about this stupid Guiding.' She snapped a biscuit in half. 'How did you know?'

'You've always sneaked through that hole in the fence to sit on that branch, pretending ours was the tree from *A Monster Calls*.'

Flo banged her right leg repeatedly against the leg of her chair.

'Although why anyone would want to hide in a monsterish tree, I'll never know. Tell me the story. Why do you love it?'

Flo put down her mug and Dolly looked fondly at the moustache of chocolate froth. Kaz and Mark wouldn't let her see the film, Flo said, they insisted she was too young, but she'd read the book and the monster didn't scare her at all. He helped the main character, Conor, accept his mum was dying, and forced him to admit that, really, he wanted the worst to happen, so that neither he nor his mum suffered any more. Flo liked the monsterish tree because he understood Conor's deepest secret and wasn't judgy. Flo wiped a trickle of hot chocolate off the side of her mug and sucked her finger. 'I know it sounds silly but that oak tree is a friend that's always happy to listen, even if it's raining or frosty or snowing. Especially if I'm talking about my big secret.'

The tree sounded like Maurice.

How could an eleven-year-old be hiding something? Greta hadn't had a single secret across her nine decades. Dolly knew that for sure because they trusted each other with the truths others might hide, like Dolly secretly fancying her boss and Greta hating hers. They knew all about each other's medical problems, including personal ones like bouts of cystitis. Even though privacy was important, Dolly used to joke that to each other, they were open books, although Greta never found the appropriate pun as funny as she did.

'Does the tree know why you ran away from Guides tonight?'

'He'll have worked it out.' Her face puckered for a moment. 'I'm not going next week and no one can make me.'

It took Dolly back to Flo's first year at primary school, how she'd tearfully counted down from Christmas to it starting again, said that her teacher was really strict and in the classroom Flo missed her mum and dad.

'How many girls were there?'

With prompting, Flo revealed that the pack had twenty-four Guides, split into four patrols. Each patrol was made up of girls between the ages of ten and fourteen. Flo would be due to take her Promise after the February half-term, the weeks before then being a trial period. She knew a few of the others from school, but not very well.

'The pack leader, Gill, said there was a really long waiting list and I must be excited to have finally got in.' Scarlet blotches on her cheeks grew. 'I didn't even know Mum and Dad put my name down. It's as if my opinion doesn't matter.'

'What did you do all evening?' asked Dolly quickly.

'Stupid stuff.'

Dolly sipped her drink and eventually Flo loosened the towel around her shoulders and told Dolly that the leader, Gill, talked about a theme the pack was working on, and the relevant badges. Everyone had to put their phones in this basket at the beginning of the meeting. The older girls looked really grown up. Dolly wanted to say how mixed ages were part of the point – Guides would build Flo's confidence and communication skills – but her parents might have already said that. The best thing Dolly could do was just listen.

'Was there one particular reason you ran away, sweetheart?' she asked, gently. 'Did something happen?'

'Maybe.'

Dolly took the towel, folded it up, and put it on the green case.

Flo exhaled deeply. 'We had to find a partner for this game, at the end. No one chose me. I had to do it with Gill and felt really stupid. Everyone was looking, just like people do at school if I talk

about how great worms are or offer to tidy the books in the
library – like I...'

'Go on, love.' Dolly placed her hand on Flo's arm.

'Like I'm a freak. Afterwards I blushed redder and redder
and...' Her voice sounded thick. 'I was worried I might start
crying like a baby, in front of them.'

They sat in silence. There was no point in telling Flo she
wasn't a freak, that sticking out Guides might eventually make
her feel more as if she fitted in; it was about how her young
neighbour felt, right at this moment.

'Was there *anything* you liked about the evening?'

Flo thought for a moment. 'The patrol I was going to be part
of is called the Bumble Bees, I suppose that's all right. I like bees.
Did you know they do a dance called the Waggle Dance?' Half-
heartedly, Flo wiggled her body. 'It's a way of telling each other
where to find the best nectar.'

'What do you mean *was going to* be part of?' Dolly pushed her
shoulder gently. 'This is just a blip. We pinky promised.'

Flo's face brightened. 'I forgot, you haven't told me how it
went tonight! Did Matilda get thrown out? Did you find Phoebe?'

With a gleam in her eyes, Dolly recounted how her speech
went. Flo giggled at Dolly's indignation that not all of the jokes
got laughs and said a naughty word when she heard about the
heckling.

'But I didn't find Phoebe. It was a silly idea. I should throw the
notebook away, sell the ring, wear the bracelet myself and that
gilet. So what if I can't do it up?'

'Only a wuss would give up now, that's what Greta would say,'
said Flo.

Dolly raised an eyebrow. 'Exactly, missy.' She looked Flo right
in the eyes. 'If we aren't in this together, there's no point me even

looking at the next challenge, whatever exciting thing might be planned for February.'

'You don't have to do it if you take a little peek,' said Flo with an encouraging nod.

'You don't actually have to take your Guide Promise at the end of your trial period.' Dolly caught sight of the time. 'Come on, it's school tomorrow, you need to get home. Oh, your present...' She fetched the cookie bag from her rucksack. Flo looked inside.

'If I leave this here, can I come around tomorrow, after school, and eat it then?' she asked, peering up from under her fringe.

'Of course. If your parents are happy with that.'

'And we'll read the notebook, find out the February challenge. I'll need cheering up if I'm going to stupid Guides until you've done it.'

10

'I'm glad Flo is okay,' said Leroy the next day, his face looming from the screen set up on her kitchen table. She hadn't used her laptop much this last year, but it had still jumped to life, as if waiting patiently for Dolly to check out the garden centre's opening hours and scroll down the café menu so that Greta could choose her lunch before arriving. The backdrop to Leroy was palm trees and a small swimming pool in the shape of a peanut shell. She knew from their last call this was Winston's garden.

'How's Maurice doing?'

She beamed. 'Eating. Swimming. Back to his usual self.'

It was a question Greta would never have asked. She treated Maurice and his tank more like an ornament, even when he once grew a funny lump. She'd rolled her eyes when Dolly got back from the vet's, calling it a ridiculous expense.

Leroy gave the thumbs-up. Then he talked about how he'd helped his cousin run his string of beachfront rentals, how he'd met a distant aunt, had become addicted to plantain chips and spotted a barracuda whilst snorkelling.

You won't want to come home, she thought. It had been over two weeks now. She was still waiting for him to mention the real reason he'd called as he talked about the jerk food, the carnival, and about how Winston treated him like an old friend already. His cousin had recounted stories about people Leroy's grandparents had mentioned in passing, from their early years before they emigrated.

'As for the rum bars...'

'I've seen on Facebook. Who was that young man leaning into you, in the tie-dye spiral T-shirt?'

'Only the barman. He wanted to be in the photo.'

'Really?' she said airily.

Leroy exhaled and threw his hands in the air. 'Okay, I might have wanted it to look more intriguing.'

'Like the photo of you last week, doing the limbo in luminous shorts, as you went under with another man?'

'One of Winston's employees. A great bloke. Lovely wife,' he muttered. 'Has Tony been around? Or called you? Asked after me and what I'm doing?'

Bingo.

Oh, Leroy.

'No,' she said gently. The letterbox rapped. Flo's secret sign. 'That'll be Flo now. You take care. I'm glad you're having fun.'

Sorry I couldn't give you the answer you wanted.

I miss you.

Ponytail bouncing, chewing gum, Flo came in. No one could have guessed that she'd spent last night hiding in a tree. She opened her palm to show Dolly an earwig she'd found on the way over, admiring its pincers. After releasing it into Dolly's back garden she washed her hands and poured hot water into the teapot. Leaving it to brew for exactly the time she knew Dolly liked, she took out her gum and dropped it into the bin. Dolly fetched the notebook whilst Flo took off her coat, hung it on the back of her chair in the conservatory and rolled up the sleeves of her red sweat-shirt. With gusto she ate her cookie. Dolly remained standing.

The second challenge, adventure, first... none of those words left her impatient to read on. Nevertheless, Dolly proceeded, whilst adding up the challenges in her head. Having started in May last year, this would actually be at least Phoebe's ninth one, tenth if she had, after all, been at the balloon debate and Dolly had somehow missed her.

'February
    This is possibly the most difficult first so far.'

The tension in Dolly's shoulders increased as she spoke.

'It's Valentine's Day this month and my dating history has been a disaster. I've never had a long-term relationship, let alone got married. I've always struggled, over the years, with letting a man get close. But I want that to change, if for no other reason than to stop Granddad from worrying – and hassling me. I don't mean to sound ungrateful, I know he means well and has been lonely since Gran died, but not all of us are meant to be half of a pair. At least that's what I've always told myself. I know it's true for some people, but deep down, in my core, if I'm honest, something's missing.

    Yet that could be because I've never been happy with who I am. Slowly, that's changing, and learning to care for myself might get rid of that loneliness. That something missing might be self-love.

    But trips to the cinema could be fun. Meals out. Walks in the park holding hands. So... I'm going speed-dating for the first time ever. My palms feel clammy just writing this. Everyone

*else there is bound to have had far more experience. They'll
know what to wear, what to say... how to breathe. At least the
event I've found seems well organised, with participants split
into different age categories.'*

Dolly's hands dropped. Anything but this. Flo almost choked
on her cookie.

*'Although I could kill Granddad. He blurted it out to Steve over
the garden fence, and now he's keen to go too, said he's put it
in his diary seeing as it's only a twenty-minute walk away.
Steve's great, but I don't want him there, as it is I'll feel self-
conscious enough.*

    *Monday 14th February. Dancing Daze, Lymhall. 7–9.30
p.m.'*

The cookie fell from Flo's fingers and, still coughing, she
jumped up. She grabbed Dolly's hands, swinging them from side
to side.

'Niiiice! What will you talk about? How will you decide who is
a good match? I could come too and—'

'No.' Dolly slumped into a chair and groaned. 'I can't think of
anything worse.'

Flo sat down too. 'Try Guides.'

Dolly had been unlucky with romance since her world fell
apart in 1975, and had always felt wary on the dates she'd half-
heartedly agreed to. Like the time she had dinner with a
colleague from work. Roy was sweet on her, everyone told her
that, and he was pleasant enough but... not her Fred. And what if
he'd let her down? That would have made her nine to five
awkward. That was the trouble with trust being broken, the

doubt stuck, like chewing gum in hair. Try as you might, you can't get it all out.

The two of them pored over the February challenge. Dolly liked Phoebe's honesty. She would never have admitted out loud, not to Greta, that sometimes she wished she had a partner, to once again fall asleep with her arms around a warm chest instead of a hot-water bottle, to wake up looking at a face that didn't have a dorsal fin above it. This Phoebe seemed to share a similar longing, despite recognising that loving yourself was more important. Dolly had learnt that the hard way, back in the 1970s.

And yet, this last year, Dolly hadn't cared for herself; she was beginning to see that now.

Dolly curved both forefingers and thumbs into circles and held them up to her face like binoculars. 'Romantic notions aside, young Flo, we've been given a couple of clues. Detective hats on, please.'

Flo hesitated and then made binoculars herself, smiling.

When had Dolly last fooled around like this?

Flo studied the words again and her face lit up. 'If this dating night is only twenty minutes away from her, Phoebe must live in Lymhall too.'

Dolly gave her a thumbs-up and typed 'Phoebe Goodbody' alongside 'Lymhall' into Google but no luck. At least she now knew the area where the case's owner lived – that was a massive step forward. Dolly pointed to the word 'Steve'. If she couldn't find Phoebe at the speed-dating night, she might find him. However, Flo was hardly listening to this theory, already planning the practice the two of them would need to put in. One speed-date after school every afternoon: Flo would pretend to be a different man each day and then by Valentine's Day...

Dolly did the maths. That was twenty-five different dates.

Whilst Flo chatted and started to think up characters, Dolly stared at a loose thread on the sleeve of her bobbled jumper. Since Greta died, the routine of doing nothing had held her hand through the worst of the grief that still popped up now and again. Opening that steamer trunk had been like finding the key to a door she'd kept shut this last year. She could close it again, but Maurice might suffer and Flo wouldn't go to Guides – she'd miss the opportunity to make friends and would carry on arguing with her parents... Dolly thought back to the small moments, in recent months, when Flo had been by her side, without realising it, pulling Dolly through that difficult time. Now it was Dolly's turn to support Flo, like she had when her young neighbour was a baby, a toddler and then a little girl, Dolly cleaning up grazed knees and wiping away tears, listening to stories about fallouts and sharing the hurt. That was the problem with caring, Greta would always say, one reason she insisted the single life was safer. However, this sense that she should help Flo had the opposite effect on Dolly; instead of feeling unsafe it gave her a solid, tangible purpose.

Flo stood up and took a bow. 'I'm ready for the first date. I'm called Ed, I've got red hair and I play the guitar.'

'I should date a man nearer my age.'

Flo wagged her finger. 'Any man would be lucky to go out with you. You don't worry about boring stuff like chores, and you listen when I talk. Not everyone does that. Did you know, insects have ears in all sorts of places? On wings in butterflies, antennae in mosquitoes, forelegs in crickets and tummies in grasshoppers. Mum and Dad must have them on the soles of their feet 'cos they rarely sit down and hardly hear what I'm saying.' She sat on the floor. 'You should borrow my latest book about chemical elements, it's full of interesting stuff, like during kissing the brain releases this love hormone; it makes you attached to what-ever you've got your lips on. We should all kiss the mirror at least once a day. Everyone might love themselves a bit more, then.'

'There won't be any kissing at this event. I'm only going to look for Phoebe.'

'Why? You might meet a special friend. Someone to spend time with. As my English teacher once said – the world is your toy store.'

11

The letterbox rapped and Flo swept in, school finished, another
fresh February afternoon, another date for Dolly. So far she'd
dated more than one pop star, an American called Buzz who
could moonwalk, and a chap in a top hat who owned a chocolate
factory. Practice was supposed to build confidence but it only
built walls around Dolly when she thought of flirting. She poured
out a glass of juice and carried it through to the conservatory,
with a large packet of crisps. Flo sipped the drink.

'Our deal isn't fair,' she announced. 'It's Tuesday again, that
means Guides. I have to go once a week. You only do these firsts
once a month. Dad's got to drop me off tonight even though he's
zonked out. Two members of staff are off with flu and he's been
on the phone all day trying to find temporary replacements. He's
still ringing. All that means Mum's got more evening work on
than usual but she insists on rushing back from a new job they've
landed in an out-of-town office block to pick me up afterwards.'
She sighed. 'Sometimes it sucks that they run a business with late
shifts. They can never switch off. I know it means nice holidays,

and we love living in Pingate Loop; I try not to be ungrateful but...'

Dolly waved the crisps but Flo shook her head, so Dolly found a pack of cards. Small moments of pleasure, this last year, had been playing Rummy and Go Fish with her young neighbour. After several rounds Flo had cheered up enough for another practice date. She turned their chairs to face each other, declared she needed ten minutes to prepare and asked if she could go into Dolly's room. Fifteen minutes later, Flo reappeared in a wide-brimmed sunhat and thick duffle coat. She sat down in front of Dolly and held out her hand, Dolly shook it.

'Good evening. My real name's Pastuso; not many people know that. May I say how lovely it is to meet you.'

'Thank you. My real name's... Dorothy. That's an unusual outfit.'

Flo took off the hat and lifted a sandwich off her head. Apparently she'd been in the kitchen too. Flo passed half to Dolly. 'I prefer marmalade but jam will do.'

Dolly stared at the bread then at the hat and coat. 'May I ask where you were born?'

Flo wiped her mouth. 'Darkest Peru. But enough about me. Do you like travelling?'

'I enjoy holidays in the UK – I don't know much about abroad.'

'But you like cases, don't you? We have that in common because I really love my suitcase and you look after lost luggage. I was lost at Paddington station until the Brown family took me in. Perhaps you could care for me too.' Flo tilted her head. 'The dark circles under your eyes look lovely; they remind me of my Aunt Lucy, a spectacled bear like me.'

'That's quite the most... unusual compliment I've ever

received,' said Dolly, wishing Greta could hear. 'And how is your Aunt Lucy?'

'She had to go in a care home, that's why I came to England.' Flo leaned forwards. 'I miss her like you must miss your sister. Something else we've got in common...'

At six o'clock it was time for her to go home for her tea and get ready for Guides at half-past seven. Dolly had given Pastuso ten out of ten, agreeing with a delighted Flo that he was the best match yet.

'Are you finding Guides any better, sweetheart?'

'It's stupid. Boring. The other girls all know each other.'

'You think the Bumble Bee patrol is cool. There must be another positive.'

'Little, microscopic bits, I suppose. We're talking the size of fairy flies – they're the smallest insect in the world, about half a millimetre long. They only live for a few days, a very short time, a bit like the good parts of Guides. Like the games where we don't have to pair up and I don't have to talk to anyone. We played the hokey-cokey lying on our backs last week.' Her frown disappeared for a second. 'It made me laugh. Like when we wrote a story, each of us contributing one word in turn.' Flo dragged her feet to the front door. She turned when she stepped outside. 'Can't *you* take me every week?'

'Flo. No, sweetheart. Your parents will enjoy doing that.'

'But I know you won't embarrass me.'

For a second Dolly felt like she used to when Greta told her she'd cleaned the bathroom so well it sparkled.

'It'll do you good. Mum and Dad are always saying it's sad about Greta but that you need to put your clogs on again, before you pop them.' She shrugged. 'I think they mean get out more. I don't know why they don't say it to your face. It shows they care, doesn't it?'

Dolly's cheeks burned. She supposed it did. But to commit to going to the church hall every Tuesday, to wait with other people, to chat, to make an effort? Knutsmere wasn't so small that everyone knew each other's business, but she'd be bound to bump into someone who wanted to know how Dolly was *doing*. Dolly had no answer because, since Greta had died, simply *being* had been more than enough effort.

'You'd have something to tell Maurice about when you got home.'

Maurice. Dolly leaving the tank lid off. She'd almost lost him because, over the last year, she'd lost focus of the important things by simply *being*. Dolly needed to sharpen the way she saw life again. Perhaps that meant breaking her safe, solitary routines.

Flo stared. 'You don't have to take me, Dolly. Sorry. I shouldn't have asked.' Mark appeared. Flo's granddad who lived in Spain was on the phone. She gave Dolly a hug and ran off.

'Thanks for having her around again,' said Mark, and he yawned. 'These days she talks about nothing else but your speed-dating. You have our sympathies. It's certainly got her using her imagination.'

'It's been a help, to be honest, and... I'd like to return the favour. Flo asked if I could take her to Guides... I think she's concerned for you and Kaz, that it's a lot of rushing around when you both work so hard,' she added quickly.

'Oh... cheers, but we like doing all that stuff.'

'Of course you do, and she'll know that, but she's a thoughtful little girl, and as she says, I need to put my clogs on more often.' She gave him one of Greta's pointed looks.

Mark blushed. 'It's very kind of you to offer, really, it's appreciated, but...' He gave an awkward smile. 'Are you sure you're up to it? It still gets dark early, and Pingate Road's always busy. Over the last year we've been worried about you, Dolly, and no one would blame you at all for letting things slide, but, what I mean is—'

Dolly shrank back. Is *that* what everyone thought?

She glanced at the overgrown lawn, suddenly very aware the clothes she wore needed washing. Well sod the lot of them. No one understood. When a sibling died people expected you to get on – it wasn't supposed to count as much as when it was a parent or spouse – but *Greta* had been her significant other; they'd spent forty-five years living together, longer than many marriages lasted.

'No problem, forget I asked. Have a good evening, Mark.' Dolly closed the front door.

She hurried into the lounge, side-stepping an empty packet of crisps, and dropped on to the sofa. A sob rattled through her chest and lost its way; she'd hadn't got many tears left these days. Instead, she stared vacantly at the carpet. It didn't help, as it was covered in crumbs, missing the vacuuming Leroy used to insist on doing. Dolly had never been much of a fan of housework, but used to keep the bungalow as neat as a pin, the way Greta liked it. Without her to please there didn't seem much point, the focus had gone, leaving life feeling blurry. This last year it was as if she'd been weighed down by a pile of bricks, and carrying that load left her little energy for even the mundane tasks like washing up dishes. The heaviness lifted now and again, like when Leroy or Flo visited, or if a beautiful blue tit or goldfinch visited the empty bird feeder. Yet sunshine had the opposite effect. It brought with it the expectation of cheerfulness. She got up, put the kettle on and reached for the remote control as the doorbell rang.

Dolly turned the television up, but the bell rang once more. With a tut, she headed into the hallway and opened the door.

Mark held out a cream cake in a paper bag. 'Kaz popped to

the baker's before work. We're trying to make Tuesday into a day for Flo to look forward to. I've just spoken to Kaz on the phone; she made me realise I've been a bit of a fool. It's only a fifteen-minute walk to Guides, after all, and we're grateful for anything that encourages Flo to go. How about this week, I walk down with you and Flo, and Kaz and you pick her up, and if that all goes well, which I'm sure it will, we'll do that again next week? And then it's half-term. If Flo agrees to go back after the holiday, then we'd be really appreciative if you'd take over completely in March – if you're still offering.'

'You're sure? I don't want to—'

'Please.' He put the palms of his hands together, the brown bag hanging down between them. 'Our life won't be worth living if we say no and Flo finds out.'

She met his eye. 'Better get polishing my clogs then.' She took the cake and shut the front door.

12

Dolly left Lymhall station. Dancing Daze was right at the foot of the high street, next to a Turkish restaurant. Unlike busy Knutsmere, which was suburban and home to many office and retail commuters, Lymhall was where Premier League footballers and CEOs lived; it was more spaced out, leafy and quiet. As one of its residents, it fitted that Phoebe would own a Zadorin gilet. Dolly hadn't visited for many years, not since Linda, a colleague at work, had moved here after a comfortable win on the lottery and thrown a housewarming party. Linda had replaced Greta as receptionist, and Dolly used to tease that her telephone voice sounded nothing like the Linda who swore in a rich Mancunian accent if anyone messed with her filing system.

Dolly navigated the high street in her brown anorak and woolly hat. Flo had tried to get her to wear a smarter jacket, suggesting she borrow one of Greta's, and offered her a new shampoo her mum had bought her, smelling of coconut. But Dolly's usual clothes had protected her from change, from facing a new life without her sister; it was hard to let go of them. As a compromise she did wash her hair, but with her own shampoo, and pulled on a pair of smart pixie boots she used to wear to work. She didn't see the point of primping; finding Phoebe was a serious business that would hopefully conclude at this event.

Having imagined disco balls and fluorescent lighting, Dolly found Dancing Daze less glam than she'd expected: a pub, not a bar, with a black-and-white sign hanging outside bearing a painting of a pair of tap shoes and a cane. A young woman appeared by her side, hair in two chestnut plaits that fell on a tailored grey coat. She gave Dolly a sideways glance and straightened her shoulders. Surely this youngster couldn't be nervous? She looked so together with her buckled handbag and confident posture.

'Like lambs to the slaughter,' she muttered. 'Come on, let's brave it.' She patted Dolly's arm as if sensing her apprehension.

More like mutton, in my case, thought Dolly, as she glanced down at her shapeless anorak. She ventured into the busy reception area that was to the left of a large room where jazz music was playing. Motifs of dance shoes and canes were printed along the coving, above oak furnishings. Wooden tables lined up in six rows of five, with two chairs at each one, opposite each other. Dolly paid her fee. A sign indicated that the front two rows were for the under-thirties, the middle two for the thirty- to sixty-year-olds and the back two for anyone older. Another section was for the LGBTQ community and two men were putting the final touches to the tables, with cloths covered in red hearts. It was a much bigger event than Dolly had anticipated. One of the organisers, in a sleek trouser suit, with big eighties hair, clapped her hands and gave a welcome speech. The first half of the evening would be more formal: five minutes with each partner. With ten chairs in each section, that would take around an hour. The rest of the evening would allow everyone to mix whilst the organisers looked at the score cards and informed people if they'd got a match.

Like a nervous teenager on a blind date, yet looking for a mysterious trunk owner, not a soulmate, Dolly studied the LGBTQ section without success. There were no middle-aged women there, unlike in the straight section, where a woman in a baggy cherry-red jumper with a picture of the Eiffel Tower on it caught her eye. Phoebe's first challenge, back last May, had been a trip to Paris. Dolly went to introduce herself but a starting buzzer rang. From behind the bar the manager stared across the room at Dolly's rucksack with the tea flask in the side. He put his hands on his hips. Dolly went up and ordered a large glass of white, deciding she'd need something stronger than a brew.

Dolly took a chair at table number two. The ladies either side of her looked immaculate, one in a twinset and pearls, with salon-curled hair and lashings of floral scent. The other boasted cat-eye glasses and a lilting foreign accent, whereas Dolly sat there in the mint-green hoodie hoping anyone called Phoebe might recognise it. She'd pulled off her woolly hat, hair now flat and lifeless. Her first date, Geoff, droned on about the estate agency business he used to run, about being president of the golf club, his voice getting louder with each mouthful of whisky. The only question he asked her was where she lived; when she said Knutsmere, he lost interest completely.

Jim was next, a bit older than Geoff, with a slick white comb-over and tweed jacket. His aftershave made him smell as if he lived in a pine forest. He seemed reluctant to sit down and took several gulps of beer before doing so. He asked Dolly what job she used to do, but didn't listen to the answer, looking around the room. Number five was the same, even though she plucked up the courage to ask a question about his favourite telly shows and microwave meals. Number six disappeared to the toilets after one minute and never returned. He didn't even present her with one of the red roses that he'd given to all his other dates. Dolly didn't share any laughter with any of the men, and their tales of cruises and grandchildren filled her with a sense of detachment. She'd rather have spent the time with Pastuso and his jam sandwich.

The hour passed almost as slowly as that first evening, alone in the bungalow, after Greta's funeral. Flo was right. She'd wished Dolly well but said no man could be more romantic than male crickets who chirped ballads to woo their partners, and a song of celebration after mating. Dolly's tenth date finally came to an end, during which she'd learnt a lot about plumbing and that the word itself, like the chemical symbol Pb, came from the Latin word for lead, *plumbum*. She'd done her best to laugh at his jokes about plum being a better word to describe bottoms than peach. Hastily she got to her feet and searched for the woman with the Eiffel Tower jumper. She finally found her leaning up against the wall at the back, joking with one of Dolly's dates. Now that she was standing, the knitted word 'Blackpool' was visible, so her jumper's design represented that English town's tower, not one in Paris. Still, no harm in asking...

'Excuse me, my name's Dolly,' she said and held out her hand.

'I'm Sheila, love, but sorry, you're not my type,' she said and grinned. Perspiring under her arms, Dolly about-turned. Feeling as welcome as a mocktail at a stag party, she introduced herself to two more sloshed candidates... both called Jane. With a sigh Dolly took refuge in her anorak and pulled up the hood. She grabbed her rucksack and picked her way through the crowd, past a policeman in uniform who'd turned up.

'What did you think to number two,' a slurred voice said.

Dolly stood rigid.

'Jesus, if that was dressed up I'd hate to see her playing it casual.'

'She needed a good splash of my aftershave.'

'I've had more conversation with a golf ball.'

'Bravo for staying put, I scarpered for the toilets.'

'In the future I'm only going to events where you register online first – let someone else weed out the—'

Dolly gulped and pushed her way past, into the reception area. She tripped and banged into the doors. They flew open and she staggered on to the pavement. A hand took hold of her shoulder and she turned around to face a man in his fifties, with greying stubble, wearing a Hawaiian shirt. His expression reflected her hurt.

'You all right, love?'

Dolly couldn't speak. A sharp pain resonated through her chest.

'I heard those arseholes – 'scuse the language.' His face flushed. 'You ignore them. Losers, the lot of them. I know their type, they won't have got a single match between them. The size of their houses reflects the size of their egos, and the space between their ears. If you want a decent night out in a pub, head down the road to the Rising Sun. I'm the landlord. Steve. There's a glass of something nice in there with your name on it, anytime.'

Hardly listening, she muttered her thanks, hurried blindly to the station and somehow got back to Pingate Loop. As she walked into the bungalow her phone rang; she took it out of her pocket. She hoped Flo hadn't run off again. A video call from Leroy? She pressed the screen to end the call but accidentally accepted it.

'Greetings,' he said and grinned. 'How's my favourite neighbour and did she meet Mr Right tonight? I couldn't wait a minute longer to find out.'

'Not now, Leroy.' She gave a big gulp. 'Let's talk tomorrow.' She shoved the phone back into her pocket. She went into the lounge and collapsed on the sofa in the dark. That was it. No more year of firsts. She'd throw the notebook out tomorrow. If Flo gave up Guides, so be it. The doorbell rang, followed by knocking. Dolly put her fingers in her ears but it didn't go away. Nor did the comments those men made; they kept going around in her head. She got up, went to the front door and opened it a few inches.

'Surprise! Happy Valentine's Day!'

Dolly let out a sob and fell into Leroy's arms.

13

Leroy took his arm away from around Dolly's shoulders and led her back into the lounge. He turned on the lights, strode over to the window and drew the curtains.

'If I jump in the car now, I can get to that bar in no time. I bet those idiots are still drinking and—'

'Leave it, Leroy,' said Dolly, and she sniffed.

Greta always said knights in shining armour didn't exist, and after the way Fred hurt Dolly all those years ago, she had to agree. In fact, the shinier the armour, the more suspicious, her sister believed. In Greta's opinion, Fred was too flash for his own good, with his bright kipper ties and exaggerated lapels, as if wearing fashionable clothes and buying fancy gifts like bottles of Rive Gauche was a crime. The Bell women had never needed anyone else to fight their battles. When Dolly was little, more vulnerable, it was Greta who'd looked out for her. Their mum was always busy holding down several jobs and her lovers didn't stay around long enough to care, including Dolly's dad and Greta's as well. Mum put her children first, Dolly could see that now. She'd always had a smart school uniform; Mum used to get her own clothes from jumble sales. Her own parents had thrown her out when she got pregnant at sixteen. Dolly never met her grandparents and her mum only spoke about Dolly's dad once, saying that he was worst kind of lowlife. Dolly's mum may not have won all her battles but defeat didn't mean she rolled over.

'Will you answer a question honestly, Leroy?' They sat down on the sofa and she wrung her hands. 'Do I smell?'

'Dolly! No, of course not,' he said quickly.

She suffered a hot flush as if she were two decades younger. His tone, the torn look on his face, it reminded her of Greta when, in 1975, Dolly asked if she thought Fred would ever return.

'Please... you're the one person I trust to tell me the truth.' Apart from Flo, but Dolly wasn't brave enough to ask her view. Yet it was one reason she was so fond of her young neighbour: she spoke and acted from the heart. It was going to be hard telling her that Dolly had thrown the lost luggage notebook in the bin. Greta had been right. Tracking down a lost case's owner was a dangerous business.

He took Dolly's hands and squeezed. 'Gal, if you showered every day, laundered your clothes more often, and put rubbish in the bin instead of on the carpet, you'd take on each day with extra gusto. It's like Maurice – he's kept perky, hasn't he, because you've kept on top of cleaning his tank? But you know all this, my love, and when the time's right, you'll act. It doesn't change how the people who matter care for you.'

Dolly couldn't look at Leroy until he talked about how much affection everyone had for her – him, Flo and her parents, people he'd bumped into over the last year, like Rosie from the mini supermarket, that dental receptionist with the pierced tongue and the dog owner who used to walk around Pingate Loop before his red Labrador snuffed it. For a moment Dolly's life grew bigger, friendlier.

'You should have seen my place those first few weeks after Tony left. I even stopped organising my food tins in alphabetical order.'

'It's not funny, Leroy.'

'Agreed,' he continued. 'I knew things had to change when I went out in underwear that didn't match my socks.'

She punched his arm.

'That's more like my Dolly.' He wiped a tear from her cheek. 'Now could be the time for you to make a few changes, this speed-dating night prompting you, like my Caribbean trip has me.'

'Yes, how come you're back? Jamaica looked wonderful.'

He leant back into the sofa. 'After several weeks of pristine beaches, blazing sunshine, beautiful sunsets, I need to get a grip on reality again. I'm glad I went, getting to know family, and as for the spices, the colours, the salty sea breeze – it's really lifted my spirits. It's made me feel young again, Dolly, and I hope, one day, Winston might visit Manchester. Clubbing in Jamaica, meeting all those new people, experiencing things I've never done before – it got me thinking...'

'That it's time to move on?'

'Exactly,' he said.

'Oh, Leroy, I'm so glad.'

'Now I understand why Tony got bored, so it's time to move on from the old me...' He rubbed his hands together. 'I'm determined to win him back.'

For a moment Dolly forgot all about Dancing Daze.

'I've already signed up to a gym. I need a new me. A Leroy who's younger, more spontaneous – *sexier*.'

She rolled her lips together. 'But the old you is more than

fine.' Charlie always thought so, but Dolly didn't like to bring up his name and, with it, the pain.

'Is it, though?' he countered. 'Tony was an excellent judge of character. Like when he had a sixth sense about that new window cleaner who turned out to be casing homes for potential burglaries.'

'But—'

Leroy's excitement didn't let Dolly interrupt; instead, he talked about how he wanted her help to redecorate, to make his place more up-to-date. He'd looked online for ideas, furnishings that were less colourful, more classic. He needed Dolly to go with him to IKEA. Leroy had never been there before and she could help him tone everything down, including his clothes on a different shopping trip...

'I need to tone down *me*,' he said with certainty.

Dolly wasn't sure how Leroy had managed it, but somehow, by the time he left, her own trauma after the speed-dating seemed almost insignificant. Leroy was about to totally re-design his home, along with his wardrobe, his diet. She sat on her hands, worried she'd throw the remote at the television thinking about how Tony had destroyed Leroy's confidence. And another burning sensation grew in her chest every time she pictured those slimeballs at Dancing Daze.

Dolly stood up and surveyed the lounge. She picked up a polystyrene box from the Chinese delivery she'd had the night before and carried it into the kitchen. Gripping a dustbin bag, she went back and filled it with empty biscuit tubes and old newspapers, with screwed-up squares of kitchen roll and empty packets of Rennies. Afterwards, she took off her clothes and instead of letting them drop to the floor, she stuffed them into the dirty linen basket. With a warm, soapy flannel she gave her face a good scrub and generously squirted toothpaste on to her toothbrush. She hadn't found Phoebe tonight, and had thrown the notebook out, but at least the balloon debate and speed-dating had sparked the idea, deep inside and tucked away, that the old Dolly might be ready to fight her own corner again.

14

Pancake Day, the first day of March and the first time Dolly would take Flo to Guides on her own. Before half-term, when she'd accompanied Flo with Mark or Kaz, Dolly had managed to avoid questioning eyes. Like those of church volunteer and former committee member, retired Edith, who was often found pottering, gleaning information about the village from the organisations that hired out that hall. She used to clash with fellow volunteer Greta, and every year they vied to see who could collect the most Christian Aid envelopes. They were part of a small team who tended to the building, weeding, cleaning windows, mending curtains, widowed Edith being one of the younger, more active members. Dolly was looking forward to seeing Flo, who had visited relatives in Wales with her parents, over half-term, but Dolly hadn't told her yet that the quest to find Phoebe was over. The letterbox rapped and Dolly left the kitchen to let her young neighbour in.

It had been exactly one year and three months since Greta had died. Her sister had only got to open the first door of her last ever advent calendar. Dolly had opened all the others, even after the funeral, even after she'd braved the lost luggage auction and burst into tears, pretending Greta had eaten all the other little chocolates. As she'd pushed the last perforated square of card, a sense of closure, not opening, had stolen her appetite.

Here Dolly was, all these months later, still expecting Greta to check if she'd stocked up on sugar and lemon. Greta had always loved the structure special days gave the year – like Shrove Tuesday today, Good Friday, May Day, Remembrance Sunday. Together, through the decades, they'd made pancakes and Easter chocolate nests, pumpkin spice biscuits and mince pies. Until the latter years when Greta slowed down; she'd watch, then.

'Are you sure you don't want pancakes with your dad?' asked Dolly as Flo sloped in.

'We had savoury ones. Bacon and cheese. He said I could have sweet ones with you.' As usual, she went into the lounge first, to call on Maurice. 'Holy Moly. Whilst I've been away you tidied up? It's always made me feel good that your room was as messy as mine. I don't like it.'

Leroy had been more encouraging. He'd dropped by yesterday to arrange their trip to IKEA and given her a high five. Good thing he hadn't seen the state of the other rooms. However, he was right: a tidier lounge brought calm to the bungalow, as if her brain were a computer that could finally process its surroundings without being bombarded with pop-ups about old light bulbs, dirty mugs and unopened junk mail.

On the kitchen unit stood a jar of chocolate spread, a tub of sprinkles and a packet of Haribos – Flo had been very specific with her instructions when she and Dolly had spoken briefly, out the front, yesterday. However, she wrinkled her freckled nose.

'Strawberries and banana slices?'

Dolly had eaten an apple with breakfast. Until then, she'd forgotten how refreshing food tasted without the addition of preservatives, sugars and fats, all the ingredients she'd found such comfort in during recent months. She'd made a jug of batter earlier, and put on one of her favourite disco records in the lounge. She didn't dance like she used to when cooking – her feet would step in time to chopping or whisking, until Greta came in and told her to turn that racket down. But this last year she had listened to the music that transported her to a different time and place, like a nightclub in the seventies – with Fred. He'd always got them seats in the VIP area with his velvet jacket and white shoes, the feathered Bowie cut and John Lennon round glasses. Other clubbers would have been surprised to see his small flat. Fred was saving hard for a bigger place.

'Sorry one landed on the floor,' said Flo twenty minutes later, and she took a big bite of rolled-up pancake, chocolate oozing like lava out of both ends. She'd wanted to eat on the sofa as she'd placed the octopus plushie on the arm nearest to Maurice and couldn't wait to see if he spotted it. 'Dad let me practise flipping pancakes but it's still tricky.' She sighed. 'I keep sneaking into the kitchen to examine our flour bags, hoping flour beetles get in; that would be utterly brilliant. But Mum and Dad recently bought these fancy airtight storage jars, so I might read up on how to get bed bugs instead.'

One of Flo's quirks, Dolly had learnt, was being serious about things that sounded like jokes.

'I'm glad you're going to Guides tonight. How did it all end before the half-term break? We haven't had a chance to talk about that.'

'What you really mean is, am I going to take my Promise after half a term of testing it out?' Flo wagged her finger. 'Don't ask me questions in code, Dolly, like Mum and Dad. You and me, we don't need to do that.'

Dolly swiped Flo's finger and squeezed it playfully.

'Gill says I must decide soon, as I'm taking up a place another girl could have. Doesn't bother me but... Mum and Dad had a word and she's agreed to let me have a few more weeks.' Flo took another bite. 'I'm not saying any more until you tell me about the dating night. You changed the subject when I asked, again, yesterday. It's been two weeks now and you haven't talked any more about the notebook either. We should read the March challenge. Are we still in this together? 'Cos if not, then I'm definitely not joining.'

Mark and Kaz would only worry if Flo refused to go, what with Mark's comments about how they both used to be shy and didn't want that for their daughter. Flo didn't need to know, quite yet, that Dolly was never reading that year of firsts list again.

'You only talk about Guides if I ask you. Is *your* heart still in our deal?'

Chocolate gloop hung from the corners of Flo's mouth. 'Yes. But I still hate it, even though I'm in with the Bumble Bees patrol.' Her face lit up for a second. 'Did you know that as bees get older, they do jobs reserved for the young ones? This makes their brain age in reverse. Imagine if that happened in humans; you and me might play hopscotch.'

Flo hopscotched her way back to the kitchen, took another pancake and went to slather on more chocolate but Dolly screwed the lid tightly on to the jar. She pushed over the lemon and sugar. Occasionally, she channelled Greta. They took their plates back into the lounge. Flo talked about the theme the pack were working on this term, that Gill had mentioned in the first meeting she went to. Everyone had to earn two types of badges – an interest one and a skills builders one – then do five hours of special activities in the meetings.

The theme was Know Myself. Lemon juice dripped down Flo's chin as she explained how the theme was stupid, that out of everything there was to find out about the world, it made them focus on themselves. They'd work on the interest badge first – it was called Personal Brand and everyone had to say what theirs was. Flo stopped chewing for a moment. According to Gill, a brand was about the stuff you like to own and do, what you believe in, what makes you *you*. Flo banged her legs against the sofa's bottom. She reckoned working out other people's brand was much easier, like her mum and dad's. They worked all the time, ate healthy, did chores; they got cross over ace things like a squadron of flying ants circling the outside drain. They recorded programmes about boring stuff like the price of energy bills or people arguing over that Brexit thing. So they had a brand that was full of rules and didn't seem like much fun.

'But me?' Flo stopped banging her legs. 'I don't know. I go to school. Read my insect books. Come around here. That's all.' She pulled a face. 'It's going to be embarrassing, talking about that private stuff with strangers. I know you won't laugh at me; I can say anything in your bungalow.' She ran a thumb over a puddle of juice on her plate and sucked it. 'Your turn now. Tell me about this dating night.'

Dolly wiped her hands on a paper napkin. She'd bought a packet from the mini supermarket. If she was going to keep herself tidier, not wiping sticky fingers on her jogging bottoms was a good start. Since Leroy had gone to Jamaica she'd got more used to doing her own shopping and had even chatted to Rosie on the till, if, 'Yes, it's cold,' counted as conversation.

Dolly described the speed-dating night's set-up, the rows of tables arranged according to age. Briefly she described a couple of the men she'd spoken to, screwing the napkin into a tight ball.

'Did you meet anyone you liked? Did any couples get together? At our last school disco two pupils kissed on the mouth, like I catch Mum and Dad doing.' She rolled her eyes. 'You'd think they'd be the last people to do that, seeing as their working day is spent killing germs.'

'There was none of that, I can assure you,' said Dolly hastily. 'Quite the opposite, in fact.'

Flo frowned. 'What does that mean?'

'Let's just say the men... weren't really my cup of tea. The important bit is, sadly I didn't see anyone called Phoebe.'

Flo's eyes had lit up. 'The girls at school talk about stuff with boys that I don't understand. Izzy reads her older sister's magazines... but I've never heard of *the opposite of kissing*. What's that exactly? It would be brilliant if I could tell them a fact.'

Dolly hesitated before giving an edited version of how she'd overheard the men talking, how she was the last woman any of them would want to kiss. She mentioned the caring man who came out to check she was all right afterwards, that he ran a pub.

'How dare they! I bet you were the best match there. Who else talks to their goldfish and understands that five-a-day should come from stuff like chocolate and tomato ketchup?'

* * *

Dolly stood at the sink and stared at their dirty plates, knowing she should wash them up instead of leaving them to crust over and eventually form mould. She might do them later. The mess in the kitchen and Dolly's bedroom wrapped her up like a security blanket. She wasn't ready to let go of it. Not yet. Not in the places where she stored food, where she had a bed. They'd been her two escape rooms this last year.

Flo was in the lounge talking loudly to Maurice, warning him that he might catch something if he kissed the mermaid with his mouth open. The chit-chat stopped and footsteps stomped as she ran back into the kitchen.

'Dolly! Dolly! The nice guy, outside the bar, the one who asked if you were okay. Did you say he was called Steve?'

'Yes. Why?' She hadn't given his name much thought, but then that was hardly surprising, she'd been desperate to leave Dancing Daze and had hardly listened to a word he'd said.

'That's one of the clues.' Flo made binoculars around her eyes. 'Phoebe wrote she was cross with her granddad for mentioning the speed-dating to a neighbour: Steve. It must be him! You need to go to his pub. He'll know where she lives!'

15

Dolly drove up the ramp, into IKEA's car park, grateful for the calm voice of the satnav, and that her car, unused for over one year, had made it there safely. She'd checked it over briefly this morning, as well as the upcycled gingham case in the boot, from the 1999 auction, that now contained a first-aid kit, jump leads and ice scraper. Dolly still had the silk Japanese kimono from when she'd opened it. At the last minute, Leroy had announced she'd need to drive her hatchback – it was only forty-five minutes from Knutsmere to Warrington in good traffic and his car wasn't starting. Since Greta died he'd been turning her Skoda's engine over once a week. Dolly parked up and Leroy explained how he'd studied an online map of the huge building.

'Wasn't the new you going to be spontaneous?'

'I'm doing up my lounge first,' he continued. 'I'll focus on that today. We could be done by one and then I'll treat you to lunch if you like. I've looked at their menu and we can have Swedish meatballs, shrimp popcorn and chips or salmon curry, and for dessert...'

They headed through the spring sunshine to the trolley rank.

Every now and then he adjusted his jeans. They were skinny style; she hadn't seen him in them before. He wore a new, sleek denim jacket to match, and gleaming white trainers instead of his favourite brogues. Dolly hadn't been out clothes shopping for years, unable to disagree with Greta's view that buying from a catalogue was far more efficient and cheaper.

Dolly ground to a halt. There, searching in her handbag by the entrance, was Edith, the church volunteer. Leroy crooked his arm and they made their way over, him pushing the trolley.

'Dorothy. How nice to see you out and about. How are you doing?'

Dolly gave a little nod.

'I was sorry to hear about Greta,' Edith said briskly. 'We didn't get on but looking back we were so alike, that's probably why. I secretly admired her play-it-straight attitude. The world would be a far simpler place if more people said what they thought.' She gave a wry smile, telling Dolly the only thing they had ever agreed on, years ago when they were both on the church committee, was a hoo-ha over what relatives should be allowed to leave at gravesides. They both thought artificial flowers and trinkets lowered the tone, and deemed the other committee members far too sentimental for voting to allow them.

'Although Greta was quite emotional herself, that day, actually.' Edith's gaze drifted into the past before a screaming toddler pulled it back to the present.

Dolly remembered that meeting because it was the day after Fred had proposed. Dolly had offered to go into work for overtime, to help file timesheets. She'd called in on Greta first, to break the happy news. Her sister was eating cereal and moaning about the decorative pebbles and stand-up wind chimes in the graveyard. Her mood dipped further when she heard of the engagement, despite managing to squeeze out a, 'Congratulations'. Dolly had hoped that her sister would come around to her news, over time.

She and Leroy entered the building and Dolly shrank back for a second, lost in the huge space, gaping up at the tall ceiling. Along with other Saturday shoppers, they passed mock living rooms, each furnished to a different theme. Dolly was all for updating, had wanted to freshen up her and Greta's bungalow for years, but the reason had to be right and that didn't include trying to win back an ex-boyfriend. Dolly's mother would reinvent herself after every boyfriend's departure, trying to create each ex's idea of perfection. When each new facade failed and crumbled away, it also eroded bits of the woman left beneath it. Dolly loved Leroy's lounge as it was, the burgundy leather sofa, the warm orange carpet, the cherry drinks' cabinet. *But this isn't about me, it's about supporting my friend*, Dolly told herself.

So she pointed out a grey sofa, white shelving, a swish new drinks' cabinet. Rugs that would suit the laminate flooring that Tony always went on about. Dolly mentioned swanky wall-fitted fires, with the simulated flames; Mark and Kaz had one. She'd forgotten what it felt like to have a project, like when they'd needed to adapt the bungalow to suit Greta's arthritis. Dolly had ordered a handrail for outside the front door, bought the slip mat in the bath and had a grab bar fitted by the toilet.

Leroy stopped the trolley for a second, wrapped his arms around her and held Dolly tight. Greta, for all her disciplined ways and dislike of public displays of affection, also gave great hugs and would always be the last one to let go. Dolly had never doubted how much she was loved.

They walked through the artificial plant section and over to a selection of picture frames, Dolly happily inconspicuous amongst the hordes of people, until a woman in a sequinned baker cap raved to her about a picture of the Eiffel Tower. She and her husband had visited the year before. Had Phoebe gone there, after all? Over the years everyone else seemed to have visited apart from Dolly and Greta, for romantic weekends, on school trips or with their job. She'd still got an Eiffel Tower snow globe that one of the lorry drivers brought back. A friend of Fred's had an apartment in Saint-Michel. Fred would have fitted in well, with his Yves Saint Laurent silk scarf and the seductive way he blew smoke rings. He'd suggested they go there to celebrate their engagement, a last splurge before saving for marriage and a home. Greta had taken the news of the trip almost worse than the engagement itself.

* * *

Mid-afternoon, Leroy yawned as she pulled up into her drive. She'd actually driven all the way there and back. He insisted a big lunch had made him tired, not the hoicking of flatpack shelves into the boot – he went to the gym every other day now, it couldn't be that. Dolly wanted to say the size of his bill must have knocked him out, but that might be hypocritical considering all the bits she'd bought. It had surprised her how much she'd enjoyed selecting items, re-imagining her bungalow. Leroy clambered out and opened the boot, mentioning how he'd drive to the garden centre the next day to look for a new hallway mat. Dolly could come if she wanted.

'I thought your car wouldn't start?' she said.

Mark shouted across from his drive, asking if they needed a hand, and Leroy hurried away to shake his hand. Flo came over, dragging her feet as the men walked past, unloading the boot. Mark offered to help him assemble the shelves. Dolly placed her two bags on the ground.

'Off out anywhere nice?'

'To do the big food shop,' Flo muttered and pushed up her knitted bobble hat with a butterfly on the side. It had come out of one of the auctioned lost cases a few years ago and used to be too big. 'When I get back Dad says I've got to start my Guides homework – that is, creating a cake, a dance or a song, to show to the other Bumble Bees what my brand is. How can I do that if I still don't know what it is?' Flo studied Dolly's bags. 'Where have you been? Have you spoken to that Steve?'

'IKEA and no. We called into his pub, The Rising Sun, but he's away for the week.'

Flo folded her arms. 'So I have to go to Guides again without you doing another challenge?'

'I for one am enjoying getting out on a Tuesday evening and taking you there.'

'You couldn't leave fast enough last week when you dropped me off. I get it. I don't want to stay either.'

Flo wasn't just a friend. She was like the extended family Dolly had never had. She hadn't said anything, but when Flo had come out of the hall last week, amongst the other girls, and one of them picked up a glove Flo had dropped and gave it to her, with a big smile, for a second Flo looked... part of something. That was important.

Flo looked at the car and managed a smile. 'You drove, Dolly. Now you're unstoppable.'

Dolly looked at the Skoda.

Yes. Yes, she was.

What's more, she wouldn't let those cruel men at the speed-dating night hold her or Flo back. She wouldn't leave Flo to flounder with her brand.

'Sorry for being a baby,' said Flo. 'It's not your fault, but I just feel our deal isn't equal any more, with me still going to Guides whilst we wait for you to talk to that Steve. We haven't even looked at the March challenge yet, just in case you have to do it.'

'You're right,' said Dolly. 'If your dad says it's okay, how about you stop at mine instead of going to the supermarket? I couldn't resist a bag of doughnuts from a baker's in Lymhall. Come on, we'll have a go at your Guides homework – together – and when that's done...' Dolly lifted her chin. 'We'll read the next page of this Phoebe's notebook.' It was still in her bedroom, in the bin that hadn't been emptied.

Flo whooped, Mark gave his approval, and ten minutes later, the two of them were sunning themselves in Dolly's conservatory. Flo opened her exercise book and bit on the end of her biro. She put both down on the basil green case.

'This is hard,' said Flo and bit into a doughnut. Jam squirted on to her chin. 'Can we think about what your brand might be first, Dolly? I'm still struggling with mine.'

Flo wasn't in the girls' football team, didn't go to dance classes or play the recorder. Her parents had made her try all of them and Dolly knew Flo couldn't wait to drop out.

'I haven't got really strong beliefs either,' said Flo. 'Not like my parents, whose voices get really high when they talk about politics. Anushka, a girl in the Bumble Bees patrol – she's also eleven – is brilliant at singing and won an award for writing. She goes to a private school in Lymhall and wears socks covered in music notes.'

As it turned out, Anushka was the girl who'd picked up Flo's glove. Dolly had chatted very briefly to her mother about the weather.

'Anushka's brand is about being creative,' Flo continued. 'She wants to be a songwriter when she's older. Megan – I haven't spoken to her yet – she's thirteen and looks after her sick mum and wants to be a nurse; her brand is about caring.'

With sugar-dusted fingers, Flo picked up her biro again. 'My brand isn't obvious like theirs, so let's start with you, Dolly. Let's light one of your scented candles; it might help.' Flo pointed to the tiered plant stand in the corner. Dolly hadn't lit a candle for over a year. Minutes later, fragrant lavender wafted their way. It was one of the few smells that reminded Dolly of her mother, who would dry wild lavender from the local park and tie it into little linen bags, to put in their underwear drawers.

With Greta around, Dolly's brand had been clear-cut. They were two sisters who lived together, retired spinsters; they baked, gardened, went to church. They helped out with Flo, took part in local charity events. They were do-gooders, Dolly supposed. Reliable. Upstanding. But Greta's death had buggered that brand, and thinking about their brand like that showed it had been more about her sister's likes and beliefs. Where had the Dolly who went dancing and flirted, the one who wouldn't tut at a dirty joke or getting drunk disappeared to? That Dolly had even tried cannabis. Routine and a comfort zone never used to be her best friends.

Yet... she'd felt happy living with Greta. Or, rather... content. Well, she hadn't wanted for anything, at least.

'Me, at the moment? I like convenience food but I'm trying to eat healthier. I've tidied up more, recently, than in the whole of the last year. I'm making the effort to go out more, taking you to Guides and shopping with Leroy. I'm going to change the lounge because... I like a project. Oh, and I still dream of going to Paris, even though I've never stepped foot in an airport.'

Flo listed everything and stared at the page, whilst Dolly fetched her another squash.

'I think I've worked out your brand. It's kind of... self-improvement. Like the influencers on YouTube who try to get fitter, try to dance quicker, one girl organises and tidies all of her friends' bedrooms...'

'I need improving? I guess that's true. I have let things get on top of me since—'

'No! You're great as you are. You don't tell me off for bringing in caterpillars and don't mind if I'm moody. What I really mean is... you are trying new things. You want stuff to change. So your brand is about... finding yourself?'

'Self-discovery... I like that.'

'You're like this YouTuber, Try Anything Tracy, one of my favourites. She says we should spend our teens doing as many different things as we can, to find out who we want to be.' She hugged her knees. 'Don't tell Mum and Dad, but she's the only reason I used to agree to try all those school activities.'

'If this Tracy inspires you so much, why did you hold off agreeing to go to Guides?'

'Because I'm fed up of Mum and Dad suggesting activities that are more like their sort of interests, not mine,' Flo mumbled. 'I don't want to talk about that any more. It's to do with my secret and something Mum and Dad did when I was born.'

What a cryptic comment. Dolly wanted to ask more but didn't want to push as Flo had closed the subject down.

'Your turn next, then, sweetheart. What do you think your brand could be?'

'Gill says, if we're stuck, to think about what would be missing if we weren't here. Mum and Dad would say bookmarks in random places and grass-stained trousers.' She rolled her eyes.

'I think that's actually a great start – you love reading.'

'Doesn't everyone?'

'Not me, and your reading interests are quite specific, to do with nature and science.'

'True. The other kids in my class like made-up stories about wizards or gangs.'

'As for dirty trousers – that's because you love exploring outside. Flo, I think your brand is about learning. You've really been bitten by the bug – literally – when it comes to studying insects. In fact, an insect could be your brand's symbol.'

Flo's face lit up. 'I could bake a cake in the shape of... a butterfly!'

'Or make iced biscuits. I can help.'

Flo lunged forwards and locked her arms around Dolly's neck.

Gently Dolly pushed her away, belly-laughing. 'Right. Let's get Phoebe's notebook.'

16

Dolly closed the door of the changing-room cubicle. It was Sunday lunchtime; morning swimming lessons for children were over. The clinical smell of chlorine suited Dolly who was on a mission. She placed her rucksack on the small bench and unzipped it. One bare foot did its best to grip the wet floor as she undressed and tugged on the threadbare navy one-piece she'd found at the bottom of her wardrobe after Flo had gone home yesterday.

March.

   Go swimming. Lymhall Pool is only a short walk away. Sunday lunchtimes are supposed to be less busy. Maisie's seen beautiful coastlines across the world, whilst eating jellyfish in Vietnam and whale watching in Alaska, but reckons it's just as satisfying seeing people having fun in the local baths.

   Fun? In water? Strangers in close proximity? Dodging collisions wearing an uncomfortable costume?

   I'd rather eat jellyfish.

So Phoebe wasn't a confident or keen swimmer; perhaps this challenge was simply to broaden her life skills. Maybe, like Fred, she had a fear of water. He and Dolly had gone to Blackpool beach once and he'd waded in up to his waist, refusing to go further, even when she'd splashed him. He'd got his own back by hiding her towel when she got out; his silly streak couldn't resist. She'd chased him up and down the beach and tripped over. He'd given her a piggyback to the promenade and bought her the biggest ice cream slathered in syrups and sprinkles.

A grin spread across her face, vanishing as quickly as it appeared. Why had he crept into her mind again? Had done, since Greta passed. Was it because her sister had banned all talk about him long ago, calling him a bad 'un? It was as if her death had given Dolly permission to think back to the only time she'd fallen in love.

This first was the easiest for Dolly so far. Just as well. She might have to go for the rest of the Sundays in the month; Phoebe hadn't specified exactly which date she'd go to the pool. Dolly used to visit it with Greta – swimming was supposed to be good for arthritis. But in the latter years her sister was often too stiff to go and dearly missed it.

As she stuffed her clothes into the rucksack, on top of the Zadorin gilet, notebook, bracelet and vintage ring, Dolly caught sight of her reflection. It had been such a long time since she'd looked at her body out of joggers and baggy jumpers. She used to take more interest in her appearance but that had waned over the decades, especially after the change. When her hormones disappeared so did the remnants of her wanting to look vital. *What's the point?* a voice in her head would ask. *This is how life is now – a quiet retirement, living with my sister.* Oh, she enjoyed looking tidy; she'd iron clothes and appreciated a smart but practical jacket that blocked out the northern gusts. She'd put on her Sunday best for church, not that she was the most fervent a believer, but it was courteous to her sister. It was only when she listened to her favourite Bee Gees that she'd experience a twinge of wanting the outside to reflect the inner Dolly who imagined John Travolta standing opposite, hips swivelling as she copied his moves in a cropped top and flared trousers.

Yet it wasn't about the clothes... Despite his love of fashion, Fred understood. Whenever they'd met up for a night out, he would always blow her a kiss and say, 'You wear it well.' She'd ask him what 'it' was and he'd reply, 'Yourself' – those twinkling eyes, he'd say, that spirited stride he found hard to keep up with, the way her hands moved up and down whilst she chatted, as if she knew sign language.

More out of curiosity, Dolly studied herself from head to toe in the mirror – the cellulite, the bingo wings. They were proof she'd got older, avoided a fatal illness or accident so far, so she wouldn't call them flaws. However, when she turned side to side a wave of foreboding filled her chest. Her stomach bulged out as far as her breasts, unavoidable evidence of what the doctor had said about her health.

In a jealous tone, Flo had asked if Dolly would shave under her arms before going – she couldn't wait for grown-up hairs to start showing and declared she'd never shave hers off. Dolly had found a razor in Greta's room, guilt washing over her as she rummaged through her sister's toiletry drawer – the hydrating bath oil, the support socks, the Tena pads, the Estée Lauder perfume that had never changed over the years, and the denture adhesive. She'd always made Dolly promise that if anything happened to her in the night the paramedics wouldn't see her without teeth in. As it was, Greta needn't have worried. That afternoon, the first of December, after a jaunt into town Dolly had knocked at the door and gone into Greta's bedroom. Dolly had planned a surprise holiday for the New Year – she'd just bought the tickets, in Manchester. It was now or never, she said to Greta, to go abroad; they had plenty of time to apply for passports and the trip was a cruise so her sister didn't need to worry about flying. All meals included, a doctor on board; Dolly would see to all the paperwork. Dolly was confident she'd addressed the concerns Greta had previously had about taking a break outside of the UK. Leaving her to digest this thrilling news, Dolly went to make a brew. But when she brought the cup of tea back into Greta's bedroom, her sister's heart had packed in. The excitement must have been too much, even though the doctors said the attack would have happened anyway.

Dolly stashed her belongings in a locker and pinned the key to her costume. Flip-flops on her feet, Greta's warnings about catching verrucas ringing in her ears, she wandered out to the poolside and scanned the water for a woman who might be Phoebe, breathing in the disinfectant smell. A pool attendant blew into his whistle as if trying to revive it. A young woman swam widths; she had two long plaits. A silver-haired man with his back to Dolly did star jumps, making big splashes. Parents fussed over children in armbands shaped like unicorns and crabs. A more serious swimmer wore a cap and goggles, and tore through the water, doing lengths from one end of the pool to the other, somehow avoiding collisions with the casual bathers. There were no formal lanes for public swimming on a Sunday. A retired couple lay on their backs on the surface, holding hands like a pair of sleeping sea otters. Leaving her flip-flops under a nearby bench, Dolly went to the ladder and dipped a toe in the water. The temperature reminded her of the warm baths she ran for Greta, and how they'd dip in temperature before Greta finally clambered in and lowered herself on to her special seat.

Dolly attempted to swim a width to start with, but almost

halfway across her lungs constricted and her breathing became laboured. Wet hair clung to her neck like strands of seaweed as she turned around and went back to where she'd started. Maurice wouldn't have been impressed. Gasping, she finally arrived. So much for muscle memory. Panting, she rested against the side. The doctor's words of warning crept into her head as the man doing star jumps came over to climb out. Dolly rubbed her wet eyes and squinted, studying him, until the friendly eyes took her back to the speed-dating evening and Dolly running away.

'*Steve?*'

He stopped. He took a moment.

'I came to the Rising Sun... you said there was a drink with my name on it.'

'Dancing Daze, of course! How are you doing?'

'It's a long story, but I need to find a Phoebe Goodbody. Seeing as you are the landlord of a pub in Lymhall, where she lives, I thought there was a chance...'

'Phoebe?' His face broke into a grin. 'It's your lucky day, love. I happen to live next door to her.'

Dolly forgot her tight lungs, the pain in her chest. At last she could give back the steamer trunk's most valuable belongings. Flo would be so excited. Thoughts raced through her head: the tales she'd tell Phoebe about the other person bidding on her luggage, about being heckled at the balloon debate and those losers at speed-dating.

'Even luckier than that, Phoebe's here in the pool today. But she was at that speed-dating night as well, you know.'

She was?

'But then' – he raised his eyebrows – 'did you think she might be? Have you been trying to find her for a while? Is everything okay?'

'I... I need to return a few belongings of hers.'

He studied her for a moment and then smiled. 'Okay, although I've tried to catch Phoebe's eye but she's dead set on doing as many widths as she can without stopping. She hasn't been swimming for a while.' He jerked his head towards the young woman with plaits. 'Now don't you forget, there's a drink in my pub with your name on it... Dotty, wasn't it?'

'Yes, that's it,' she said, staring across the pool, not even registering that he got her name wrong. Steve said cheerio and climbed out, wearing banana-yellow swimming trunks. *That* was Phoebe? A woman in her *twenties*? Goosebumps formed on the top half of Dolly's body. She couldn't take her eyes off the young woman as she pushed off the other side and swam back in Dolly's direction. Oddly, she looked like a competent swimmer. Why then was this challenge such a difficult one for her? This stranger almost felt like a friend. They'd both had a hard year; both wanted to change. Phoebe reached the side of the pool and stood up, taller than Dolly. Her eyes fell to the woman's inside wrist. A tattoo. It was the same symbol as on the white T-shirt.

Phoebe met her gaze, looked away, and then turned back. Dolly had never seen that shade of green eyes, like the fresh, fragrant herbs that used to sit in pots on her kitchen windowsill, when Greta was alive.

'It's rude to stare,' said Phoebe and those eyes sparked.

'I'm sorry but it's just... I've been hoping to meet you for so long. Phoebe Goodbody?'

'Who's asking?' She frowned. 'Haven't I met you before?'

'I thought you'd be older,' Dolly said, still fixed on her face with its prominent cheekbones. 'The year of firsts... you talked about dropping out of university a lifetime ago... and one of your friends, Susan, has grandkids. You know Gene Kelly, then there's the way you talked about how you'd never had a long-term relationship, let alone got married, I assumed...'

Phoebe gasped and crossed her arms. 'Who *are* you? How have you got hold of my notebook? Why would you read it? All those thoughts, they're... *private*.' Her voice stuttered.

'Believe me, I didn't want to, but I've been trying to find you,' she replied and beamed. 'The notebook, the stunning pearl ring, that nice gilet, the bracelet, they're in my locker.'

'My Gran's ring – you've got it?' Phoebe's hand flew up to her chest.

'I've been doing the challenges since January, you see, hoping to find you, to return those items. I took part in the balloon debate...' Dolly thought back to the group of youngsters there – a couple had long chestnut hair too. 'The speed-dating night...' Of course, Steve was right. 'I realise now our paths crossed.'

Phoebe stared at her. 'Yes. Outside. I remember now.'

'This challenge was a relief as I like swimming. In fact, I might come every Sunday, and—'

'You've been *stalking* me?' Phoebe's nose wrinkled and she backed away, water circling around her.

Dolly shrank back against the swimming-pool edge and shivered. She... she'd thought they'd laugh about Matilda and the stupid man on the date night who kept going on about plumbing, and joking how Pb stood for *plumbum*. Instead, Phoebe glared at Dolly as if it was her fault she'd lost her luggage. Dolly slid down into the water, wanting to hide herself.

'How did you steal my luggage?' Phoebe's frown deepened. 'Not having my things ruined my trip to Paris. I especially needed everything in that little compartment and I've been so worried about losing Gran's jewellery. I had to change my flight and come straight home the next day. It was the first challenge I tried and it nearly put me off doing the whole thing. I assumed my case had been lost in transit and the cardboard label had got torn off, or that someone had taken my case by mistake. But it never turned up. I gave up ringing the lost luggage number and left my details. They never rang back. Were you at Charles de Gaulle airport? Did you see me, looking frantic as the baggage carousel went around?'

'No. I've never been abroad.' Dolly stared at the blue water. She was still getting used to talking to anyone who wasn't Flo or Leroy, and her words weren't coming out right with Phoebe.

Phoebe jerked her head towards the ladder. 'You've got ten minutes to hand over my things, before I call the police.' Her voice shook.

'But it's not like that! You see, every December—'

'Ten minutes,' she hissed.

Feeling sick, Dolly climbed up the ladder.

'I'll be in the reception area, waiting,' said Phoebe and she sped past, heading for the lockers, having wrapped herself up in a giant towel from the bench.

Dolly fumbled with the locker key and pulled on her clothes without drying off. She didn't bother with socks and the water dripping down her back as she left the changing room hardly registered. Phoebe stood by the vending machine and stretched out her hand. Dolly passed over the folded Zadorin gilet, with the notebook on top and ring necklace, the bracelet too. Phoebe hugged them to her chest. She stared at Dolly's feet and an angry shade of red flooded her face.

'Those too,' she said in a cold voice. 'What a sad little life you must lead, poking your nose into someone else's year plan and wearing their clothes.' Her top lip curled. 'You're pathetic.'

Dolly gave her the trainers with the rose-gold caps and, flip-flops on, walked outside, hand curled tightly around the tea flask in her anorak pocket. Without looking back, she got in the car and drove home.

17

Dolly sat in the lounge, tea flask unopened in her hands. It was late afternoon and the moon crescent was visible. She'd switched the lamp on but hadn't fed Maurice, nor herself, and twice she'd ignored knocking at the front door. Flo and Leroy had caught her on the way in. She'd mumbled that yes she'd met Phoebe, no they weren't going to be friends and without answering any more questions had hurried indoors. Carrying out a year of firsts had given structure to the months ahead, but now... Dolly glanced through the window and into the sky again. She'd read once that the universe's shape was determined by its density. Perhaps that's why her future looked so shapeless, as without Phoebe's notebook there was nothing in it.

She was about to turn away when... she jolted. Two faces bobbed up above the windowsill; she could just make them out through the nets. A small hand waved. A large one pointed to the door. With a sigh, Dolly got up. Flo and Leroy stood on the doorstep.

'Mum and Dad...' Flo looked sideways at Leroy. He nodded. 'They took me for a woodland walk in Alderley Edge this morning, said spring was finally here and the outdoors was important, probably for good health, but I like spring for other reasons...' Flo reached into her pocket and took out a small cardboard box with holes pierced in the top. She opened it to reveal a glossy black beetle. 'I took this box in case and tempted this beetle in whilst Mum and Dad were looking at their Fitbits. Its back shines like liquorice painted with clear nail varnish. I wanted to keep it for a while, but I've had trouble identifying it, so I don't know what it eats. Lots of beetles on the internet look similar but don't come out until it's warmer.' She let it run over her hand. 'But now you've seen it I can let it go.' Flo crouched down by Dolly's front border and said goodbye as it clambered on to the soil.

'That's very responsible,' said Dolly.

'It's important to be responsible, isn't it?' said Leroy brightly. 'Like answering the door so that your friends don't worry and—'

'I'm hungry after cycling and tea isn't for ages yet,' interrupted Flo. 'Leroy talked about some pink sandwich biscuits you'd bought from IKEA yesterday.'

Leroy stood behind Flo, hands on her shoulders. 'And I've got a thirst on me like you wouldn't believe, after doing more work on my new lounge.'

Dolly drew the curtains and collapsed on to the sofa once more, doing her best to avoid looking at the octopus plushie. Leroy went to the thermostat on the wall, above Maurice's tank. He switched the heating on, even though it hadn't fallen below sixteen degrees. Flo headed into the kitchen and filled the kettle. Maurice darted to and fro, before swimming upwards, near to the tank's feed hole. Still in her flip-flops, Dolly went over and dropped in a few flakes. Flo came in and handed Dolly a mug. She came back with another for Leroy, who sat in the armchair. Flo put her juice on the table next to Dolly, and gave her the packet of biscuits that had been wedged under her arm. Dolly tore it open and took out two before handing the packet back. Flo sat cross-legged on the floor and asked why Dolly was wearing flip-flops.

As the buttercream filling melted in her mouth, Dolly's body relaxed. 'I've had a shock but that's no excuse. I should have answered the door earlier. Without you two this last year... if it hadn't been for you both...'

'I think you're trying to say you love us more than... those doughnuts you bought yesterday,' said Leroy.

'More than the ones with squirty jam,' said Flo.

'Even those dipped in chocolate,' added Dolly. She cupped her hands around the hot tea mug and opened up about her disastrous meeting with Phoebe.

'But you didn't steal the notebook,' said Flo and clenched her fists, 'and your life isn't sad – I think you've been brave taking on those challenges.'

'She wouldn't let me explain. It's strange, she was nice at the speed-dating evening, patted my arm and everything.'

Leroy thought Phoebe sounded nice in the notebook as well, and explained how, the day after Tony ended things, a delivery man had accidentally tried to deliver flowers to his door. Giant daisies. Leroy had slammed the door in his face. When he'd stopped crying he rang up the company to apologise. He'd explained he'd been upset, said that person wasn't the true him. Dolly wished she'd been there for him the last year. Oh she'd listened when he came around, made him cups of tea, albeit in grubby mugs, but she should have taken him out, distracted him with trips to the cinema and shopping. Instead all she'd been able to think of was herself. Flo had clearly been struggling too, arguing more with her parents – and what could her secret be?

Her universe wasn't empty at all. She had Leroy, Flo and Maurice to care for.

'Phoebe might have recently suffered a break-up, like I had, or be facing some other difficulty,' said Leroy.

Dolly hadn't thought of that.

'You could always make your own list of firsts,' said Flo, hopefully.

'I wouldn't know where to begin,' muttered Dolly.

'Suppose. Oh well. That's our deal over with. Can you tell my parents?'

Dolly gazed at Maurice, who was swimming around his mermaid ornament, and at the lounge, more homely without stale food smells. Leroy might be right. Maybe Phoebe was in a bad place, today. Goodness knows Dolly could relate to that – and how creepy to have a complete stranger track you down and talk about things you thought were private; she could see that now. What's more, it was clear from the notebook's March entry that Phoebe hadn't been looking forward to the swim in any case. Dolly smoothed down her hair and sealed the top of the biscuit packet. Flexing her toes, she stared at her friends. Friends who'd needed her support but instead had done their best, for months, to cheer *her* up.

'So, you're happy with the changes you've made to your lounge so far?' Dolly asked Leroy.

He nodded and beamed. 'The light, airy decor of Winston's beachfront rentals gave me ideas on how to place furniture and make the room look spacious. And this is just the beginning. No more moping. Action instead of navel-gazing. Pining for Tony was never going to win him back. My new diet and gym workouts are going to prove I'm still vital and interesting.'

'Who'd want to gaze at their navel?' asked Flo and she pulled a face. 'Belly buttons are full of fluff and bacteria.'

'Agreed,' he said. 'From now on, eyes forward.'

'It sounds like you're taking on one big first instead of lots of smaller ones like Phoebe,' said Flo to Leroy.

Dolly tilted her head and thought for a moment. 'Me too. I'm going to continue tidying this place. Tomorrow I'll put out the knick-knacks I bought for this room. I'll carry on eating more healthily. I used to love swimming with Greta – I'll try going every Sunday, as a starting point.' Dolly sat upright and plumped a cushion next to her. 'How about you carry on going to Guides, to be fair to Gill who's given you those extra weeks to decide about your Promise, Flo, and I'll do all these things, and I'll continue to walk you there every week?'

'Not really the same, though, is it?' Flo screwed up her face. 'I know! What if you do the Personal Brand badge with me? For the first part I'm cooking those caterpillar biscuits at yours, to take in this Tuesday – I think you should bake something for *self-discovery*. Then, for the next part of the badge we'll have to...'

Dolly reached out with her little finger.

18

For the third time, Dolly reached the other side of the pool, the shallow end, and stretched out her arms. She held on to the edge and bent her knees, her whole body looser than it had been for months. She turned around and a mum threw her toddler up into the air, catching the little boy as he squealed with delight. One of the rare, clear memories Dolly had of her own mother was when she'd taken her and Greta to Manchester's Victoria Baths. Usually the two sisters would go without her once a week – they didn't have a bath at home, and had continued the ritual for a while, even after Dolly and Greta moved out. The pool's baths were on the balcony, above the second-class men's swimming area. You'd get a free cup of tea and bar of soap. But this one time their mother also came, in between her two cleaning jobs' shifts. Laughing loudly, the three of them splashed each other. As she relaxed, the years fell off their mother like drops of water.

Dolly glanced at the large clock up on the white-tiled wall. Half an hour's breaststroke was quite enough. This afternoon she and Flo were due to discuss the next stage of the Personal Brand badge. Leroy had invited them over; he'd baked a cake and wanted to show off his revamped lounge. Flo's green caterpillar biscuits had gone down a treat at Guides last week and she'd given Dolly a cupcake made by Anushka, with musical notes piped on the top. Dolly had also baked biscuits, in the shape of a magnifying glass to represent self-discovery. She'd chosen a recipe using oats and raisins. Flo said they tasted like breakfast and had taken two for her parents. Despite his extravagant ways, Fred used to love plain biscuits. But Dolly wouldn't think about him.

She crouched down to push off the side when... her eyes narrowed as a woman came out of the changing rooms. The woman unwrapped a large towel and placed it on the bench, near Dolly's flip-flops, before hurrying into the water. Wishing water wasn't transparent, Dolly ducked down lower. Next week she'd come at a different time, Saturday, even. The March challenge must have been to swim every Sunday. At least Dolly had finished and could get out once Phoebe started her front crawl. Except the young woman fixed her eyes on Dolly and then headed in her direction. She swam the last few metres underwater and popped up next to Dolly, remaining submerged in the water, up to her shoulders, blinking.

Don't say anything. Wait for her to talk. 'I bought your case at a lost luggage auction.'

'What?'

'It's held once a month in the Northern Quarter. People bid on lost cases the airport passes on. If you don't believe me—'

'I do. It makes perfect sense why someone like you... Granddad said there'd be a logical explanation. So did Steve.' Phoebe exhaled. 'How much, out of interest?'

'How much, what?'

'Did you pay for my case?'

'Forty pounds.'

Phoebe let out a low whistle. 'You could have sold my Zadorin coat. Or the ring. Made a massive profit.'

'Some things are more important than money.'

'Agreed. Like manners.'

'My sister always used to say that. I am sorry if I came across as nosy, you see—'

'No. I'm sorry,' Phoebe said stiffly. 'I was dead rude the other day.'

Dolly tipped her head to one side. 'Oh. Right. I haven't read the whole notebook, you know. Just challenge by challenge since January, hoping each month that I'd find you. Apart from the first Paris one. I read that when I was trying to work out what the notebook was.'

Phoebe fiddled with the end of one of her plaits. 'If it was me I'd have sold the coat and read the whole thing straight off.' A toddler floated past on an inflatable turtle. 'Have you thrown away everything else?'

Dolly explained what she'd done with the other belongings. 'I don't think I saw you at the balloon debate.'

'Tonsillitis. I was holed up in front of the telly being fed ice cream by Granddad. He still thinks I'm two, not twenty-two. Steve told me about your date night. If it's any consolation, my evening there went no better. I quite liked one bloke, but then the police turned up...'

'I saw an officer.'

'My date had paid for his drinks with a stolen credit card.'

'He never! One of mine was a plumber and kept telling me that the word plumbing comes from the Latin *plumbum*. He made terrible jokes about bottoms.'

'He sounds like a right plumbum to me,' Phoebe said.

Blink and you'd miss it: Phoebe had dimples.

Dolly told her about Flo and the deal they'd made but

skimmed over how the last year had been difficult. She didn't mention Greta, didn't say how she'd hardly gone out, how the bungalow was a mess, how the doctor was worried. Instead, she talked about Guides, the Personal Brand badge, Leroy and their trip to IKEA. Sculling her hands through the water, Phoebe listened.

Dolly's ears turned red. 'I don't think I've said that much in one go to anyone this last year. Not even Maurice.'

'A friend?'

'A fish. He likes frozen peas and the Bee Gees.'

Those dimples hung around a little longer this time.

'Have you completed all of your firsts so far, apart from the balloon debate you missed and the trip to Paris you had to cut short?' asked Dolly.

'Yes, but it's not been easy. One was a taster day at a martial arts centre. That was especially difficult for someone like me.' Phoebe jerked her head towards the silver ladders and suggested coffee, hastening to add it was her granddad's idea. But Dolly was running late for her afternoon with Flo and Leroy. Phoebe's shoulders sagged very slightly. Dolly's world had grown so small this last year, she saw the tiny things.

'But how about... only if you want to... lunch this week, in the Rising Sun?' suggested Dolly. 'Say, Wednesday, midday? Steve says there's a drink there with my name written on it.'

'Dotty, isn't it? I don't know... I only came back to apologise. I actually work in the pet shop around the corner but I don't take my break if it's busy. Lunch wouldn't be possible.'

'No break? That's illegal. You should tell your boss you've got an appointment. You don't have to ask for what's due to you.'

'I'm not always hungry at lunchtime,' Phoebe said, arms curling around her body.

'Then order a snack.'

'Steve's food doesn't suit me.'

Why was she making excuses when she'd been happy to go for coffee and the Rising Sun was local?

'I'd love to tell you more about that balloon debate. For a start, I got heckled...' Dolly gave a small smile. 'I'll leave my name and number at the pool's reception desk. Text me if you want to meet. Oh, and if Steve puts pen to glass, my name's actually Dolly.'

19

'Dolly might meet Phoebe for lunch this Wednesday,' Flo informed Leroy, swinging her backpack as she trotted into his hallway.

'Can't see it happening,' said Dolly.

The three of them walked into Leroy's lounge. The red leather sofa had been replaced by the grey one from IKEA, punctuated with cream cushions and with an armchair to match. The orange carpet was now beech laminate. Abstract pale colour prints hung in place of the rich still life oil paintings. The new smart drinks rack showed off military lines of wine, its frame free from scratches, unlike the old cherry wood one.

'Wow,' said Flo. 'It's all so... vanilla. That's a word Mum uses for—'

'Things that are really... classy, right, Flo?' said Dolly quickly.

At least the new fire looked cosy. Leroy flicked it on and the simulated flames did a rumba. Flo wanted to know where he'd put his board games. They were tidied away in the loft. Minimalism was the modern way. Leroy had read up on it, and would buy white cabinets to go under the window, for his LPs. The room may have looked simple but actually everything was thought through. Clutter slowed you down, he explained. This more spacious approach was the best way to live for busy people who had deadlines.

Dolly refrained from pointing out he'd retired. He strutted into his kitchen. Skinny chinos today. The three of them sat at his kitchen table. Leroy dished out large slices of carrot cake. A piece of grated carrot stuck in Dolly's teeth. The cake was full of vitamin A, he explained, low in fat, and that cream on top was dairy-free. In no time at all Leroy's new clothes would fit. He'd bought everything one size too small, to motivate him.

Flo wiped her mouth. 'To become what? Minimalist like your lounge?' She took another bite. 'Carrot aphids are really cool, you know, and if gardeners blast them off with water' – she enacted holding a hose – 'often ants will lift them back on, because when aphids feed they produce honeydew. That's like the creamiest ever chocolate to ants.'

'Dolly tells me your brand is learning.'

'Yes and hers is self-discovery. What would yours be, Leroy? Playing games? Dancing? Going out with friends?'

After much thought Leroy announced it was similar to Dolly's, now that he was on a journey.

When Flo left to go to the bathroom Dolly said, 'Except your journey isn't quite the same as mine, is it?' She stared at his unremarkable taupe shirt. 'When I think back to the Leroy I knew before Tony and what you've said about your life over the years, the partying, the music, the extravagant wardrobe, none of that ever changed, not when you two were still dating. It's only since Tony has left that you're re-thinking.'

'But that's the same with you, since losing Greta.'

'No... I think I lost myself years ago, when I first moved in with my sister, after I… was hurt. I don't want that to happen to you. Tony's a fool. The old you deserves better.'

Leroy pushed away his plate. 'I don't blame Tony for leaving. I've turned into a boring old fart. I stopped moving with the times. Are you saying I can't change? You had a wake-up call when Greta passed. Aren't I allowed one too, thanks to my trip to Jamaica that made me feel really alive again?'

'Of course you are – as long as it's for the right reasons.'

Leroy's eyes glistened and his hand stretched across the table.

'Sorry, I didn't mean to upset you.' She gulped. 'I'll shut up.'

'You haven't. It's bloody brilliant, seeing *my* Dolly back, I've missed the one who loved a debate.'

Flo appeared in the doorway and Leroy beckoned her in. 'Come on, tell me about the next stage of your badge.'

'Only if you tell me first about getting Tony back. Have you got a plan?'

'Were you listening at the door, madam?' asked Leroy.

Flo grinned and sat down again. She wanted to know about Dolly's last boyfriend, if she didn't mind talking about it. Dolly shrugged. Leroy jumped in and said it was a postie. He'd asked Dolly out the day she retired. 2016. David Bowie had just died. The postie had asked Leroy's advice, having suddenly realised life was short. Leroy told him to go for it. Dolly dated him for a month.

'Yes, Derek was a lovely chap. We'd always enjoyed a nice chat when he delivered my letters. But like with the other men I've briefly dated, as I've got older, the chemistry wasn't there.'

'Did you never want to get married?' Flo pushed.

'Only once. When I was young. That was the one long relationship I've had but it didn't work out. He was called Fred. You don't decide you want to get married and then it happens, you see… it's all about meeting the right person. And for me, whether

I like it or not... it's always been Fred.' Dolly had never admitted that to herself before.

'Whereas for some people there's more than one soulmate out there,' said Leroy. 'I want to get back with Tony, but perhaps I'd still be with Charlie if he hadn't moved back to the States.'

'Charlie was fun,' said Flo and she grinned. 'I was only small but remember him kneeling on the floor and pretending to be a rodeo bull whilst I sat on top.'

'Charlie knew how to have a laugh, for sure,' said Dolly. 'He was a great dancer, too, just like Fred.'

'Like Fred Astaire, a famous dancer,' suggested Leroy, and he got to his feet, swirling around, gyrating his body. With a comment about grown-ups being embarrassing, Flo took out the Guide badge book. The next stage was to consider how she communicated her brand and how different aspects of her life showcased it.

'I guess I like practical clothes, and I like pop music but am more a fan of wildlife soundtracks – bees buzzing, whale song. There's a brilliant app my science teacher told me about, it's called Nature Noises.'

Whilst Leroy tackled the washing-up, Dolly read the badge book. 'It says to think about the language you use to communicate your brand, when speaking to different groups of people, to put together lists of words and phrases. How do you chat to your friends about bugs?'

'You already know that, Dolly,' said Flo. 'I talk about all the fun stuff. How violin beetles are shaped like violins.' Flo mimed playing that instrument. 'How caterpillars are awesome as they have twelve eyes.' She made her eyes bulge. 'How bonkers it is that butterflies taste with their feet.' She held her nose. 'And how slugs can stretch to almost twenty times their length, like a piece of chewing gum.' She extended her arms into the air.

'So you make jokes, use vivid comparisons and hand gestures, and your face, to express your enthusiasm. You choose descriptive words like awesome and bonkers...'

Flo jotted everything down.

'Next, teachers... Do you communicate your brand to them in the same way? Or are they a different audience?'

'Hey, this sounds like a business meeting,' said Leroy, drying his hands on a tea towel.

'Welcome to Guides, boring as office work,' muttered Flo in a monotone voice, yet her eyes had lit up as she scribbled. With her teachers she talked about how, say, cockroaches were more like termites than beetles, how they were such survivors because their bodies could last for ages without food or water. She enjoyed talking to Mrs Johnson who knew loads about bugs, and agreed with Flo they shouldn't be called creepy-crawlies, because insects weren't scary and did a whole lot more than crawling. Flo put the end of the pen in her mouth, concluding that she communicated her brand in a more... grown-up way, with facts and figures, like how in its lifetime a ladybird would probably eat around five thousand insects. And Flo might show her teachers a picture she'd done.

'I love flicking through your sketch book,' said Dolly, 'so that's another way you communicate your brand, through drawing.'

'What about with your mum and dad?' asked Leroy as he sat down again.

Flo snorted. 'I avoid talking about bugs with them. My parents hate insects because of their work; daddy long-legs especially freak my mum out. Dad goes mad if flies get into the kitchen, and he uses naughty words if they find a cockroach at one of the offices they're cleaning. I've got nothing in common with my parents apart from an obsession with banana cake. But that makes sense because recently I worked out that they've been lying to me about something really big...'

'Go on,' said Dolly gently.

Flo paused then rolled her lips together.

Flo used to keep secrets when she was younger, too, like when she was five she went through a phase of hiding objects such as the TV remote control. Dolly and Greta cottoned on it was because she enjoyed pretending to help them look for it, so they'd play along whilst she giggled. However, Dolly had a feeling that this latest secret was something much more significant.

'You've never shared your expert knowledge about insects with your mum and dad?' Leroy asked.

'What's the point?'

'Open up to them a bit, love... as if you are speaking to your teacher, then they might understand it's a serious interest,' said Dolly. Her phone buzzed and she reached into her coat pocket. Her pulse quickened as she showed the message to Flo. 'Well I never, Wednesday's lunch is on.' Dolly had so many questions after meeting Phoebe. Why was a martial arts day so challenging for *someone like her*? And parts of the notebook didn't make sense since finding out Phoebe was so young, like how could some of her friends have already passed? 'If I'm brave enough to face this Phoebe again, missy, you've got what it takes to dazzle your parents with insect facts.'

20

Steve winked across from the bar and Dolly tentatively raised her glass of wine, surrounded by chatting voices and the bustle of food being brought out of the kitchen. The pub suited Steve, with its welcome sign over the entrance, the shelves of board games, the cheerful music playing in the background. It had a brickwork interior with hanging artificial ivy, a wooden floor and solid rectangular tables. It was down-to-earth, practical, despite its high-end bistro feel. Dolly had slipped into a newly washed polka-dot jumper and slacks free from stains. Also, she'd come straight from the hairdresser's – her salt-and-pepper roots were blonde again. The split ends had been cut away, the layers spruced up. Dolly had forgotten how a good hair day could lift spirits. Greta had sworn by a shampoo and set, every week, and when she walked out of the salon, for a few seconds, she looked more like the Greta from Dolly's childhood. Dolly had said as much to her stylist this morning, the one she'd ignored in the park a while back.

Steve pushed a drink that looked like lemonade towards Phoebe, who picked up a menu and strode over. Dolly reached down, under the table, to her rucksack and checked she'd brought her tea flask.

'We'd better choose from the snack menu, it'll be quicker. My boss is tight about breaks and will kick up a fuss if I'm a minute late.' Phoebe brushed strands of hair out of her face, sat down and took off her sporty fleece revealing a dark green shirt with a logo that read *Lymhall Pets*. Dolly ordered a three-cheese platter with baguette on the side, then changed it to a wholemeal ham salad sandwich. Phoebe did the same but in reverse.

Looking flustered, Steve came over, promising to put their order through as quickly as possible. Two members of staff had handed their notice in yesterday, so he was short-staffed. Graduates, both of them. He was pleased they'd found the jobs of their dreams, but it had taken Steve long enough to find them. Getting new staff was harder than ever. He suggested Phoebe might prefer to work with humans.

'They're too undomesticated for me, sorry,' said Phoebe, and she downed half her drink.

'Busy morning?' asked Dolly.

'Nothing I'm not used to,' she said, without making eye contact. 'A stock delivery – compressed hay, dog and cat food... and this afternoon we've got new fish tanks arriving.'

'You sell actual pets?'

'Only fish. For everything else we direct customers to animal shelters. How many have you got?'

'Only Maurice.'

Phoebe met Dolly's gaze. 'On his own?'

'No, he's got me. So... you live with your granddad?' Dolly asked swiftly.

She folded her arms. 'What of it?'

'Nothing. I lived with my sister my whole life. Family's important.'

The lines between Phoebe's arched eyebrows softened. 'I dropped out of university a couple of years ago, when my second year ended in the June. I spent almost twelve months after that... dealing with stuff. I mean... I had some therapy,' she mumbled.

Then Phoebe began her year of firsts at the end of last spring, in the May. She talked about university loans and how her granddad had helped with costs. As she started to get better, thanks to the counselling, Phoebe wanted to start earning and got her part-time position. Now she worked Wednesdays, Fridays and Saturdays.

Dolly tried to read Phoebe's appearance – she looked so healthy, so together. But then, many people suffered from invisible illnesses. Perhaps she was depressed or something had happened to give her post-traumatic stress.

'Have you lived in Lymhall long?' Dolly asked.

'Granddad and Gran moved here when they got married.'

'What about your parents?' It was out before Dolly could stop it.

'I've lived with my grandparents for as long as I can remember,' Phoebe said abruptly. 'Isn't it enough that you've read my private notebook? Why all the questions as well?'

'Sorry. I'm out of practice – you know, talking to people. It's hard to offend a goldfish.' Cheeks flushed, Dolly picked up one of the colourful napkins Steve had put down and ran a finger over the picture of half a sun above a horizon. 'My situation hasn't been that different. I've lived with Greta for most of my life and moved back after a difficult time too, after being let down badly, in the seventies.'

'A man?'

She explained about Fred. All the plans they'd made. The proposal, the trip to Paris – and how he'd up and left out of the blue for greener pastures.

'That Fred sounds like a right selfish bastard.'

'That's what Greta always thought – without the B word. She didn't swear, ever... What about you?'

'Granddad's always telling me off for using the F word, so I only use it now in the most extreme circumstances.'

'No. I mean, this last year. Was it to do with a boyfriend? If you don't mind me asking?'

She looked away. Their meals arrived. The two women stared at their plates. Then at each other's.

Dolly sighed. 'I'm on a health-kick.'

'Me too,' said Phoebe and she picked up her fork. She pushed the lumps of cheese around before she took a deep breath, broke off a chunk and put it into her mouth.

Dolly had never heard of a cheese diet.

'The ring in the trunk is so beautiful, the way the pearl is set inside a ring of diamonds,' said Dolly.

'It belonged to my gran's mother. I only wear it if I'm going somewhere special. I'm so grateful to have it back.' She ate another small mouthful of cheese. 'The July challenge, last year, was to keep a gratitude journal for a month. I never thought I'd manage it but persevered. It taught me to appreciate the small things like a beautiful sunrise or friendly smile from a customer.'

'I'd love to hear more about your year of firsts,' said Dolly, unable to bear another minute of the silence that fell as they each forced down their meals. 'I was scared stiff at the balloon debate and can't believe I put myself through speed-dating. You're so brave.'

'The notebook was the idea of my friend, Maisie, who reckons the worst pain, on death, would be from regrets. Despite her having travelled far and wide, despite having children, I get the impression Maisie has several *if onlys*. Swimming has been the worst one so far.'

'It's been the easiest for me,' said Dolly. 'Water is so... freeing.'

'Don't you feel... exposed?'

'As Greta used to say, you come into this world naked; we're our true selves when swimming.' When having sex, too, not that Greta would ever have said that. Dolly pictured Fred, how under the covers, with him, she used to feel more like the inner Dolly that not everyone else saw. 'Why have you found it the hardest challenge so far?'

Phoebe took a moment. 'I don't like... being the centre of attention, and at a pool everyone in the water looks to see who is coming out of the changing room. In fact, I don't like people looking at me at all, even with my clothes on. It's why I hardly left the house for so long.'

Steve came back with steaming coffees, each with a biscuit on the side. Having only eaten half the sandwich so far, Dolly tore open the plastic packet and ate the Biscoff rectangle in one go. Phoebe stared at hers for a moment, before opening it and nibbling a corner. Dolly glanced at the clock above Steve's bar. Fifteen minutes left.

'You said in the introduction to your notebook that you needed change, that you'd been hiding away, like you've just said... I could have written that. I suppose that's one reason I took on the challenges. You see... my sister died, the year before last.'

'Oh. That's crap.'

'I shut myself away for a good twelve months.'

'Did...' Phoebe paused. 'Did hiding away help? Did anyone try to intervene?'

'At first. Then the visits tailed off. It didn't bother me. I'd stopped replying to texts and calls. But I've come to realise how my close neighbours were superstars. Little Flo next door with her chatter that made a change from the television. She didn't worry about the mess, didn't expect entertaining conversation. Same with Leroy on the other side. Is your granddad like that?'

Dolly took a mouthful of coffee, for one moment stepping back from the scene, looking at herself out socialising – lunching with someone who'd felt like a friend through the notebook, in the way characters did when you read a story. Dolly had actually got out, drunk wine and made conversation. How had this happened?

'When things were really bad he gave little nudges.'

Dolly pulled a face. 'Sounds like Leroy. I used to put my earbuds in.'

Phoebe smiled. 'I've lost a lot of friends. Like you, I stopped replying to messages. I don't blame them for giving up.'

'I thought you were middle-aged... You mentioned, in the notebook, that not all of your friends had made it to your age, but you're only—'

'Twenty-two.'

'You said that dropping out, after doing the second year of your French degree, felt like "a lifetime ago".'

'It does.'

Time was funny like that. Some years dragged, others raced. Now and again Dolly still made tea for two, as if Greta had only been gone a few hours.

'Did something happen? Were those friends in an accident?'

Phoebe's face hardened.

'Sorry. There I go again.' Dolly cleared her throat. 'Right, I'd better settle the bill. Thanks for meeting me. Good luck with the next challenge. I'm grateful for having done a few.' She told Phoebe more about the deal she'd made with Flo and how her young neighbour was going to miss the excitement of finding out the next month's first. Phoebe couldn't help laughing over the practice speed dates.

'You're a great role model, Phoebe Goodbody, and this Maisie must be a good friend.' Dolly held out her hand.

A pained expression crossed Phoebe's face before she slipped her fingers into Dolly's. Dolly went to get up but Phoebe didn't let go.

'The next one is going to be even harder. It might... I mean, only if you want... it's no big deal... but it would make it easier to see someone else suffer as well.' Dimples appeared.

'It's not wild swimming is it? I once got bitten by a crab.' It was on one of the weekends she and Fred had gone to Blackpool. He'd been more upset than her.

'Do you watch bake-off programmes on telly?'

'Greta and I used to. When she was alive I enjoyed baking, although the taste was always more important than the appearance, to me. I would never have the patience to make a showstopper that took four hours.' Although pride flowed through Dolly when she thought of the knack she used to have for turning out tasty cakes, biscuits and pies. Dolly's baking never failed to make Greta close her eyes and utter a heartfelt sigh of delight.

She hadn't baked without her sister around. What was the point for one person?

'My gran was a huge fan, a prolific baker and always tried to get me into the kitchen to help her out,' said Phoebe. 'But I only bought ready-made stuff at university. Maisie read about a bake-off experience in the Trafford Centre and we both reckoned my gran would have loved me to take part. It's popular for hen parties, birthday celebrations, for team-building exercises. The ticket includes all the ingredients. You bake in pairs.' Phoebe twisted the bobble on one of her plaits. 'Five pairs are given the same recipe and two hours to complete it. Then they sit down for afternoon tea, eating what they've made, trying everyone else's... The winners get a trophy and their tickets refunded.'

'Me? Go in for a bake-off?' Dolly clenched her teeth. 'I'm not sure I could make a cake rise, these days.'

'I'm not keen either. I don't mind making a fool of myself baking but... for other reasons, this is more of a challenge than speed-dating, a balloon debate or heading to Paris on my own. Even more scary than swimming.'

Dolly had thought meeting Phoebe would answer all her questions but it had only thrown up more.

'When is it?' Dolly asked.

'The middle of April. Thursday the fourteenth. I booked it months ago. It's the day before Good Friday.'

To Dolly's surprise, Greta used to enjoy visiting the Trafford Centre, with the extravagant decor, the Roman pillars, the palm trees, the massive food hall built around a steam ship. Everything about the place was over the top, but Greta would say going there was more like a holiday than just a trip to a shopping centre. And being under cover, it became practical with the wheelchair. Dolly used to like people-watching and missed their visits. And the Lindt chocolate shop had the most amazing pick 'n' mix counter.

'I suppose I could drive...' Dolly said.

A wide smile crossed Phoebe's face.

'Blimey, our kid,' cut in a gravelly voice. 'I'd almost forgotten what a good investment those dental braces were. Now, introduce me, lass, to the wonderful lady who returned your notebook.'

Phoebe rolled her eyes and pulled out a chair as a man approached in shoes that looked well polished but not especially stylish. Dolly lifted her head to the khaki parka. 'Give over, Granddad. What are you doing here?'

'Taking an interest in my granddaughter's life. No law against that is there? I also fancied a stroll and lunchtime pint. If you can't do that in your retirement, it's a sad old life.'

'Same as usual, Wilfred?' called Steve from behind the bar.

The man nodded and took off his flat cap. Dolly stared at the streaks of white in his hair, the strong nose slightly slanted to one side. She gripped the table as his smile flatlined.

'*Dolly?*' he said.

'Fred?' she whispered back.

Phoebe's jaw dropped. 'Holy fuck.'

21

Dolly tried to keep down a cup of tea but rushed to the bathroom as soon as she got home. She retched into the toilet – the ham sandwich was spent. As the letterbox rapped, she wiped her mouth and washed her hands. She took a moment in the hallway before opening the door, her dry, salty cheeks pulled tight, eyes swollen. Flo and Leroy stared as Dolly explained that she wasn't feeling too well and there was nothing much to report about meeting Phoebe, they'd simply chatted about the firsts, eaten, had coffee. Dolly suggested Flo went home, had tea and then popped back later to do more work on the Guide badge.

However, Flo remained on the doorstep and crossed her arms. 'Friends tell each other everything. You must have a bit of gossip.'

'We'll come back later,' said Leroy, gently, and went to steer Flo away.

Dolly paused and gestured for them to come in. They sat in their usual places in her lounge: Dolly on the sofa, Leroy in the armchair, Flo on the floor.

'Did she tell you about any of the other challenges?' asked Flo. 'Did you arrange to meet again?'

'Yes. One was filling in a gratitude journal for a month. And no, I had to leave quickly due to... this stomach upset.'

Leroy moved to the sofa and put an arm around Dolly. Flo left the room and came back, trying not to spill a tall glass of water. Dolly drank a few mouthfuls and Flo put it on the side table, next to the tea flask. She sat cross-legged on the floor again and looked up expectantly.

Dolly reached for Leroy's other hand, on his lap. 'He was there. He's her granddad.' Dolly's voice wavered. 'All this time he's been living in Lymhall.'

Flo hugged her knees. 'Who?'

Dolly's breath hitched. 'Fred.'

'*Your* Fred?' Leroy let go of her hand and turned to face her. 'The one who buggered off all those years ago?'

'If you don't mind, I can't face talking about it at the moment. I need to...'

'Digest it? It's like when Dad eats garlic. It keeps him up all night but by the morning he's fine.' Flo stared for a few moments and then jumped up. 'That quiz show's on that you like. I don't have to go back home until half-past five.' Flo passed Leroy the remote control and sat the other side of Dolly, snuggling up like she used to, when she was a toddler.

Sitting in between them took Dolly back. It was that day after Fred proposed, in the afternoon, a Saturday, she'd done overtime at Hackshaw Haulage. That morning, when she'd rushed around to Greta's, Dolly had been bursting with talk of Paris. Said the wedding wouldn't be for a couple of years but they were going to have one last splurge before settling down to save. Dolly rang Greta again, later in the afternoon, but she'd only just got back, in a bad mood after her church meeting, said it had overrun and she had a headache. At six o'clock, wearing the lipstick Fred especially liked on her beaming mouth, Dolly had called at his flat for dinner, as arranged.

Dolly leaned into the memory and it filled her with emptiness. She could picture Fred's landlord now, the tie-dye top and long hair. In between puffs of pot he'd explained Fred had moved out, packing as quickly as he could, a couple of hours before. He'd left no forwarding address and hadn't even asked for his deposit back. The landlord didn't think much of it, tenants came and went. As long as they paid their rent and didn't mess up his salamander bathroom, he didn't ask any questions. Fred had left behind his velvet-upholstered turquoise cocktail chair, and the smoked-glass coffee table he'd been so proud of. Turned out, he was moving far away from Manchester. There were no mobile phones back then. She had no way of contacting him. He'd grown up in children's homes and had no known relatives. In floods of tears she'd visited Greta. Dolly had moved out of her sister's place when she'd got her job, craving independence, loving a flatshare with women her own age. But suddenly Dolly felt so alone.

To her surprise, their mum had been making a rare visit. She didn't look well. At the time Dolly and her sister hadn't known she had cancer. Dolly told them about Fred and the three of them sat squashed on Greta's small sofa, Dolly in the middle. It was the only memory she had of her mother holding her hand, as an adult, and wanting to know all the details.

'Mark my words, Dorothy, you're better off without men,' she had said. 'I've given up looking for Mr Right. Only ever found Mr Left. Left me once he'd had what he wanted. Left me if money got tight. Left me if a prettier, younger woman came along. Left me because he was scared of settling down. Your father was the worst.' She and Greta had exchanged glances. They often did that.

That evening was the only time Dolly could remember her mother taking a close interest in her. She'd been such a vague presence throughout her childhood. Her mum said Dolly should move back in with her sister. Forget Fred, forget romance, forget naive ideas about marriage. Greta agreed and a couple of weeks later took Dolly on holiday to Margate. The sea breeze blew away any remaining doubts. Dolly's new life would not be one of romance.

After the quiz show, Leroy and Flo left. Dolly sat on the sofa and stared at Maurice. An ugly expression had crossed Phoebe's face when she'd heard Dolly only kept one goldfish. She didn't understand how the relationship between Dolly and Maurice was special. He'd swim excitedly to and fro if she went near the tank's lid, and if she ran her hand around the glass he'd often follow it. Yet seeing Fred again took Dolly back to the days of having a companion with lots in common. Someone who understood your wants and needs, your hopes and humour, the reason you liked mashed-up bananas on toast or didn't mind losing at darts. Whereas Dolly would never understand why Maurice sometimes ate his poop, and likewise he'd dart to the bottom of his tank if she sneezed loudly, not understanding that noise wasn't a threat.

With a shudder, she knelt by the tank.

'I thought Greta and I were enough for you,' her voice croaked. 'But now I realise what you've been missing all these years. I'm sorry, little chap. How lonely you must have been, especially during hours in the dark.' Those nights when she had laid alone in bed, wishing the other side of the mattress was occupied with comforting arms and soft words, with lips that erased problems of the real world, Maurice had probably been doing the same, floating in water that only moved if he did.

Tail swishing from side to side, he swam up to the glass. They stared at each other for several minutes, both with water in their eyes.

Dolly stood outside the bottle-green shopfront. She'd intended on visiting this morning but talked herself out of it. It was now half-past four, thirty minutes until the shop closed. A bell rang as she pushed the door. Dolly inhaled the smell of wood shavings and algae. The room was crammed with stacks of hay and sawdust, with colourful pet toys, food bowls, hamster cages, and leashes. To the left was a row of tropical aquariums with lights on, and the sound of bubbling water relaxed her. Each tank was home to a different type of fish. As she walked along she finally came to an unlit one at the end, home to several that looked like cold-water fish, like Maurice, except with large patches of white as well as the gold. A till drawer slammed shut behind her. Phoebe said she was in on Fridays. Dolly could have come on a different day. It was too late now.

Phoebe looked up as the other customer left. She came out from behind the counter. The weather was warmer today and Dolly had put on the berry-red jacket she used to wear for work.

'I... didn't know whether to text you,' said Phoebe. 'How are you doing? I had no idea... Granddad has hardly spoken since Wednesday.'

'No change there, then. He left without a word all those years back. But he's not the reason I'm here.'

'I'd not heard him be called Fred before. Gran called him Will.'

'He once told me that he used to get called Wilfred by the staff when he was in care. Secretly he always wanted to have someone special in his life who'd care enough to shorten it.' Dolly didn't know why she was telling Phoebe this, as if Phoebe didn't know her grandfather better than her. 'I was a bit older than you when he disappeared. People got married younger in those days. I knew straight away he was the man I'd settle down with. Or thought I did.'

That was one reason she'd agreed with her mother and Greta, about giving up on romantic notions. Oh, most of the men she'd dated over the years were decent, but as well as the spark missing, something always held her back. Fred had proved how easy it was to make a mistake. Not a mistake like in maths where you simply got marked down, or a mistake with the wash where a white shirt might come out pink. Mistakes of the heart left an indelible mark that couldn't be erased with a rubber or bleach. They made you question and doubt and hate yourself, even though the damage wasn't your fault. That was why she'd woken up yesterday and decided the best option was to pretend seeing him in the pub had never happened. Leroy had come around last night with a bottle of wine and they hadn't talked about Fred. She'd spent the day cleaning the kitchen; now it matched the lounge in terms of order and cleanliness. She needed another trip to IKEA, very much liking her new additions to the lounge, like the neat storage boxes, one for post and stationery, another for old magazines and cut-out coupons, and the cerise throw to cover her stained rose-pink sofa – and the artificial succulent plant that graced the windowsill and added life to the room. Last week, in Knutsmere, she'd bought a plastic-leaf fern for Maurice's tank. The interior design of his home was no less important than hers. She couldn't help smiling when he'd tried to eat it.

'I'm here to find a friend for Maurice.'

Knutsmere pet shop didn't sell livestock and Dolly didn't fancy carrying a bag of water back on the train from Manchester. Plus she trusted that Phoebe would sell her a healthy fish. The last thing Maurice needed was to find a partner and then have it ripped away from him. Dolly knew how that felt. Nothing had amused her last year when she'd stayed inside fending off company, not even Maurice's antics. That was the only thing worse than losing a loved one – losing your zest for life.

Losing yourself.

Had Maurice lost his way over the years, even though his surroundings hadn't changed, swimming to and fro with only Dolly's face and the beat of the Bee Gees for company? For a second she closed her eyes, unable to bear the sense that she'd let him down.

'What made you decide?' asked Phoebe, the tips of her ears reddening.

'I realised a mermaid statue wasn't enough company for him. Fish might not have the powers of make-believe, like children do with toys.' Or like Dolly did with daydreams. The first years after Fred left she'd spent sleepless nights imagining their reunion. There'd be tears. Apologies. A fancy, candle-lit dinner. She'd never imagined a ham sandwich and a granddaughter. 'Not that I think fish are unintelligent and as Flo pointed out, even if the mermaid were real, Maurice might have preferred a merman and...'

'I don't know about that... although I did read an interesting article once, about how less impressive, smaller males flirt with the bigger ones because that behaviour makes them more attractive to the opposite sex.' She stood next to Dolly and pointed. 'Do you think he'd like to meet any of these beauties?'

Dolly peered forward. 'I like that one at the back, with the white underbelly. Can you tell if it's a boy or girl?'

Phoebe's face appeared right next to Dolly's. 'There are various ways of sexing goldfish. See the pectoral fins? The ones at the front. They're a bit short and stubby. Whereas in males they are longer and thinner. What are Maurice's like?'

Dolly stood up straight again. 'Yes, his are slimmer.'

'I think she's a bit older than the others.'

That would suit him, then. Dolly asked what the best way of introducing her to the tank would be. She'd investigated online this morning and already knew she'd have to acclimatise her to the water temperature first by floating her plastic bag in the tank. What if Maurice attacked? He was a gentle soul but... well... Dolly wouldn't appreciate a stranger suddenly turning up in her lounge. Dolly wanted to get it right.

Phoebe offered to help. No, she wasn't going out, even though it was Friday night. So Phoebe held the goldfish bag whilst Dolly drove them to Pingate Loop in silence. Dolly made a brew and they floated the bag in the top of the tank, adding the tank's water to it, bit by bit. Maurice darted to and fro underneath. There was a chance he might chase the new fish, or the other way around. It was a territorial thing.

'Right,' said Phoebe. 'Do you want to do it? Tip the bag gently sideways so that she can swim out and then all we can do is watch out for signs of aggression.'

Palms sweaty, Dolly held the plastic. 'There you go, Fanny.' She held her breath as the white-and-gold fantail slid into the tank, before flapping her fins as she neared Maurice. He shot away and went downwards, towards his bridge, hovered for a second and then went back up. Talk about a face-off. However, their top fins were upright – Dolly always took that as a good sign. The two fish weren't chasing each other or biting. In fact, they aligned side by side.

'Do you think I've done the right thing?' mumbled Dolly. 'He is very set in his ways.'

'Even titanium melts if the temperature is hot enough, and Fanny looks pretty hot to me.'

Phoebe and Dolly exchanged smiles.

'The name suits her, by the way.'

'Maurice is named after one of the Bee Gees, it's his favourite band. "Fanny (Be Tender With My Love)" is one of their tracks.'

Fred hadn't been tender with Dolly's love. The letterbox rapped and provided a welcome distraction. Flo grinned hello, side-stepping as an evening breeze rocked her ginger ponytail.

'I saw Phoebe,' Flo hissed. 'It's her, right? Can I come in? Pleeease?'

Dolly opened the door wider and gave Flo a sharp look as she forgot to wipe her feet. Flo went back to the doormat, scraped her school shoes across them and then slipped them off. She lolloped into the lounge.

'Isn't Maurice handsome?' said Flo and knelt on the carpet. 'I especially love how he always...' She gasped. 'Who's that?'

'Flo, it's Phoebe. She works in a pet shop.'

'No, silly. In the tank.' Flo pressed her nose against the glass. She turned to face Phoebe. 'I'm Flo, Dolly's best friend – apart from Leroy.' She gave Dolly a pointed look. Dolly nodded. Flo gazed at Fanny, then Phoebe again, who left to use the bathroom. 'All these new faces. Dolly, please can we invite Anushka too? I've told her how cool this place is, with the tree out the back, with your conservatory, with Maurice. Can I ask her around at the weekend to prepare for the final bit of our badge? Her mum says it's okay if you agree. You have the best snacks.'

'So, missy, did you forget your manners and already ask her before me?'

Flo grinned again. 'It's ages since you've told me off. You must be getting better. I'll do your washing-up for a week or help with the ironing, if you agree.'

Phoebe appeared and hung at the lounge's doorway. 'I should get going.'

Flo wouldn't hear of it. Phoebe needed to try Dolly's pink biscuits and help work out how Maurice was going to make friends with Fanny. Flo charged into the kitchen to fill the kettle, suggesting they give the fish peas as they might bond over Maurice's favourite treat. He looked so happy; Dolly wasn't imagining it. His body swayed with the grace of a ballroom dancer and every now and then he swooped down to pick at the gravel, like he always did when the record player crooned 'How Deep Is Your Love'.

'Please, stay,' said Dolly to Phoebe. 'I don't think I can bear Flo's excitement, on my own, if she finds out you and I are entering a bake-off competition.'

23

'What's an elevator pitch?' asked Flo, studying the Guides book. She looked at Anushka, who shrugged.

Last week on Tuesday, outside the church hall whilst they were waiting to pick up the girls, Anushka's mum had told Dolly her daughter liked Guides a lot more since Flo had started going. Anushka's family had moved to Knutsmere during Dolly's year... inside. That made her sound as if she'd been in prison – a good description. Until recently being locked away had offered reassurance and security, but Phoebe's notebook had reignited a desire for more. So Anushka's family didn't know about Greta. Not first-hand, anyway – her dad did know Mark; they were both members of the local gym.

'For the last part of this badge we've got to tell the story of our brand in a quick way that' – Flo read from the book – '"makes a lasting impression".' She and Anushka sat at Dolly's kitchen table. The aroma of a Sunday roast filled their nostrils, Leroy humming as he peeled carrots.

Dolly explained 'elevator' was the American word for 'lift', her chest full and warm as the she and the two girls relaxed in her kitchen, with its gleaming surfaces and folded piles of laundered tea towels. This time last year she was three months into living alone, without Greta, the clutter and mess acting as company. Yet this recent orderliness and space didn't feel empty because her life was now filled with Flo's adventure of going to Guides and Leroy's love life, with Maurice and his new girlfriend Fanny, and with Phoebe and her monthly challenges.

She didn't include Fred.

Fighting off a headache, Dolly suppressed a yawn, having not slept properly since that lunch with Phoebe in the Rising Sun. 'A pitch is a persuasive speech you give to get people interested in whatever you're doing – to really grab their attention. Imagine stepping into a lift. Your speech shouldn't last longer than it takes to travel to the floor you want.'

Flo raised her eyebrows. 'I'd have to choose a floor at the top.'

'It's why your pitch has to really focus on the important elements.'

'To kick off, why not draw up a list of words to do with your brand?' suggested Leroy.

Gill said they could record their pitch on their phones and play it next week, if nerves took over at the prospect of talking in front of everyone. Flo stuck out her tongue as she concentrated hard, writing a list of words on a notepad. By the time the chicken was ready, both girls had a rough draft. After the last mouthful of apple crumble, they helped clear the table then snuck into the lounge to check on Maurice and Fanny. When Flo and Anushka returned they wouldn't let Dolly help with their pitches, wanting their speeches to be a surprise. So Dolly wrote a pitch about her own branding instead.

Anushka went first and the others applauded – she'd given her speech in a sing-song tone that suited her words about music and lyric writing. She didn't want a video made, confident that at least Flo would clap at Guides if no one else did. However, Flo did want filming. Just in case. She stood up, holding the notepad in front of her. Dolly positioned Flo's phone and then counted down from five with fingers, mouthing *go* when she got to one.

'Without insects we'd be dead. They break down poop and are food for animals. They also pollinate, are designers and are faster than Olympians. Like the Darwin's bark spider whose web is twenty-five metres wide, and the tiger beetle that runs at nine kilometres an hour. I will never stop watching and learning their ways. My life is going to be spent working busier than an ant, studying insects. Who knows, they might be able to fix climate change. Think of that next time you step on an ant or kill a spider. I love Ed Sheeran and Ariana Grande, but insects are the real rockstars of the future.'

Leroy clapped. 'Brilliant. You go, girl!'

'Dad killed a fly with a newspaper yesterday,' said Anushka. 'I'm going to tell him it was like murdering his favourite singer, Chris Martin.'

'Also tell him flies clean up waste. Help dead things rot. It's not their fault if they think poop smells like pizza.' Flo took back her phone. 'Now it's your turn, Dolly.'

She stood up and glanced at the sheet of paper Flo had torn out of her notebook for her. Thanks to doing her speech at the balloon debate, Dolly's pulse didn't race. She smiled at the other three and smoothed down her jumper. 'Life is like a pickpocket, slyer than a violent criminal, it steals things without you even realising, like that sense of knowing who you are. So, refreshing the lounge, trying new recipes, even speed-dating, I'm prepared to face any challenge. You see, self-discovery is my thing. It's never too late to work out the next *me*. That could be life's plan all along. Nature goes through cycles, wilting, regenerating. Why should humans be any different?'

Leroy listened intently.

'That's so cool – and true,' said Flo. 'Like the daffodils in our garden. The flowers disappear after a couple of months but come back the next year in bigger numbers. What about you, Leroy? You said, before, that your brand was a bit like Dolly's; that your changes meant going mini... minimalist, taking the colour out of your lounge, and trying to get into smaller clothes... What would your pitch be?'

'Dolly's hoping to find herself, whereas I'm hoping to find love. I know where I want it from, and to be a better fit I need to be a different person.'

'Leroy split up from his boyfriend, Tony, but is trying to win him back,' explained Flo to Anushka.

He thought it was working. Last Thursday he'd posted a photo Dolly took of him in his new chinos and dark green leather jacket. Tony had liked the post, then messaged him, saying Leroy's outfit looked great. Dolly did her best to smile as Leroy spoke about how it was early days, but he was going to ask Tony to meet up for a drink in a sophisticated bar he'd found online, called The Alchemist, in Spinningfields. It served drinks with fog bubbles on top and jelly shots. Tony was bound to be impressed. Boring it was not.

Anushka put down her biro. 'No one at my school liked me when we first moved here last year. My ears aren't pierced and my shoes are sensible, and their parents are always buying them stuff. One girl's got a pony. Whereas I have to do chores, and I don't mind not having much pocket money 'cos I like spending time with Granny – anyway, going to the Arndale shopping is boring. But I begged Mum to let me get earrings for my last birthday, even though I was afraid it would hurt, so that the girls in my class would like me more. And fancy trainers they all had, with wheels on the bottom, even though I was worried about falling over.'

'What happened?' asked Flo.

'Granny told me the most important thing is being yourself, because otherwise it's all pretending and that's not living, it's hard work, like a twenty-four-hour job. She said I should only ever change for *me*, not for anyone else.'

Leroy stared at Anushka before lifting his cup to his lips, even though Dolly knew he'd finished his coffee.

Anushka drew a heart on the table with her finger and talked about her great-uncle, her granny's brother; he'd always been shy but, in his twenties, pretended to be louder and went to parties the whole time. Her granny said that make-believe was exhausting and always ended badly. It got you in the end and got her great-uncle; he became really ill and had to go to AA to get better.

'AA?' asked Flo.

'Dunno what it is, Granny didn't explain.' She looked at Leroy. 'AA sounds like a good place but you'd miss Dolly and Flo, wouldn't you, and the flight there could be expensive?'

'Talking of travel,' said Dolly speedily, 'has Flo talked to you about the notebook I found in a piece of lost luggage, Anushka, with the challenges in?'

'Yes! I love swimming.'

'The April challenge is to take part in a bake-off.' Dolly's stomach clenched at the thought. 'That's why I made apple crumble today, to practise. I want you three to act as judges.'

'Stop! A bake-off? You didn't tell me that!' Flo jumped up and floss-danced, whooping loudly.

'I've been waiting for the right moment,' said Dolly, and put her hands over her ears.

Anushka giggled and got up to join her friend. Dolly revelled in every laugh and move, knowing such lack of guile might disappear at high school next year. Leroy put down his coffee cup and his chair scraped back. Suddenly his favourite TV show was on. The girls sat down and talked about how *The Great British Bake Off* was one of their favourites, whilst Dolly took Leroy's arm and gave it a squeeze. He kissed her on the head and waved goodbye to the girls.

'Let me judge the crumble first,' said Flo. 'It had a soggy bottom.'

'It's meant to, silly,' whispered Anushka.

The girls rated the flavours and textures of the dessert, whilst Leroy stopped outside, in front of her garden, chatting to a dog walker. His middle bulged slightly over his tight trousers. He'd had his hair shaved closely at the sides – Dolly quite liked that. But it wasn't Leroy; he kept running his fingers across the tops of his ears, as if he missed the curls. When Fred first left, it had made Dolly question everything about herself. Was she not funny enough? Too talkative? Too curvy? But her mother had unwittingly taught her a lesson. How changing yourself to keep a partner was a pointless battle. Each time a man left, her mum would go on a diet, try a new perm, scrape together enough money for a new dress, but the ex never came back and the weight would go back on, and more than before. So, with Greta's help, Dolly accepted Fred wasn't for her.

The doorbell rang and Flo and Dolly saw Anushka to the door. Flo packed up her things.

'I'm not in the mood for the park today, but Mum and Dad insisted. They're obsessed with fresh air being the answer to everything – as long as it hasn't got insects in it.'

Dolly pulled her close for a hug and then gently pushed her away and met her gaze. 'Show them the video, sweetheart. Promise me that.'

Back in the kitchen, after Flo had left, Dolly dried the dishes. As she finished, the doorbell rang again. Her eyes dropped to Flo's pencil case on the kitchen table. Holding it in one hand, she opened the front door.

'You'll forget your head one of these days, sweetheart. Here—'

The case dropped on to the floor and pencils rolled across the carpet as Dolly stared at Fred.

24

Dolly picked up the pencils, dropping a couple in the process; she took her time before standing upright. As their eyes met again, time rolled back, taking with it his hearing aids, the wrinkles, the bushier eyebrows, until she was looking at the Fred she fell in love with – a Fred with thick, styled hair and designer labels, cigarette hanging sexily out of the side of his mouth. He used to be such a sharp dresser. A cocky bugger, too, according to Greta.

Fred was here. On her doorstep. Fate had brought them together in a different millennium. She wanted to run away and bury her head in a pillow, as the crushing pain his disappearance had caused ripped through her once more, along with precious romantic details she'd never dared think about for fear of falling into a spiral of sadness. Like the chocolate he'd buy her when she got her monthlies. How he'd always prepare her favourite Salt 'n' Shake crisps.

Now he was shaking his head. 'So it's true. We've been living close all these decades.'

'We're hardly neighbours and I've never had any reason to visit Lymhall. Greta always said the people there must be daft to spend that much on property.' She held on to the door. 'What exactly do you want?'

'I wouldn't say no to a hot drink.'

'You've got a nerve,' she snapped, annoyed that somehow she'd opened the door further.

'No pluck, no luck and... I'd be the luckiest lad in Manchester if you let me in to talk.'

'Lad? Hardly. Almost half a century has passed since we last met – or have you forgotten?' She'd been twenty-five in 1975, him three years older.

'I forget a lot these days... where I've put my glasses, what Phoebs said to me five minutes ago. But you? I've not forgotten one detail of our life together.' His voice was quiet. 'Looking good, Dolly.'

For the briefest of moments she felt as if she were in her twenties again.

'Whereas you look as if your exciting new life, away from Manchester, didn't bring the treasures you'd hoped for. What happened? Did you limp back with your tail between your legs?' It was as if his presence, after all these years, wrapped a tight band around her chest that constricted with every word they exchanged. 'What is there to discuss? It's history. Said and done.'

'I wanted to... I need to... fill in any gaps.'

'This is about easing your conscience?' Her voice wavered. 'Picture me, turning up to your empty flat. At first I imagined all horrors... that you'd lost the job you loved, that you had a terminal illness or had suffered, I don't know, a psychotic episode. But I'd already decided, in my head, that I'd stand by you, whatever it was.' She gave a hollow laugh. 'Then the landlord told me the truth – an opportunity you couldn't refuse had come your way.'

Fred lowered his gaze. 'Let's not discuss this out here. If I could come in and—'

'You think I care that the world hears how you left me wondering what was wrong with me? Was that opportunity a new job offering, a more exciting life, or another woman who was prettier, more successful?' Greta wouldn't approve of airing her distress in the street. The door swayed as she longed to close it in his face. Trouble was, curiosity infused her body like a powerful drug and she gave in. Dolly hung up his unremarkable parka – it would have never earned a place in his old wardrobe. She showed him into the lounge and, hands unsteady, Dolly filled the kettle. She moved the turquoise flask and reached for a tin. But he didn't deserve biscuits. *Come on, Dolly, get it together*, she told herself. When she entered the lounge, he was staring at the one dependable man in her life.

'That's Maurice – and his friend, Fanny.' She passed Fred his drink, not knowing what else to say. She didn't offer him sugar; in her experience a person's tea habits never changed, regardless of what life threw their way. Greta had drunk hers very milky with two sugars when she was eighteen and eighty-six, Dolly's had always been stronger. Tea was a constant in a world you couldn't rely on to stay the same.

'Maurice and Fanny,' he mumbled. 'The Bee Gees.'

They'd both loved 'Nights on Broadway', 'Massachusetts', all of that band's early disco top hits. When *Saturday Night Fever* came out at the end of the seventies, three years after Fred had disappeared, it had brought back all the memories of the afternoons the two of them had spent listening to LPs, slow dancing, kissing, both proud that the Bee Gees used to live down the road, in Chorlton. Dolly sat down in the armchair and pushed her back right into it.

'How have you been?' he asked, in that familiar gravelly voice.

'Fred... Will... whatever you go by now... I didn't invite you in for a great catch-up. You wanted to explain why you ditched me. You've got as long as it takes for us to finish our drinks.'

He flinched as she picked up hers and took a large mouthful, not caring that the liquid scalded her tongue. Courting had been a happy whirl of new experiences for Dolly; she'd never eaten out in the Chinese quarter before dating him, nor drunk a Harvey Wallbanger. She went to her first concert with Fred too, he bought tickets to see 10cc at the Hardrock nightclub in Stretford. She'd insist on paying for their cinema trips whenever she could afford them. He'd especially loved *The Sting* with Paul Newman. Fred worked hard as a salesman, in cameras when she first met him, then he moved to a new company that was at the forefront of the digital industry. A few months before they split up he'd been part of launching the first video game console. She'd been so excited playing Pong, the table-tennis game that by today's gaming standards was so simple. Greta could never understand the appeal, saying the crossword taxed her brain more. Fred enjoyed spending his commission, buying Dolly flamboyant bunches of peonies and boxes of Milk Tray chocolates, whereas she'd bake him his favourite pineapple upside-down cake.

Dolly put down her cup quickly; it clattered on the saucer. She'd blocked out these memories for so long, considering them a luxury to dwell on. In fact they were the opposite, as they left her feeling depleted. She stared stonily at him.

'Look, all this... it's been a shock for me too,' he muttered.

'How? It was your choice to scarper.'

'I wasn't given a choice.'

'What do you mean?'

He got up. 'After seeing you in the pub, I wasn't going to visit... and then Phoebs mentioned Greta had died.'

'That was over a year ago. I'm stronger now, so don't worry on my account,' she said, and folded her arms.

'No, what I mean is...' Fred walked up and down. His pace didn't betray his age; he always had been fit. It was tennis back in the day; he'd belonged to a fancy club. They had been to a winter ball there once. Fred had chatted with Mr Hackshaw, her boss; he'd sounded so confident, talking to him about his sales career and where he saw digital technology going. Occasionally, over the years, looking at her digital bedside clock had made her think of Fred, then the timely ring of the alarm would remind her that it didn't pay to look back at what might have been.

Fred stood still. 'I... needed time to sort myself out, before I could get back in touch. However that took a while and by then a few years had passed. From time to time I once again considered tracking you down and telling you the truth. But I couldn't do that, not with the possibility that Greta was still around. I knew you two were close.'

'You aren't making sense.'

'The afternoon after we got engaged' – his voice faltered – 'Greta visited my flat.'

No she didn't. Her sister had gone to a church meeting, the one that ran late and put her in a bad mood. Could Fred be senile? Was that why Phoebe had spent last year as a hermit – as well as having therapy, had she been looking out for her granddad?

'Greta warned me off. It's because of her I left. You see—'

'What a load of rubbish. In any case, Greta would have told me. We respected each other's privacy but shared everything important.' How dare he imply her principled sister had gone behind Dolly's back? 'There's no way she'd have kept something like that secret. Why on earth would she interfere? We both knew Greta wanted me to date a man in a more regular job' – Fred didn't work nine to five and his job took him away some weekends – 'but she always said it was up to me who I dated, that it was none of her business.'

Fred looked every second of his age. 'Dolly, listen, please, just for a minute. Greta said that if I didn't call off the engagement and leave, she'd—'

'Whoa.' Dolly held up her hand. 'You can stop that right there, Wilfred Taylor. Greta had a sharp tongue, but a good heart. She'd *never* threaten anyone. And threaten you of all people, when she knew we were planning a future together? It's pretty low that after finding out my sister is dead, you decide it's the perfect opportunity to blame her for the fact you couldn't commit, didn't even deem me worthy of an explanation or a goodbye. After you left Greta said she'd always thought you a chancer, and your visit today confirms her theory.' Dolly jumped up. 'I won't have my sister's name tarnished, especially when she's not here to defend herself.' She marched into the hallway and grabbed his parka off the hook, pushing it against his chest. She pulled open the front door. 'Don't contact me again.'

'She did visit, Dolly. I'm sorry. It's true. She came straight over from a church meeting because she'd found out that—'

With great satisfaction, Dolly got to slam that front door.

25

As she and Dolly walked along Pingate Road, on the way to Guides, for the umpteenth time Flo chatted happily about the elevator pitch she'd given at the meeting last week. She hadn't even used her video, and Dolly asked her to tell her again how some of the girls asked her afterwards about the big spider's web and fast tiger beetle. Her young neighbour's boosted self-esteem warmed Dolly' heart. Despite the setting of the sun, tepid spring rain had stolen the chill. Dolly hadn't told Flo or Leroy about Fred's visit the weekend before last. Yet she'd thought of little else as she'd completed the house's restoration back to how it was before Greta passed. Every room stood pristine and dust-free. Dolly had continued with small changes as well. At the weekend, after Dolly went swimming, she and Leroy had gone to IKEA again and she'd bought a new duvet set for her bed, and the lamp in the shape of a flamingo standing on one leg that she'd seen there before. Leroy also bought more sober sheets, to replace his vivid sets. Tony had agreed to meet him at the fancy bar in Spinningfields tomorrow.

'Aren't you jumping the gun?' Dolly had asked as he'd placed grey silk pillowcases into the trolley. Vigorously Leroy shook his head. Tony had signed off his last text with a kiss. Leroy also bought two velvet cushions, black trimmed with gold, Tony's favourite colour combination. Dolly had pushed him further. 'You heard what Anushka said about her uncle... Is it really worth pretending to be someone you aren't to get Tony back? Is being on your own for a while so bad? You weren't dating for a year or two before you met Charlie yet I don't remember you being unhappy. The same during the years between Charlie leaving and you meeting Tony, once you'd got over him going back to America.'

'It was different then. The future still seemed full of opportunities, but since I've retired and my seventies are looming... since visiting Jamaica, hearing stories about relatives who've passed, whom I've never met, and never will, it's made me realise life really is finite.' He'd shrugged with a dismissive air. 'Anyway, who's to say I'm pretending?'

Trouble was, Dolly knew that if you told a lie often enough, it felt like the truth. All these years she'd become the expert and not allowing herself to miss Fred, she'd done her best to rewrite her feelings and had accepted the ending, that she'd never wanted, to their story, insisting it was all for the best. But now he was back, she'd couldn't deny that there'd always been a part of her that hadn't accepted those lies.

Her thoughts shifted back to her own house and the one item in the kitchen that had stayed dirty since Fred visited. His cup stood on the kitchen unit, staring at her, proof that the unimaginable had happened, even though her first inclination, after he'd left, had been to throw it in the bin. The mould that had formed on his cup was a reminder of how poisonous his visit had been.

Phoebe had rung, apologising for giving her granddad Dolly's address. Fred had kept the details of what happened to himself and simply told her secrets were best kept in the past. But secrets were only secrets if they were based on the truth. Dolly had ended the call swiftly. She needed to put Fred firmly back in the past and that meant that he took Phoebe with him. At the thought of losing that growing friendship, a heaviness spread through Dolly's limbs. There would be no bake-off happening in April, not for Dolly.

'Tonight I'll find out if I've won my first badge,' said Flo, an arm linked through hers, a gesture Dolly treasured. She'd missed that closeness with Greta, even though, as her sister's arthritis had worsened, linking arms had been more out of necessity.

'Did you show your elevator pitch to your parents, like I suggested?' She hadn't liked to ask before, not wanting to make a big thing of it.

Turned out Flo had practised in front of them too. They'd clapped the first time she did it without messing up the words. Said it sounded good, and when she got back last Tuesday, from doing it for real, they asked what other bug facts Flo knew. Her mum nearly agreed cockroaches were amazing when Flo told her they had almost a million brain cells. As for the park trip they went on, Flo's parents declared she was very clever, recognising all the different species by remembering what she'd seen on the computer.

'I didn't tell you any of this,' said Flo, "cos I wanted to wait and see if they'd really changed, and today they asked if I'd like to visit Manchester Museum this weekend – an end-of-term treat. I've got two weeks off school from Friday. It's got a massive room full of insect displays. Also... I'm going to take my Promise and stay at Guides. But don't say I told you so,' she added and glared.

'I know you... held back because of your secret. Is that all sorted now too? You can always talk to me about it, you know.'

'It's okay... I've come to a decision.' She took a deep breath.

'I'm going to live with what they did. They might believe telling me the truth will hurt. And me questioning them might hurt them too. No one wins and I've decided that maybe it doesn't really matter.'

Flo reckoned some secrets were so small you forgot them, like hiding her lunchbox raisins. Whereas other secrets seem huge at first and you don't forget, but you might get used to them over time. Flo talked about that sound in the trees in the jungle, a kind of buzzing, a singing – well it was made by cicadas. They were a bit like grasshoppers and lived for ages underground, some for seventeen years. When they crawled out they didn't bite, didn't sting, some didn't even eat, they just searched for a partner, made babies and died. That had made Flo think... secrets could be like that. If they were kept hidden long enough, there was a chance they wouldn't hurt anyone if they ever came out.

They approached the church hall and Flo ran off to greet Anushka, turning to wave at Dolly before she disappeared through the side entrance to the building. Dolly smiled at Anushka's mum before turning to go. Edith approached in the opposite direction. She clutched a plastic bag to her bosom.

'Spare kettle,' she said. 'The one in the hall is playing up. I wouldn't want the Guides leaders to go without.'

'Can I ask you a question, Edith,' said Dolly. 'When we met at IKEA you mentioned that one time you and Greta agreed on something... the meeting about what parishioners should leave at gravesides.'

'What of it?'

'Could you tell me what time it finished? I... I've been going over that day in my head for other reasons and can't help fixating. You know what it's like when you live on your own, you mull over the past.'

Edith raised an eyebrow.

'Greta said the meeting went on longer than she thought it would...'

Edith took a few minutes. 'Only a little. It finished at half-past eleven. My husband and I always had a pub lunch out on a Saturday and that day was his birthday. He banned all talk about gravesides, said it was morbid, he was feeling old enough having turned twenty-six.'

Dolly frowned. 'Are you sure?'

'I'm not much older than you, Dorothy, I haven't lost my marbles yet,' she said curtly.

'No of course not, sorry. So... did she mention where she went after that?' Now and then Greta stayed after a meeting to mend pew cushions and choir robes, or to have coffee with other committee members.

'What's all this about?'

'I met an old... someone I used to know, recently, and they insist they spent the afternoon with her. But, like you, I distinctly recall that day and Greta telling me the meeting went on a bit and that's where she was. My mother visited that evening, you see, that didn't happen often and that's another reason why I've never forgotten. But I don't want to call this person a liar if they're right and I'm wrong.'

Edith broke eye contact. 'If Greta was lying, she must have had good reason.'

'Please. It's important.'

Edith hugged the bag tighter.

'You said Greta was emotional,' continued Dolly. 'I assumed that must have been because the meeting got heated.'

Edith snorted. 'A few strong words over church issues never bothered your sister, you should know that. We both told the other members of the committee exactly what we thought of them letting people litter the graveyard with all sorts of fripperies like mini fluorescent windmills.'

'What upset her, then?' Dolly shivered.

Edith put down the bag, as parents filed past, back to their cars. 'Greta broke down, if you must know. I wasn't sure what to do – your sister never was my cup of tea, and I wasn't hers. It was all a bit embarrassing. Everyone else had left and she was pacing up and down. She said her worst nightmare was coming true, about receiving bad news, she mumbled about a holiday that mustn't happen. All I know is that she was off to a confrontation that would cause a lot of hurt. Other stuff...' Edith cleared her throat. 'Greta was rambling.' She picked up the kettle again. 'After that day our relationship became even more prickly. I thought the opposite might have happened but I think she regretted opening up to me.' Edith went to go. 'I've never forgotten Greta's last words, about the Eighth Commandment that says not to "bear false witness", how it meant that as evil is opposite to good, so was lying to being honest – she reckoned it wasn't always that straightforward, that sometimes lies were better than the truth.' A tide of red rose up Edith's neck as she gave a clipped smile and hurried away.

26

Dolly didn't see the woman outside her bungalow who wore joggers and headphones; a hand on her arm didn't register either. Dolly put her key in the lock, stepped inside and was about to close the door when the breeze delivered her name.

'Dolly! Would you like me to leave? I still regret giving Granddad your address...' Phoebe's words hung in the air between them, Dolly not taking them in. Headphones removed and around her neck, Phoebe bounced up and down in the cool evening breeze. 'Is there any way I can change your mind about the bake-off?'

Greta had lied.

Dolly stood frozen so Phoebe took a step forwards; she rubbed Dolly's back and guided her inside. Phoebe strode ahead to the kitchen. Dolly placed Greta's photo face down, on top of the record player, picking up the octopus plushie to make room. She turned it to the blue side and sat down with it on her lap. Phoebe came in with two mugs; she settled in the armchair and sipped her drink.

'Ah ha, there's Ozzy.'

Dolly gave an apologetic look and handed over the octopus but Phoebe shook her head.

'You can borrow him if you like.'

'Bit keen, isn't it, running after work?'

'No. I love jogging.'

'Lymhall is reasonably close to Knutsmere, in the car, but it must have taken you ages on foot.'

Phoebe pulled a face. 'Susan says I'm not allowed to do more than half an hour and it sucks. I caught the bus into Knutsmere centre and ran from there.'

'There are biscuits in the kitchen, by the toaster. Help yourself.'

Phoebe fetched them and sat down in the armchair. 'I love that cupboard to the right of the kitchen window. Is it a genuine suitcase? The authentic handle is brilliant.'

'It's the lot I bid on in the... 2012 auction. It has three shelves fitted inside. Our old cupboard kept getting loose at the hinges, and the suitcase's colour matched our other wooden fittings exactly. A polish and lick of varnish left it looking brand new. It contained a lovely pair of leopard print stilettos. We gave them to Kaz next door.'

Phoebe offered the biscuits to Dolly who took out three. Phoebe stared at the tube, put her hand in, then took it back. She sighed and then took one out after all.

'You don't have to. More for me,' said Dolly.

'I promised Susan.'

Why would this Susan, a friend she'd mentioned in the notebook, care about something so insignificant, and why the limit on jogging time?

That evening, years ago, when Dolly had visited Greta after finding Fred's flat empty, sitting on the sofa with her mum and sister she'd worked her way through a whole packet of digestives.

Normally Greta would have taken them away, said one was enough. Dolly had thought she was being sympathetic but now she knew Greta had let her eat them due to a guilty conscience. Her sister had pretended to be surprised by the news of Fred's disappearance but according to him... and now Edith...

What else had her sister lied about?

'... so I couldn't resist buying a packet for your tank.'

'What?' asked Dolly, and she stared at the small yellow box in Phoebe's hand.

'Fresh bloodworm treats. They're new stock, today. The store's fish love them, they'll be sold out by the end of the week. They are bloodworms preserved in vitamin-enriched jelly. I thought they might act as a romantic dinner for Maurice and Fanny.' Phoebe got up and dropped a few into the tank. The two fish eagerly chased them.

'Is it to do with Granddad?' asked Phoebe and she sat back down. 'I don't know what all this is about but... after the last year or two, I do know that talking helps.'

'You first, then. Why does Susan care about biscuits? Why can't you jog for as long as you want? Why exactly did you leave university?'

Phoebe shuffled in the armchair.

Dolly took another biscuit. 'See. Talking isn't always easy.'

Phoebe put down her mug. 'Susan isn't a friend. She is... or was, my therapist.'

Oh. Dolly thought back to their pub meal and how Phoebe had initially made a fuss about not wanting to meet for food out. A digestive disorder like Crohn's disease might explain that. An assistant at the garden centre that she and Greta liked most once explained how she could be laid up for weeks with it, how she had counselling to deal with the pain.

'I shouldn't have pried. I hope any treatment you've had has helped.'

Phoebe fiddled with the drawstring hanging from the hood of her sports top. 'I've... had problems with eating. I don't expect you to understand,' she added. 'Trust me, I've heard it all from neighbours, mates, even GPs – "Just eat normally, three meals a day," "You look fine the way you are," "It's mind over matter..."' Her face smarted. 'Even, "Some children are starving, you should be ashamed of yourself."'

'Oh, Phoebe... I'm so sorry to hear that, love. I had no idea. But suffering isn't relative, is it? It's like someone who's lost their whole family telling me losing one sister is nothing.' Dolly patted the seat next to her. Arms folded and hugging her own waist, Phoebe went over. 'I've read about it in magazines. I can see now why swimming, why the bake-off, might be extra difficult for you.' How quickly Phoebe had got into the pool once her towel was off, how she'd told Dolly it was rude to stare... and in the notebook, the trip to Paris, how Phoebe's biggest concern had been if she would look chic...

'That was the first time I'd been swimming in ages. I wish I could be more like you and not care so much about my appearance,' said Phoebe.

'Is that supposed to be a compliment?' Dolly smiled and put her arm around her. Dolly explained how her mum pulled out all the stops to look attractive. She'd spend hours on the loo – Dolly worked out when she got older that her mum had been taking laxatives. But it never did her any good, she only attracted losers, and the harder she tried, the worse they seemed to treat her. So Dolly could never be much bothered about what stared back at her from the mirror.

'Fred and I were opposites from that point of view. He loved keeping up with the latest fashions, all those big lapels and flares.'

Phoebe's eyes widened. 'But he's always dressed so conservatively.'

'He had this bright turquoise cocktail chair.'

'No!'

Phoebe should have seen the silver satin suit he'd wear to nightclubs. He put it on in his flat once – they hadn't been dating that long. It was December 1973, a power cut, he said to go around for a candle-lit sandwich dinner. He reckoned his suit would reflect the light. His battery-run radio worked and they danced together, singing along to the current chart number one, 'Merry Xmas Everybody' by Slade.

The two of them sat for a while, Phoebe leaning into Dolly like Flo did if she'd had another argument with her parents or got told off by a teacher at school. Eventually Noddy Holder stopped singing in Dolly's head.

'So, how are you doing now, darling?' she asked Phoebe.

'Better. I've got my job. I've done these monthly challenges. The martial arts day pushed me to the limit. Tai chi is an exercise that doesn't burn a huge number of calories – Susan said I should find hobbies that weren't connected to my problems. In the past I've always used exercise as a means of compensating for overeating, and therefore it's enabled my most harmful behaviours. Maisie thought the judo would test me as well; I've always found physical contact with people difficult.' Phoebe leaned even closer. 'Now that's not such a big issue.'

'It sounds as if this Susan – and Maisie – have really helped your move forwards.'

'They've both been amazing. It was a joke getting help at first. If you've got a normal BMI there's not much out there. Lots of eating disorders are invisible illnesses – bulimia, binge-eating disorder like I've got, or rather had. As I've headed into recovery it's become more a pattern of sporadic disordered eating. Even anorexia can be invisible in some cases, as the fashion these days is to be so thin anyway... sorry. I'm probably boring you.'

'Don't stop.'

Phoebe tried hard, now, not to class days as good or bad. In the past, if not bingeing, she'd only eat super healthy foods. Take the pub lunch – it's why she forced herself to order cheese, when she'd normally only allow herself a low-fat food like lean ham. Susan had taught Phoebe to be kind to herself. That had made all the difference. To never speak to herself in a way she wouldn't let other people.

Dolly wanted to know how it started. A surname like Good-body opened the gates for comments from the other kids in her class, Phoebe explained; she had been a little overweight. However, school was okay once she realised that the so-called cool people were dickheads. But that first term at uni, she was having so much fun, she didn't eat properly. The weight fell off and she got loads of compliments. Phoebe thought no one would like her if she put it back on.

'The pressure of not wanting to put on weight made me binge. Human nature, I guess. Susan says it doesn't do any good to deprive ourselves. When I think I'm failing at how I look, and at life, the misery increases and so does my urge to dive into food. For a few seconds, those carbs, the sugar and fats, they pass as the best friends in the world. Like when you're little and someone you love gives you a hug and makes everything better. But after-wards I hate myself even more. It's a vicious cycle, or used to be, my eating habits are much better these days.'

'It's a top priority to be liked?' asked Dolly, genuinely curious.

'You've seen social media. That's the way it is nowadays. I keep well away from it now. It's all about follows and likes. I've talked a lot with Susan. I think it goes back to my parents not being around.' Phoebe's mum died in a car crash when she was five. Her dad couldn't cope and sought refuge in drink. His liver packed up in the end. It was as if Phoebe couldn't stop talking now she'd started. 'I wasn't enough to keep him here. He chose death over me. When I went away to uni the damage that had caused surfaced. Looking back, Granddad and Gran had always said I was no trouble... it's because I thought I had to be perfect, because me being me wasn't enough. Then when I lost weight, in the eyes of certain people I reached a level of perfection. I was scared of losing that.'

Dolly's eyes dropped to Phoebe's wrist. 'I have a confession. I did wear that yellow crystal bracelet a few times. It's such an unusual colour.'

'Citrine. It helps you stick to your goals. The only place I go online, and that's anonymously, is in a support forum. Several of the friends I've made there... they haven't made it. Eating disorders have the highest mortality rate, you know, out of all psychiatric illnesses.' Her voice wavered. 'The members have introduced me to lots of helpful things, including healing crystals.'

'Is that symbol to do with your eating? The one on your tattoo and T-shirt.'

'It's the eating disorder recovery symbol. For me the curves of the lines remind me that curves are okay, eating healthily is the most important thing, not being skinny. The overall heart shape represents self-love and kindness. It probably sounds silly but on really bad days, wearing the T-shirt, looking at my tattoo... both of those give me strength.'

'Oh, love, it doesn't sound silly at all.'

Poor Fred, He'd suffered too, lost a daughter, and a son-in-law, then his wife. 'Did you ever used to talk to your grandparents about this?'

'Granddad grew up in a children's home with no one and hated it. At least I had family. How could I complain?' Her cheeks flushed. 'I can't believe I'm telling you all this. No one knows this much about my eating apart from Susan and Maisie. I really miss Maisie. She used to really listen and made me laugh.'

'Is she a friend from university?'

'No. The library.'

'Greta loved reading too and would go to the library in Stockport in Wellington Road. I could never see the appeal of having a head in a book myself. But she made a friend, too. Harry, he was called. I met him once.' Greta's arthritis had been especially bad that day, so Dolly drove her in. Whilst Greta checked out her books, Harry asked Dolly if she thought her sister would appreciate being asked out. Dolly said to go for it, Greta often spoke about Harry and he seemed like such a nice man. But a few weeks later she stopped talking about him and changed the day she went to the library.

'It's an impressive building, I think people from all over the region visit it. Libraries are great places for making friends, even though you aren't supposed to talk, you've got common ground before you even open your mouth. Maisie was... special. That year I was at home, having treatment, we'd meet up and go for a coffee, in between her trips abroad. She's travelled the world. I loved listening to her stories. One reason I wanted to go to Paris was because she spoke of its amazing bookshops.'

'She must be very proud of how you've done.'

'I don't know. We lost touch a while back.' Her mouth drooped. 'As I'm not on socials, she couldn't have found me and we never exchanged phone numbers. I don't even know her surname. So stupid. But, then, life happens. I left uni with no warning, didn't contact any friends from there for ages, I couldn't face explaining. I'm hoping she'll reach out again when she's able. The librarian got to know us both and I've asked her to pass on my contact details when Maisie comes back.'

Dolly gave Phoebe a hug. She'd never forgotten, one of the drivers where she worked, Phil… they were good friends. He came in, in a bit of state one morning, in the early nineties. Princess Diana had talked publicly about her bulimia the day before. It inspired his daughter to open up. Phil and his wife were trying to understand. Their daughter had been vomiting up food for months.

Phoebe said she'd always tried hard to hide her problems from her granddad, but he used to notice that suddenly all the biscuits were missing, or how anxious she was about going out. He offered to pay for private counselling, if that was quicker; said he'd support her whatever she decided about going back to university.

Fred always had been supportive – when Dolly had been given a rough ride by a customer at work, had scratched her car or argued with Greta.

'I miss Gran. Every day. For as long as I can remember we'd talk about books together. She made the best rice pudding and always made time for me. Gran just seemed to know when some-thing was wrong, if a friend had been mean at school or I'd got a bad mark and was feeling down. Now my best friends are all away at college. Granddad, Susan and Maisie, they've been my rocks. Granddad letting me talking things through, even if he didn't always know what to say. Susan's mindset advice and Maisie's idea to create the year of firsts. She helped me think up all twelve. I was supposed to start them the January before last, six months into leaving university and having counselling, but Christmas was a nightmare food-wise and set me back. In retrospect six months of therapy wasn't enough. So I delayed starting it until May, throwing myself in the deep end with a trip to Paris.'

'Maisie sounds like a wonderful friend.'

Phoebe believed a sense of sadness had drawn them together – Phoebe with her eating issues, Maisie with her past. She'd endured difficult times as a young woman, but said having children made that better. Phoebe reckoned the travelling might have been a distraction from painful memories for Maisie, in the same way that the bingeing was for Phoebe. For whatever reason, they clicked straight away.

'Maisie has her quirks, like we all do. I lost my library card once, one of the last times I saw her. Maisie said she was always forgetting where she put things, so really important documents she kept hidden... now what was it... in an object that looked happy on the outside but was really sad.'

'What did that mean?'

'No idea. She teased, enjoying trying to get me to guess, and then I suddenly found my card and the moment passed.' Phoebe sat up and eased the yellow crystal bracelet off her wrist. She took Dolly's hand and pushed it over Dolly's fingers. 'I want you to have this. It's helped me. I want to pass that on. I got it from Afflecks in town, from a crystal stall there. I could take you, if you want.'

'I'd like that very much.' Dolly held her arm in the air. The lumps of citrine burned brightly as light hit them. They might help her like they'd helped Phoebe. This past year Dolly had dived into loneliness and binged on it. Avoiding everyone else had offered huge comfort, an escape from reality and the need to build a future without Greta.

'So... why were you so upset, outside, just now, Dolly? I've talked enough.'

'I bumped into an old... acquaintance of Greta's today,

Edith...' Her face crumpled and she covered her eyes with her hands, a sob catching her unawares. She told Phoebe how she now believed Fred's explanation that he left without warning, all those years ago, because her sister threatened him, said he needed to call off the engagement and leave. Edith said Greta was worried about a holiday... that must have been Dolly and Fred's imminent trip to Paris.

Dolly shook her head. 'I could always tell if Fred was planning a surprise or had bought me a gift, he'd get this silly grin on his face – he was useless at keeping secrets. Or so I thought. Whatever my sister knew about him, it must have been one hell of a dark secret for him to hide it so well.'

Phoebe's body stiffened.

'You don't seem surprised by me thinking that? Phoebe?'

'I can make a guess. There are things about Granddad that... might surprise you. But it's not my place to say. You need to talk to him. For both your sakes. Come around to our house, Dolly. I'll make food. I'll be there if it all gets too much. How about tomorrow night?'

27

The next evening Dolly and Leroy each stood on their own drive, suited and booted, Greta would have said. Dolly in her red jacket, checked trousers and polished shoes. Fred wasn't a friend, not any more; this meeting was formal. Having not slept well again, she rubbed the back of her neck. Emotional ill health was easier to spot as she aged and left its mark physically. Looking back over the last year she'd ignored the signs, the stiff joints, waves of nausea, the chest pains, the constant tiredness. Leroy was off to Spinningfields to meet Tony, wearing his leather jacket and more than a splash of aftershave. Old Spice used to be his signature scent – nostalgic, reliable, an agreeable fragrance. His new one's grapefruit notes smelt acrid.

Dolly took out her car keys. 'Sure you don't want a lift to the station?'

'I could do with the exercise. A six-pack won't create itself.' He patted his belly before striding over to give her a hug. He stepped back and took her by the shoulders. 'Don't let anything you hear tonight knock you off course, gal.'

'And don't you let Tony mess you around,' she said and gave

him a beady look. He rolled his eyes, kissed her on the cheek and, humming, headed off. Dolly drove around Knutsmere several times before taking the road to Lymhall. The satnav directed her to a cul-de-sac, not far from the village centre, and a large detached house with a fancy bird bath in the front garden. Black metal rails ran across the front border, with gold painted spikes. Fred always had coveted the high life. He'd dreamt of owning a Ferrari and a second home in Spain.

She pulled up the handbrake, turned off the engine and checked herself in the mirror. She hadn't bothered putting on make-up, apart from a cursory slash of pink across her lips. The curtains twitched. As she approached the oak door Phoebe opened it. Fred stood behind in a nondescript jumper and grey slacks. Dolly wiped her hands on her trousers.

'I've made cottage pie. Hope that's all right,' he said.

The old Fred didn't cook much and used to prefer meals that sounded more cosmopolitan like chicken Kyiv or tikka masala, or Black Forest gâteau, dishes that nowadays were considered thoroughly British. She followed them along the hallway and into the living room, reassured by the homely cooking smell. Dolly expected to see a level of luxury she could never afford, with studded chaises longues, Jacquard wallpaper, heavy swag curtains, panelled walls...

Oh.

The sofa by the front window looked comfortable, in fact sunken in the middle. There was a teak, electronic ignition gas fire – she hadn't seen one of those for years – with... a tabby cat stretched out in front of it? Bookshelves were cluttered with political and sporting memoirs, a guide to vintage cameras, and many well-thumbed novels. Framed photos, too, and an old-fashioned carriage clock. The television looked top of the range, with a gaming box and two consoles near it on the floor, plus she spotted an Alexa device on a glass table – all reflections of the man she used to know.

Phoebe directed her to the sofa; Fred sat down in an armchair and ran a hand through his thinning grey hair. He took off his large slate framed glasses, so different to his old round, John Lennon ones. He rubbed his eyes and put them back on, jigging them from side to side as he did. Perhaps some things never changed.

'Wine, Dolly?' asked Phoebe.

'Better not as I'm driving. Any soft drink will do. Thanks, love.' She fiddled with the citrine crystal bracelet around her wrist.

'Where are my manners... Can I take your jacket?' Fred went to get up.

A flicker of heat tickled her insides. He never used to be so polite when it came to removing clothes, undoing buttons and zips with ease. Not nearly quickly enough, she'd jokingly complain, in between kisses.

'You said Greta threatened you...'

Hand through that hair again. 'Why don't we enjoy dinner before we talk about that?'

Phoebe came in and passed her a lemonade. 'I'm dishing up. I thought we'd eat in the kitchen.'

Dolly shot her a grateful look as she left and then turned back to Fred. '*Enjoy?* You assume I'm pleased to see you again.'

He went over to the cat and ruffled its underbelly. 'No Dolly. I'm simply trying to make this less of an ordeal, for both of us.'

She followed him into the kitchen – sleek and white, with digital displays flashing in all corners, on the cooker, microwave, the fancy American fridge-freezer, on the coffee machine, the scales, a Bluetooth player on the windowsill. In an instant she was closer again to the old Fred – until she looked outside at the garden. It had well-maintained borders with a wildflower patch in one corner. A fence at the bottom separated it from an overgrown field behind. A stroll in town, around Cathedral Gardens, was as near as he used to get to nature, back in the 1970s. As for a cat, shedding hairs on his furniture, he often used to shoo away the landlord's. Although he'd get angry when the lad in the flat next door blew pot smoke into its face for a laugh.

Dolly must have changed too, even if she was still a foodie, still liked flicking through magazines and soul music. She no longer wore jumpsuits and maxis, nor coats with fringed edges; she'd got over her crush on Kojak. She sat down at the kitchen table, bigger than her dining-room one, and helped herself to cottage pie, being careful not to watch Phoebe eat, not wanting to make her friend self-conscious. The three of them talked about the weather, climate change, Middle Eastern politics, how back in the 1970s the issues were the Vietnam War, the Troubles in Northern Ireland and gay liberation.

'Decimal Day was in 1971,' said Fred.

'D Day, as Greta called it. She supported the Save Our Sixpence campaign. She was furious when the milkman had trouble converting prices and rounded up the cost of a pint, and then when the local payphone jammed with the new coins.'

'Didn't the UK join the European Union in the early seventies?' asked Phoebe.

Fred nodded. Was he pro Brexit or against? What did he think to the current government? Or immigration? Inclusivity? Would he consider the modern world too woke or be worried about far-right nationalism? He and Dolly used to be like the hung parliament that resulted from the February 1974 general election between Heath and Wilson – neither of them would win when it came to an argument about politics. They both had strong views but respected each other's right to embrace different beliefs, as did most of their friends. These days, society felt so polarised.

'Arctic roll for dessert?' asked Fred, and he gave a tentative smile.

Dolly wiped her mouth and stood up, chair legs scratching against the natural stone flooring. 'Sorry, Phoebe. This was a bad idea.' She stalked into the hallway and put her hand on the front door handle.

'Wait... Dolly...'

She turned around.

Fred threw his hands in the air. 'I'm sorry. I don't know how to handle this.'

'You expect me to be charmed that you've bought in a dessert we used to love all those years ago, when I had dreams of a shiny future? You think a sponge roll will make me forget how you upped and left? And how dare you blame *you* letting me down on *my* sister?'

'No, I don't. Everything was my fault. Hear me out, then I'll never contact you again.'

Dolly filled with a gush of emptiness. 'There you go again – you think the answer is to drop a bombshell and then disappear, leaving me to pick up the pieces, like before?'

'Please, Dolly.'

Phoebe hovered in the kitchen doorway, twisting a tea towel. Fred disappeared into the lounge. Phoebe beckoned to Dolly and the two of them went into the kitchen. They stood by the window. She explained that her granddad had never been that good with words. Like when her gran tried a fancy duck recipe once. It didn't look the best and he asked if it was something the cat had turned down. He was mortified when she put his in the bin, couldn't apologise enough – he'd meant to be funny.

'That rings true,' said Dolly. 'I had a yellow floral mini dress when we were together. The first time I wore it Fred said it showed off my huge bottom. He didn't understand why I was upset as he loved my curves.'

'This last year, talking's really helped me, but I was ready. If you aren't, Dolly, I wouldn't blame you for leaving. I love Grand-dad, he's held my family together during tough times. But you and him sorting out the past, you've both got to want it.'

Dolly stared out of the window, right into the field. Her heart-beat slowed. She left the kitchen and headed in the direction of the front door... stopping by the living room. She went in. Told him to keep it brief and perched on the edge of the sofa, as the sound of distant clattering plates and running water joined them. Fred closed the door and sat down again.

'That afternoon, after you proposed...' Her cheeks burned. 'Why did Greta call on you?'

'She said I mustn't take you to Paris, with a vehemence that I didn't think could simply be down to just a fear of flying. Greta hadn't ever visited France, had she, not gone by ferry? There was no chance of her having... left a scandal behind in the capital?'

'Are you for real? No, Fred. Firstly the word "scandal" would never appear in the same sentence as my sister. She's never been abroad, not then, not ever.'

'Well, she was adamant, looked as if she might lose it when I insisted the trip would do us both good. I'd never seen her like that. Yet she kept saying she didn't want to interfere, didn't want to hurt you...'

'But?'

Fred put his elbows on his knees, leaning his chin on his hands. 'She'd hired a private detective to follow me during previous months.'

'Greta didn't even like detective shows like *Harry O* or *The*

Streets of San Francisco.' Dolly jumped up. 'I'm not staying to listen to this nonsense.'

'She said it didn't add up, that a young man like me had so much cash.'

'But you worked long hours, evenings and weekends, at the cutting edge of technology.'

Silence filled the room, every corner and crack, urging Dolly to open the door to let it out.

'At the cutting edge of the black market, more like,' he mumbled.

Dolly dropped back down on to the sofa and listened. He had his nine-to-five jobs selling cameras, then in the field of early video technology, but the money wasn't enough. Not for the life-style he wanted. So he went into a different kind of sales... Greta found out. Threatened to tell Dolly if he didn't leave immediately.

'And... quite rightly,' he said. 'I'd have done the same if a loser was dating a person I cared about.'

Loser? Not Fred. He was dynamic. Hardworking. Fred was going places.

'You could have come clean to me,' she stuttered. 'We all make mistakes. We'd have worked it out.'

'She said she'd go to the police as well.'

'But it wasn't her place... she should have told me. *You* should have.'

Fred had come back to Manchester two weeks later, but Dolly had gone from her flat. Greta had said if she ever saw Fred's face again she'd dial 999, so he didn't dare go to hers, or write. He wouldn't have found Dolly there either. At that time she and Greta were away in Margate.

'But we had lots of mutual friends. I could have tried them, or contacted you at work,' he mumbled. 'It's no excuse but I was scared Greta would find out, scared of jail, so... I gave up.' The door creaked open.

'Everything all right?' Phoebe came in and sat cross-legged on the floor, stroking the cat. 'Have you told Dolly where you met Gran?'

Dolly bristled. 'I don't think that's necessary.'

But Phoebe nodded at Fred encouragingly.

'It was 1990. Angela and I were both taking part in a volunteering programme.'

What... wait... so Phoebe's mother couldn't have been his biological daughter? Fred took a deep breath and explained. He'd been in his early forties, settled in a job. He'd been in relationships from time to time and was earning good money, had a nice house, top-of-the-range car, he took trips around the world, but none of that satisfied him. Not in the way Fred thought it all would when he was a young man. Something was missing from his life. Angela had buried her first husband a couple of years earlier and felt the same.

'We met at a charity that' – his voice faltered – 'helped ex-prisoners to read.'

'You hate reading.'

'I discovered a love of books when I was sent to prison.'

Dolly sat stock still. Fred, a convicted criminal?

'My petty crimes caught up with me in the end, a couple of years after I left Manchester, and resulted in a sentence longer than I'd hoped for. I did the time, hated every minute. Prison reform hadn't come in back then, the lack of sanitation, the crowding... mentally, I was in a bad place. Then my cellmate lent me *The Great Gatsby*. He was a lifer and said he'd have ended up in the psychiatric wing if it wasn't for stories. He'd murdered his uncle and didn't care what the other inmates said about him reading a "poncy" romance, he knew, deep down, they feared him. Jay Gatsby's millionaire lifestyle whisked me away from my cell's squalor.'

Fred, in a cell? Locked up with a murderer? Her hand covered her mouth and a sense of losing control transported her back to 1975 and the landlord telling her Fred had left, how everything had stopped for a few seconds, her surroundings had blurred, the landlord's voice had become muffled. How everything she'd thought was real about her life disappeared in a puff of disbelief. She stared at Fred as he carried on talking, hearing nothing but blood whoosh between her ears.

'...and a lot of the people inside re-offend because they can't get a job afterwards,' he said. 'I wanted to make a difference.'

'Why did Angela get involved?' she muttered.

Angela. She sounded glamorous.

'She had an uncle, knew him as a little girl, he was always kind to her but not a well man. He got thrown in prison for trying to take his own life. That's how it was before the law changed in 1961. He managed to do it inside.'

'Oh, how sad,' said Dolly.

'Yes and it always stayed with her, so she looked at volunteering and as she loved reading she chose the literacy programme. She was all for people having second chances. Like my best mate who had set up his own business, right at the forefront of the CD manufacturing industry. He offered me a job after I came out, when no one else would.'

Fred's head dropped for a moment, and he stared at his lap, fastening and unfastening his watch strap.

'You expect me to give you a second chance too?'

He shook his head. 'Of course not, and all these years later I respect Greta for what she did. But I would never have chosen to leave you, Dolly. When I came back, I trekked around all our favourite haunts – Rafters nightclub on Oxford Street, and that café we loved with the lava lamps and lime linoleum floor.'

Dolly could still clearly picture that café and the coffee and walnut cake they often ate there.

'I've only got your word for all this – you lied to me, easily enough, back then, and it still doesn't make sense. Why would she care so much about us visiting France?' She jabbed at him with her finger, in the air. 'You risked everything for the sake of smarter clothes, trendier haircuts, for, what, the attention you got as we'd be whisked into clubs' VIP areas?' Her voice rose. 'It's all so shallow. And a private detective? Greta lived a simple life. I don't understand why you'd make up this story.'

Phoebe looked from Dolly to her granddad. A tide of purple filled his cheeks and, arm shaking, Fred reached into the magazine rack by his side. He pulled out an envelope, faded brown and worn at the edges.

'I don't know why I kept this,' he said, barely audible. He handed it over. Dolly turned it from side to side, before opening it. The envelope smelt musty. She looked inside and drew out two large black-and-white photos. One was Fred as she remembered him, with the John Lennon glasses and cigarette hanging out of the side of his mouth. He was surrounded by a crowd, selling watches off a trestle table. The other was of him accepting something in a paper bag from a man in a trench coat.

'It wasn't solid evidence,' said Fred, 'although that man in the photo was known to the police. He'd been inside several times for fraud and assault. But the note inside the envelope...'

Dolly looked again and pulled out a piece of paper, instantly recognising its Basildon Bond watermark. She placed it on her lap, reading the familiar, distinctive italic writing, the capital letter t that always leaned to the left at the top, the curly apostrophe and comma – Greta would always write those with a flourish.

'There's more photos where these came from, don't ever forget that. Stay away from Dolly,' she read out, and with those words, the straightforward line of the two sisters' past snapped in half.

28

Dolly sat in her kitchen, still wearing her jacket, a bottle of wine on the table. The doorbell rang and she loped into the hallway. Leroy stood, blinking in the darkness, a bottle of rum tucked under his arm.

'Saw you rush in. Figured you might still be up.'

'You're back early.'

'So are you.'

'Doritos?' she asked.

'Lumps of cheese mixed in?' Leroy shot back, hopefully, as he stepped inside. 'It's like a hothouse in here.' Leroy fanned his face as they walked past the lounge.

Stuff Greta's policy of being frugal with the heating. As soon as Dolly had got back from Lymhall she'd gone straight for the thermostat dial and rammed it up, even though outside it was mild.

She prepared snacks, opened the back door and kicked it shut, before they settled at the oak loveseat, each with their own bottle.

'I watched a programme about Ancient Egyptian gods once,'

said Dolly and tipped her head back, gazing at the oily night sky, thousands of stars transforming it into an old master's painting. It reminded her of a pair of the sequinned black satin hot pants she'd owned, back in the 1970s. 'The moon god was called... Khonsu. They believed he could aid healing.'

Dolly had often wished a god were on the internet and had a Frequently Asked Questions section. Does The One really exist? What was she supposed to do without her sister? Is a Jaffa Cake really a biscuit?

'I'd better stay out here all night then.' Leroy drained his tumbler and topped it up with rum again.

She studied him over the bowl of crisps and Red Leicester cubes. His eyes looked puffier than usual.

'Tony. I misunderstood his Facebook photos,' said Leroy. 'Those younger men were colleagues from work. For once he's kept his love life more private – proof it's serious. He was always posting about us.'

Dolly took another crisp.

'The *he* I thought he'd been dating is a *she*.'

'Okayyy, but you've always known he dates men and women.'

'It's not that... He's fallen in love, Dolly, for the first time in his life, he said.' Leroy picked out three lumps of cheese and put them all in his mouth at once. 'What's more, she's pregnant. Tony's ecstatic, even talked of marriage, laughed about forty being the new thirty. He agreed to meet me because he wants to stay friends, said both their dads are dead and I'd be a brilliant grandfather figure to the baby.' His eyes glistened under the moonlight that had first introduced him to Tony, by the canal in the gay village, all those months ago. 'Imagine, me a granddad, sitting there in my tight chinos, drinking a jelly shot and looking at him through fog bubbles.' She reached across the table and placed her hand on his. 'I've never seen Tony like this before,

Dolly. It's as if someone's struck a match and lit him up from the inside.'

'Pity he didn't explode. Thoughtless bugger.'

Leroy gave a hollow laugh. 'I didn't know what to say, tried to be grown up about it.'

'Fuck that,' she said, taking a leaf out of Phoebe's book, not caring if Greta was frowning down.

Leroy couldn't help laughing, for real this time.

'I'm serious. He wants his ex to be his baby's grandfather? The ex he hurt deeply? The man with the biggest heart in Knutsmere, who shakes his stuff on the dance floor better than anyone I know?' She put her drink down. 'Indoors. Now. I'm in the mood for a boogie – that'll heal us far more quickly than Khonsu.'

'Not until you tell me how your evening went.'

She paused, knocked back her wine and set the glass down again, before words tumbled out about Fred's dodgy past, the incriminating photos, Greta's threats.

Leroy gave a long whistle. 'That's some big sister, looking out for you to that extreme.'

'If Tony was involved with petty crime would you have preferred me to ward him off in secret, or let you confront him?'

'Fair point.'

Greta had loved Dolly when her own mum couldn't be bothered, but those photos, that written threat, now numbed Dolly's affection towards her sister. As did the wine. Greta hated people getting drunk and Dolly's words slurred, as if they were on Dolly's side. She held out her hand and pulled Leroy up.

'"I Will Survive" by Gloria Gaynor to kick things off,' he said.

An hour later, they flopped on to the sofa, old LPs and singles scattered across the floor.

'I hope Maurice and Fanny enjoyed the show,' she said, articulation perfect now. Dancing had cleared her head and given her absolute clarity about her life from this point forwards.

'How's it going with those two?' asked Leroy, catching his breath.

'If I bend near the tank, Maurice doesn't swim up to my face quite as quickly as before. I'm taking that as a good sign. I know he must have been lonely sometimes, and I'm sorry about that, even though before he was never ill, had an excellent appetite and enjoyed swaying to the disco beats of "Tragedy".' She patted Leroy's arm. 'But you and I, we don't need another person to be fulfilled. I've lost Greta, you've lost Tony, but we've still got friends, we've got each other and, unlike Maurice, trips out and hobbies. And Doritos. So, from now on, let's make the most of what we've already got, and let's promise to put ourselves first.'

Leroy's hand shot towards hers and their little fingers held on to each other. 'I'm in. From tomorrow. Let's go out for lunch and on to the movies. Popcorn all round.' He undid the top button of his chinos. 'Can't say I'll be sorry to throw these away.'

Arms around each other, they stumbled into the hallway. Dolly picked up the local paper by the front door – she hadn't it seen earlier. Underneath was a folded piece of paper.

Dolly scanned the words written in a black marker pen.

I HATE MY PARENTS. Can I have tea at yours tomorrow night?
Flo X

29

Dolly sat opposite Leroy at the kitchen table.

He burped. 'That steak and the mango colada are still repeating. Good thing we didn't have them until after the movie.'

'The jumper you're wearing is almost as bright as that drink's paper umbrella. I've missed it.'

'Me too. I'd forgotten what a lift it is, to pull on a cheerful colour in the morning. It's a little baggier than it used to be. I've lost a few pounds. I was thinking – this putting ourselves first business, I'm going to carry on healthier eating, for *me*. I might even come swimming with you.' He put his hands behind his head and stretched out, in a pair of comfortable trousers.

The letterbox rapped and Dolly opened the door to a pale face and hooded eyes. Flo slumped in and followed her into the kitchen without taking off her coat or shoes, or bobbing into the lounge to say hello to Maurice and Fanny. She dropped into a seat at the end of the table, elbows on it, not budging a millimetre when Dolly placed a juice in front of her.

'How was school?' asked Leroy.

'It's all about exams this year. We may as well be at high school already. We keep repeating the same old work.'

'At least you've got your visit to the museum at the weekend,' said Dolly. 'I can't wait to hear about those bug displays.'

Her shoulders sank lower. 'We had a big argument. Then Mum and Dad cancelled the trip after I told them they'd get bored, said there was no point going and slammed my bedroom door.'

Leroy and Dolly exchanged glances.

'How's Guides going, sweetheart? Still okay?' she asked.

'Yeah. We're working on the second badge now, the skills builders one, for the Know Myself theme. We've got to do the work over the Easter holidays. I'm on the bit about *putting your best feelings forward*. I've got to think about if I ever overreact and which reactions are good and which are bad.'

Dolly raised an eyebrow.

Flo sighed. 'I know. But I felt so cross.'

'We all overreact sometimes,' said Leroy. 'Usually because we are hurt or scared.' He winked at her. 'How about a game of Go Fish?'

'I think I'll go and sit in the tree for a while.'

Dolly and Leroy stood by the window. Flo climbed easily halfway up, stopping at a bough wide enough to rest on. It wasn't raining and the sun hadn't quite dipped beneath the horizon, having wrapped the day up in its arms, a promise that summer was coming. Yet Flo looked as if it were the middle of winter, arms wrapped around her body, face tucked against her knees. Leroy got on with peeling potatoes for mash – without butter. Dolly grabbed a favourite green gilet from her bedroom; it had been a while now since she'd hidden herself in her brown anorak. She glanced in her full-length mirror. If Dolly were Phoebe, or rather if she had the young woman's illness, she'd wince at the bulges around the middle, and rue the loose jowls. She turned to one side, imagining Fred's view: did he miss the thick brunette hair, now wispy and blonde? Did he note the lips that had shrunk, that smooth hands were now mapped with veins? Finally, Dolly as Dolly stared into the glass, nothing but grateful for a reflection so much more cheerful and confident than the one she'd avoided for months. The yellow crystal bracelet caught her eye. She stood up straight. Not looking bad, Dolly, not bad at all.

* * *

'I'm coming up,' she called to Flo.

Flo looked down through the branches. 'You can't make it up here. Just getting up from the sofa you make grunting noises.'

'I'm not like that cockroach you found that had lost a leg.'

'But cockroaches' legs grow back. What if you fall?' Flo gave a dramatic sigh. 'Stay there, I'll come down to you. But I'm not going inside. Not yet. We can sit on the garden chairs.' Dragging her feet over the lawn, Flo joined her at the loveseat.

'Leroy and I sat out here late last night,' said Dolly.

'After your meal with Fred. How did it go?'

'Not good.'

'Is Leroy back with Tony?' she asked eagerly.

'No.'

Flo stared at her through the dusk and simply nodded.

'How did your evening go?' Dolly asked, against the backdrop of starlings' twilight chorus.

'I found a giant house spider and seeing as my parents liked my elevator pitch, and suggested that museum trip, I thought things had changed so I caught it and took it into their bedroom to show Mum. Her scream surprised me and I dropped it. I told her not to worry, I'd get one of my jars, to catch it.' Flo zipped her anorak higher. 'My mistake. I'd forgotten they didn't know about any of the containers where I keep insects. She marched me into my bedroom and had a look around. She grabbed Lacey.'

Flo explained that Lacey was a two-spot ladybird. She'd flown on to Flo's shoelaces in the front garden when she got home from school. Flo took her inside, wanted to draw her; she'd never found a two-spot one before. She was going to release her out the back later but her mum emptied the jar outside straight away, said it was *unsanitary*. Flo folded her arms. Kaz and Mark had demanded to see all the containers, asked what Flo had been keeping. She tried explaining it was never for longer than a couple of days, but the more she talked about ants and worms, about beetles and caterpillars, the more horrified they looked. Her mum insisted on vacuuming Flo's bedroom from top to bottom. Another spider appeared and Flo called her mum a murderer when she sucked it up.

'Oh, love. Did you apologise?'

Flo pursed her lips. 'The real apology should be from Mum to that spider. She's the one who overreacted but I'm the one who gets punished. I thought they understood me more, but turns out the only reason they were impressed with my pitch was because I was confident speaking and showed a good memory. In the elevator pitch I'd talked about wanting to study insects, but they just thought I meant as a hobby. Dad said I'd understand when I got older that there was no point going to college, not with all the costs and loans these days unless I chose a subject that was... *concrete*.'

'Like what?'

'Business studies.' She threw her hands in the air. 'Not that he has any right to decide my future, he's not even my proper dad.' Flo's cheeks flushed. 'And I don't want to talk about that.'

Dolly's eyebrows shot into her hairline. Flo had a different father? Someone Kaz knew before Mark? But they'd been school sweethearts. Unless Kaz had an affair or... She bit her lip. It was none of her business. This must have been Flo's secret.

'Mind, university does cost a lot these days,' Dolly said gently. 'I was shocked when Phoebe told me how much.' She squeezed Flo's arm. 'I'm sorry, love.'

Leroy came to the back door. 'The fish fingers are on. Potatoes boiling. How about that game of Go Fish?' He shook a pack of cards.

Flo won and perked up enough to wolf down dinner. She played around with the last forkful of peas.

'It's like Mum and Dad don't know me at all.'

Dolly paused. 'I didn't know everything about Greta. But that's because she hid things. You still haven't made your passion for insects clear enough to your parents. It's all very well talking about wanting to go to university to study them, but you need to show your parents that it's a genuine, serious intention.'

'Look at it from a business point of view, like they would,' said Leroy. 'You're twelve soon, aren't you? Why not put your name down for a paper round. You can never start saving too early for college. You could research courses, too. Find out practical facts, so that your parents know this isn't just a daydream.'

The doorbell rang and Flo followed Dolly until they reached the lounge where she bobbed in to tell Maurice and Fanny how much her life stank. Dolly pulled open the door.

Arms full, Phoebe glanced back at the road, looking flushed. 'I've been to the corner shop after finishing my shift. I don't normally work Thursdays but offered to help with a stocktake. Logging today's date into the computer so many times made me realise, the bake-off is two weeks today. They could choose an Easter theme. We need to practise. I've got all the ingredients for a traditional simnel cake, whatever that is. I looked up Easter baking online. Next Thursday you could come to ours to practise making Easter biscuits – we could do them in the shape of bunnies and chicks. Granddad's agreed to go out. What do you think?'

'Cake?' Flo's face appeared at the lounge doorway. 'Can I help?'

Dolly looked between the two of them. 'Help Phoebe carry these ingredients into the kitchen. Then wash hands.'

Flo rushed up to Phoebe and paused before shyly taking several items.

Leroy beamed as he stood by the sink, having finished the last of the dishes. 'Happy to gofer and act as DJ.'

Flo held up an orange jar, stepping from side to side. 'It better be that "Lady Marmalade" song you like so much, then.'

'You sure this is okay?' asked Phoebe when Flo and Leroy headed to the record player.

'Yes. I need to get my head around everything but I'm done with putting my life on hold. And your granddad doesn't need to be out of the house. He can't hurt me any more than he already has. This competition is about you and me, Phoebe. I'll bring the ingredients next week.' Leroy and Flo came back in, him strutting to disco beats.

'Great, I'm looking forward to us baking together,' said Phoebe. 'Next Thursday is the seventh; I'll make sure I put our practice session on the calendar.'

Leroy's face dulled for a second, before he picked up the sink sponge and wiped down the work surface.

'Why don't we make a night of it?' said Dolly, with a side-ways glance at her neighbour. 'Steve's pub does decent grub. Flo, if your parents allow it, and as it's school holidays, do you fancy having tea there with us, next Thursday? If Leroy doesn't mind, he could drive you home whilst I go to Phoebe's for the baking.'

'Wow! Yes please!'

'You could meet us there after work, Phoebe – just have a drink if you don't fancy eating that early.'

Phoebe shot her a grateful look.

'Leroy?' Dolly shot him a pointed look.

His shoulders loosened. 'Wouldn't miss it for the world.'

Last year Tony had taken Leroy out for an evening picnic on his birthday, the seventh, saying it would be romantic. The weather had been unseasonably hot for April. They'd driven to Alderley Edge and parked up, before walking to the popular sandstone ridge with its spectacular views of Manchester and the Peak District. Strawberries dipped in chocolate, rich cheeses, grapes, Leroy had talked about the food for days afterwards, and the horizon, streaked with yellow, red and orange.

Dolly hoped that this birthday's Rising Sun would help erase the memory of the one that had set.

30

'Didn't you book a table for half-past five, when Phoebe finished work?' asked Steve and he checked his computer till. The Rising Sun had earned a reputation for the best food in Lymhall. A whoosh of savoury fried smells escaped through the kitchen swing doors.

'I'm here early to give you this...' Dolly slid a bag across the bar. Flo stood on tiptoe as Steve looked inside. She'd helped Dolly ice it.

'Cake, candles...' Steve looked up.

'For our friend Leroy. I was hoping you wouldn't mind if...' She pulled out decorations.

'Go for it,' he said. A woman stood tapping her long nails on the bar's natural wooden counter. Steve shot her a tight smile.

'Still got staffing problems?' Dolly asked in a low voice.

'I don't know how much longer I can cope, to be honest.' He straightened himself and picked up the cake. 'But don't worry, I'll make sure you have a fantastic evening. Music choice?'

'Leroy likes a band called Earth, Wind and Fire,' said Flo.

'Anything you can dance to,' said Dolly.

Steve explained how one of his favourite playlists was a 1970s disco medley and despite a sour look from the woman waiting he started doing the Funky Chicken. Flo covered her mouth with her hand, unable to hide her laughter. He pointed to table in the far right-hand corner of the room, the brickwork interior there almost hidden by trailing ivy. Flo scattered the multi-coloured glitter, whilst Dolly tied a silver balloon to a chair. The cardboard centrepiece looked as if a firework had burst into stars and suited the animated chat from the crowd at the neighbouring table drinking champagne.

'You must like the drinks in this place, Dolly,' said Flo, bopping the balloon. 'You haven't brought your turquoise tea flask.'

At that moment Phoebe appeared, wearing a bold striped sweatshirt and jeans, hair let down, long and glossy – no one would ever guess she'd been so ill. Greta had always taken people at face value. If a stranger was rude she thought it was because they were simply uncouth, whilst Dolly preferred to look deeper, to work out the hidden reason. Yet with Fred, Greta hadn't trusted what everyone else saw, the kind smile, the popularity, the courteous manner. Or was it only Dolly who'd been blind to the designer clothes his day job could never have afforded, to the mysterious weekends and evenings away he never really talked much about?

Flo announced she'd already decided to have the beef burger; her mum only bought veggie ones these days. She showed the menu to Phoebe and the two of them sat down. Leroy appeared in the doorway, wearing his favourite lime-green anorak, as the song 'Midnight Train to Georgia' came on. Flo looked up and waved. He came over, moving his hands in a chugging train motion.

'Great moves,' called Steve from the bar. Leroy looked over and gave a little bow.

'Wow! I should have worn sunglasses,' he said and stared at the table decorations before giving Dolly a hug. He smiled at Phoebe and said, 'Nice jumper, Flo.'

Flo looked so grown up in her pink-and-blue animal-print top, with jeans and a little suede jacket. Over the last year a change had taken place: cute bobbles and hair slides had disappeared, Disney character clothes were replaced with more adult options. The little girl who liked long cuddles and chats with Maurice was slipping away to make room for a confused teen.

'Happy birthday, Leroy!' Flo said and shyly pulled out a parcel from her rucksack. Leroy took off his coat, dark shadows prominent under his eyes.

'I'll go up to the bar and get drinks, it'll save Steve having to come over,' said Phoebe.

Leroy sat opposite Flo and tore off the shiny paper.

'It's a card trivia game about music in the seventies,' she burst out. 'You could play it with Dolly.'

'We haven't had a games evening for a while.' He raised his hand in the air and Flo high-fived it. 'I'll put it with my other games. I've brought them all back down from the loft.' Dolly pushed over a thin envelope. Leroy ran his finger along the seal and tugged out... 'A voucher for... *Jammin'*?'

'It's a Jamaican food restaurant. I didn't know we had one in Manchester. It's not far from The Printworks. They've got takeout sweet treats, like that rum cake you were saying Winston baked.'

'Here's my present,' said Phoebe, arriving with a tray of drinks. 'I told Steve about your trip to the Caribbean and he made you a Jamaican Breeze cocktail, with honey, vanilla, spices and orange.'

'Thanks. All of you.' He looked around the table. 'These presents are spot on.' Leroy closed his eyes as he sucked on the straw, then took off the chunk of fruit and bit off the flesh. Flo jumped up and stuck the paper parasol behind his ear. He twirled it with his fingers. 'The new sophisticated me really didn't last long.'

'You could order a fancy meal instead... like Steve's pesto salmon,' said Phoebe.

Leroy looked at the options. 'Scampi and fries in *a basket*? I'm impressed. I haven't had that for decades. It's far more *me*.'

'Steve likes to play around with the menu, keeping it relevant but sometimes going retro.' Phoebe pointed on the menu. 'There's even a prawn cocktail, jazzed up with sticks of avocado.'

Rubbing his forehead, Steve came over. He kept glancing back at the bar.

'Happy birthday, train man... Leroy, isn't it?' He gripped a handheld electronic order pad. 'I'll have to duck if "Heaven Must Be Missing an Angel" comes on – you might take flight.'

'Can't resist a catchy beat, I'm afraid. Are' – he scrutinised Steve – 'the eighties more your decade?'

'Any decade that gets my feet moving. If there are hand movements to boot, all the better.' He walked to and fro, doing the hustle dance routine, clapping his hands in the appropriate places.

Phoebe rolled her eyes. 'I should be used to this, by now.'

Leroy got up, pulling Dolly to her feet too. He suggested the bump, so the three of them put their hands in the air and bumped hips together, in time to the music.

'Maybe minimalist Leroy was better after all,' whispered Flo to Phoebe.

'What do I have to do to get a drink around here?' called a voice from the bar.

Quickly Steve took their food order and left.

'You've known him long?' Leroy asked Phoebe, concentrating on his drink.

'Steve's lived next door, like, for ever. He and his husband, John, used to babysit me when my grandparents went out.'

'I didn't know he was married,' said Dolly, Leroy listening intently. 'The speed-dating evening...'

'John died four years ago,' explained Phoebe. 'Steve has thrown himself into work since then. An insurance policy on John's death meant he could update the pub. The two of them had been discussing a refurb for a while, so that felt like the best way to spend the money. Steve updated the menu, redecorated, and eventually it worked; business has really taken off this last year. Local companies often bring clients here for lunch. Then there are the themed evenings – for Valentine's, Saint Patrick's, Easter... they always go down a treat. He's been able to relax more lately, think about his personal life – at least, until he had the staffing problems.'

Phoebe stirred her drink with the straw.

'He regularly asks me if I'll consider moving jobs, offers me good money. He went away to a conference for a week, recently, all about how pubs are having to reinvent themselves. He's thinking about meal delivery. But however busy he is, Steve still comes around to ours to eat, once a week, and we play card games. He likes to cook and insists on taking over the kitchen and' – she looked at Dolly – 'he doesn't take offence if I can't finish the meal.'

'Sounds like the perfect parent,' said Flo, and glugged her Coke.

Leroy studied the queue forming at the till. Steve was red in the face and perspiring as if the pub's temperature reflected its name.

'Doesn't surprise me he can't keep the staff,' said Leroy. 'I got a call from work yesterday, asking if I'd be interested in going back to run the restaurant part-time.'

'What?' said Dolly. 'I can't imagine going back to Hackshaw Haulage, not now.'

'Me neither. They threw me a big retirement party and everything. But my successor has left. They sounded desperate. The hospitality industry still hasn't recovered from—' The sound of shattered glass interrupted him. Steve stood behind the bar, looking flustered.

Flo questioned Phoebe about university – the cost of accommodation, something called a maintenance grant, how you didn't begin paying loans back until the April after you graduated, how the monthly amount depended on your earnings. Phoebe thought it was cool that Flo wanted to study insects. A woman on her course had dated a guy studying entomology. In the summer of the first year he did a volunteering trip to Peru and monitored butterfly species. He came back satisfied he'd made a difference.

A waiter appeared with their food. Dolly had gone with the salmon, which prompted the conversation to move to Maurice and Fanny. Flo asked Phoebe how goldfish ate without teeth, fascinated to learn they had them at the back of their throats. She disappeared to the loo whilst Phoebe and Dolly planned their trip to Afflecks and then Leroy struck up a conversation with Phoebe about Man City's latest game, when shouting cut through, as Flo came back.

'This place is a joke! I'm not waiting an hour to eat,' hollered a man by the till. He stormed out of the pub, his laptop case swinging from side to side. Steve's gaze followed him as he flounced out, not hearing more patient customers ask him for a drink. Leroy chewed carefully as he finished his scampi, put down his knife and fork, then got to his feet. He collected his friends' empty plates and marched over to the bar. He chatted to Steve for a couple of minutes. Steve shook his head vigorously but Leroy kept talking, until... he rolled up his sleeves and disappeared into the kitchen. Moments later Leroy reappeared and started taking drinks orders.

'But Leroy can't work on his birthday,' said Flo. 'What about birthday cake? I've got to be home, at the latest, by nine. We're up early to go to Wales for the weekend. Dad reckons the school holidays traffic will be bad, and it's a Friday.'

Leroy pretended to throw a glass over to Steve and the two men laughed.

'Why don't you help me and Dolly with our baking practice? We're doing biscuits this time.' said Phoebe. 'And if we hurry, we can still get back here by nine and do Leroy's birthday cake then, when it's less busy. I only live five minutes away by car. Biscuits don't take long, it'll be icing them that needs more attention. Dolly could ring your parents, see if they'd mind you staying out a little bit longer, just in case you're a few minutes late.'

Flo gave Phoebe a hug and the two of them linked arms as they headed outside, waiting in the porch for Dolly to tell Leroy of their plan. The baking session flew by and Phoebe said she'd tidy the kitchen later. The icing had been tricky. They'd put in too much colouring, the yellow chicks looked blinding, and the shortbread was so crumbly several biscuits had cracked. But Flo had announced they tasted as good as shop-bought ones. When they arrived back at the Rising Sun the food order rush had abated. In fact Leroy and Steve were sitting at their table in front of Jamaican Breezes. As the three of them went over, Steve headed for the kitchen, beckoning to Phoebe and Flo to follow.

'How did it go?' Leroy asked as Dolly sat down. 'Was Fred there?'

'He stayed in the lounge. Flo showed incredible restraint. I could tell she was dying to go in and introduce herself.'

'And Flo is allowed to stay out a little later?'

Dolly nodded. She'd spoken to Mark. She still hadn't told

Leroy about him not being Flo's real dad – it was obvious her young neighbour hadn't meant to let that slip out. It didn't make sense to Dolly; she'd always thought how alike they'd looked, with the same shaped nose.

'But let's talk about you.' She jerked her head towards the bar. 'What was that all about?'

'Just helping out.'

Dolly pushed his shoulder. 'Leroy Robinson, what aren't you telling me? You look as if you've had the best birthday ever.'

'I'm truly alive again Dolly, for the first time since Tony left. Work phoning me last night. I hardly slept afterwards. Their offer excited me – not the prospect of going back to them, but the idea of mucking in again, the buzz of serving customers, having a place to go where I'm valued...' He ran a finger around the rim of his glass. 'If I'm honest, I can see now that Tony and I were never a good fit. He'd call board games "bored games" and thought disco music naff. But when the initial physical attraction loosened its grip I held on tighter than ever because I was scared of... retiring. Of becoming irrelevant. Helping Steve tonight has confirmed what I figured out in the early hours of this morning. I'm not ready to retire. Steve jokingly offered me part-time hours and couldn't have been more surprised when I accepted.' His face shone. 'It'll mean I get to enjoy the aspects of work I used to love – chatting with customers, pulling pints, delivering food – without the managerial responsibilities. It's made me realise... my personal brand... it's not self-discovery, like yours, after all. I think my brand is that I'm a people person.'

A fizzing noise interrupted them. Steve appeared, carrying the cake that had a sparkler candle in the top. Phoebe carried plates, Flo forks and napkins. The other tables joined in with singing 'Happy Birthday'.

'Well done for having a slice,' Dolly whispered to Phoebe.

'Well done you for just having a small one,' she replied.

They smiled at each other, a smile that acknowledged there were more layers to the sponge than simply the two stuck together with cream. Dolly took her last mouthful when fingers tapped on her shoulder. She turned around.

'This is stupid, Dolly,' said Fred.

'What on earth are you doing here?' He hadn't even got a coat on; his wispy hair was tousled.

'Us not talking. We're acting like a pair of teenagers.'

'I think you took the medal in that in 1975,' she replied in a stiff voice.

'Granddad. You promised,' hissed Phoebe. She stood up. 'I'm sorry, everyone. We'll leave.'

Steve got up and came back with a box of dominoes. 'Bet I can beat you two hands down,' he said to Leroy and Flo. 'The bar's quiet for the moment. We can fit in one game if we're quick.'

Flo stopped staring at Fred and she, Leroy and Steve busied themselves laying out pieces.

Dolly got to her feet and wiped her mouth with a napkin, folding it up neatly and placing it back on the table. Leroy wasn't the only one who'd not slept well last night. With the prospect of potentially seeing Fred during the bake-off practice, thoughts had spun around and around in her head, like a washing machine that made its contents dirtier, not cleaner.

She stared at Fred. 'I'm finally going to clear out Greta's room. First thing tomorrow, I'll get stuck in. I'll be looking for anything that explains why she didn't want me to go to Paris. Come around at three. We'll discuss what I've found, if anything.'

He touched her shoulder but Dolly shook him off and crossed her arms.

'You didn't fight hard enough for what we had, Fred. For us, there's no going back.'

31

Six o'clock. An early start, weighed down by a dark atmosphere and pummelling rain. Dolly opened the door to Greta's room, opposite hers. Despite the dust and stuffiness, it still looked tidy. She stared without going in, at the shelves with books in alphabetical order, the dressing table with toiletries neatly aligned on its top. Greta bought the cheapest products, apart from when it came to perfume. On a shelf, above the dressing-table mirror, she'd placed a collection of beautiful bottles, different cut-glass shapes, oval, rectangular, tall and sleek, some with atomizer bulbs. The shelf was actually the shallow lid of the small case Greta had bid on in... 1997. Peach material lined the inside, a totally impractical colour but Greta always had loved pastels. Its gilt trim did look smart. With a deep breath, Dolly walked into the room, clutching a roll of black dustbin bags and a sheet of stickers. She wrote *Charity Shop* on several, *Bin* on others, and stuck them on to bags. After a large mouthful of strong tea, she went over to the chest of drawers.

Underwear, petticoats, socks, tights, nightdresses, it was easy to stuff them into a bag for the tip. Her breath hitched as the smell from the scented paper drawer liners rose into the air. They still smelt of sandalwood. Still smelt of Greta. Fingers digging into the floral duvet cover, she took a moment on the bed. Pangs of emptiness seeped into her pores, deeper than any perfume could. Despite the decades spent in the bungalow, Greta's room was new territory. Like a nosy child, Dolly lifted the lid on a small pot-pourri bowl, tried hand cream, examined jewellery. She stood in front of a framed black-and-white photo, the only one of the two sisters and their mother. Dolly had been around two years old and held their mother's hand. Greta would have been eighteen. The snap was taken in front of deckchairs on a beach. Their mother had saved every penny for weeks and taken them to a boarding house in Lytham. Greta had been through several difficult months and needed a break. She'd been blamed for an incident at work that wasn't her fault and had to leave, and on top of that had to see Mum through another break-up. The three of them looked happy enough in the photo, until you inspected it closely – Greta seemed strained.

Greta had had a few boyfriends when she was younger. Dolly had met one when she was five, an image in her head of a khaki uniform. His conscription had ended but he'd been bullied in the forces; Greta talked about how he'd go days without talking. Greta never dated as she got older – unlike Dolly, unlike their mother. Her sister's reading choices were eclectic and included romances. Didn't she crave a love story of her own, Dolly had once asked, or at least a few dates, to have a bit of fun? But Greta had rolled her eyes, said fiction was fiction, and in any case she had her job, her books, gardening was fun and, of course, she had Dolly.

Dolly took down the frame and stripped the walls, putting the pictures on the bed for the moment. In the corner, Greta's notebooks caught her eye. She picked up a handful of the ones containing book reviews and sat on the bed again. The covers were pastel, no fancy patterns, and she flicked the top one open. The first review was fairly recent, from 2018, and about *Less*, a Pulitzer Prize-winning novel focusing on a failed novelist. The review spoke solely of the character's trips to Mexico, Italy, Japan, other places... the food, landscape, the weather. There was no comment on character development, nor plot twists, nor prose. She flicked forward several pages to one about *Captain Corelli's Mandolin*. Greta wrote only about the Greek Cephalonian island setting. Dolly picked up another notebook. Each one might have a different theme, the next could focus on historical eras, but yet again, foreign countries were the focus. The review of *The Color Purple* was all about Georgia. *The Little Paris Bookshop* one, France, *The Kite Runner*, Afghanistan, *The Girl with the Pearl Earring* was set in Holland, *Loser Takes All*, Monaco. Dolly threw that notebook to one side and picked up one more that began with a novel called *The White Tiger* – the review talked about the sights and way of life in India. Dolly turned to the pile of recipe notebooks and leafed through one before standing up. She flexed her fists in front of the wardrobe, and went to open the doors but her stomach rumbled. Breakfast first.

She drew open the curtains in the lounge. The room brightened enough for her to see Maurice and Fanny. She crouched by the tank and they swam over before darting to the top of the tank. She missed her close relationship with Maurice, the daily staring contests, but she wanted the best for him. Greta might have been afraid of losing her closeness to Dolly. Or was she genuinely afraid her younger sister might get hurt? Greta once read a book about penguins, the review of which had no doubt focused on Antarctica. She learnt that bird species were sixty to ninety per cent monogamous. Bald eagles wouldn't look at another partner unless their mate died. But in mammals, Greta announced, the percentage was three to five.

After dropping a pinch of flakes into the tank, Dolly put on the kettle and reached for the Tupperware container of Easter biscuits, left over from last night. However, her mood, her aches and pains, her mobility, all had improved so much with her eating more healthily and getting out and about, swimming as well, and the chest pains had eased. Therefore, instead, she made a bowl of porridge, with berries on top and a modest squirt of honey. The meal filled her with reassuring warmth, and after washing up her bowl she returned to her sister's bedroom.

The wardrobe's doors swung open and a wave of nostalgia caught her by surprise as she touched Greta's favourite tweed coat. It had always been so important to her sister to look respectable, with rigid lines down trousers, sparkling brooches and hats positioned at just the right angle. Dolly had thought Greta might relax once retired, but that gave her more time to focus on the appearance of herself and the bungalow. Dolly pulled out the tweed coat and slipped into it. She did it up. Right to the top. Then she filled dustbin bags with clothes until the rail was empty. She took off the coat and buried her head in the material for a moment, before putting it into the bottom of a charity shop bag. At the bottom of the empty wardrobe was a portable box file. Dolly would examine that later. Dolly lifted up a small wooden chest and sat down on the bed. Carefully she opened the lid.

Of course. Mum's special things. Her favourite ivory pendant, the most expensive item she'd owned, a present from a boyfriend before he revealed he was married. Her decorative powder compact with flowers engraved on the top; a small pile of birthday cards. Dolly flicked through them. Her eyes pricked. They were all from Greta. She was about to close the lid when poking out from underneath a lace handkerchief was a yellow knitted bootie with a tiny orange bow. There were two of them. Their mum always did say that Greta looked good in sunshine colours. As the rain fell in torrents outside, Dolly sorted through her sister's shoes, on a rack under the windowsill. She'd filled seven dustbin bags, two of them full of bedclothes. For the moment, she'd leave the perfume bottles where they were.

Fred used to buy her L'Air du Temps perfume by Nina Ricci, and if he went for a weekend away would ask her to spray it on his handkerchief, to have a bit of her by his side for those two days. Her jaw set. She stood on tiptoe and removed a bottle from the shelf. She loosened her grip and let it fall into a newly opened dustbin bag. The others followed, then toiletries, the creams and lotions, packets of unused tablets. The doorbell rang.

'Shit.'

Swearing. In Greta's room. The ultimate sacrilege.

Right at this moment, it felt brilliant.

She glanced in the mirror. Her hair was a mess, perspiration shone on her brow, dust covered her jumper. The woman in the reflection shrugged back at Dolly. She didn't owe Fred anything, and that included a pristine appearance.

* * *

They sat at the kitchen table and the kettle whistled like a referee foreseeing a fallout.

'Terrible weather,' he said as Dolly got up.

'But good for the garden,' she replied.

She put his tea down in front of him, and sat with hers, accompanied by a late lunch – lightly buttered toast. The crunch as she bit down sounded magnified.

'Phoebe's really pushing herself doing this bake-off trip. Angela wouldn't believe it,' he finally burst out.

'She's a lovely girl.'

'Yes. I'm very lucky.' He held his mug with both hands. 'So, did you find anything in Greta's room that might help us?'

Us? He had no right to use a word that ignored the last four decades apart.

'A box file I'm going to go through, but apart from that just clothes, personal items, all of her notebooks.'

'Did she carry on writing book reviews? You said once how she always had her head in a novel and wrote up her thoughts afterwards.'

'There are piles of them in her bedroom. The reviews are unusual, each one focusing on the story's setting.'

Fred jigged his glasses from side to side. 'May I see? Being a reader and all...'

Dolly brought in as many as she could carry and placed them in front of him higgledy piggledy. Fred opened one randomly and shook his head. '*One Hundred Years of Solitude*. A classic.' He scanned the review. 'I see what you mean – it focuses on Colombian life. This book was one of the first...' Fred shifted. 'I read it in prison. A bit of a challenge for a beginner but I became gripped by such a saga, a story about so many generations. Jealousy ran through me with every page. I never did find out anything about my biological parents.'

He always did love *The Waltons*, the ultimate telly show about generations of families living together. Dolly's shoulders relaxed as he picked up another notebook.

'*Live and Let Die*... Yes, Harlem... Jamaica... was she a fan of James Bond movies too?'

'Goodness, no. They were far too commercial for her tastes. She found the books much more acceptable.'

A flame of humour flickered between them before loud knocking on the front door snuffed it out. Dolly returned a few moments later.

'Do I want my drive resurfacing,' she muttered and sat down. Fred didn't reply; he was going through the notebooks, at speed, one by one.

'The... love that comes across about the landscapes and cultures... It's incredible that she never holidayed abroad.'

'Not really. She was never interested in actually travelling the world, considered it a waste of money, said the UK had everything we needed. Greta did fill in notebooks after our breaks but only listing the places we visited.'

'Could I see?'

Dolly fetched a couple.

He turned the pages. 'York – she lists the Viking Centre, Moors Railway, a stately home, the... Angel on the Green?'

'A pub. Lovely homemade pizza.'

'Llandudno... the North Shore Beach Promenade, Happy Valley Botanical Gardens, the cable car... The Cottage Loaf.'

'I've never forgotten their chocolate orange baked Alaska.'

Fred closed the notebook. 'Such practical lists, nothing like the flowery, emotional reviews of places in the novels she'd enjoyed. Greta was clearly passionate about new sights and places, yet that doesn't come out of the notebooks referencing UK holidays. It's as if foreign climes excited her most. Surely she could have overcome her fear of flying. It doesn't add up. She went on a cable car in Wales. Wasn't she at all nervous?'

'She loved it. Insisted on going up twice.'

'That doesn't strike me as a woman who's scared of heights or vehicles she has no control over driving.'

Dolly read the Llandudno list herself and sat up straighter.

She lifted the portable box file on to the table. 'I'll see if I can find any clues.'

'You always did like the Pink Panther movies; a big Inspector Clouseau fan.'

'You called me Pink Panther for a while. It was the name of a diamond. You said that's what I was, and like that gem your love for me would last for ever.' Dolly's cheeks burned and she got up. 'I need to get on, Fred. I'll let you know if I find anything.'

'It was because of growing up in care,' he blurted out.

'What?'

'Diamonds, cars, top meals out... I thought no one would love me unless I had all that.' He met her gaze and she sat down again. 'That's why I sold stolen goods, to get the extra cash. You called me shallow the other day, but it wasn't because I wanted to look good or show off... You know how I got moved around different children's homes. No one ever wanted to adopt me. It's no excuse Dolly, but I thought if I had lots of... of *stuff*... fancy clothes, a motor, eventually a big house... people would want to stick around. Unlike my own mum who left me by a park bench, like a scrap of litter only worthy of being incinerated.'

'But I'd have lived in a shed if it meant us staying together, Fred,' she said in a hurt tone. 'Couldn't you tell?'

'I know that now but I was young. Stupid.'

'I'm sorry you never found out more about your parents,' she said, gently.

'Too many dead ends. I gave up trying in the end.'

'Your mum was probably young. Scared stiff. Thought you were bound to be spotted by a bench. She wouldn't have been thinking straight; certainly wouldn't have associated you with rubbish.'

'I try to tell myself that. The love you showed me back in the day… and more recently Angela, Phoebe, it's all helped.' He took off his glasses. 'I consider myself lucky. I've squeezed far more out of life than many manage. People have been kind, given me opportunities.' He put his glasses back on again. 'Greta may have got it wrong, Dolly, but at least she cared. Don't be angry with her.'

'She lied to me.' Dolly's voice hardened. 'Tomorrow I'm taking her belongings to the charity shop.'

'Take a tip from me. Don't donate to a local shop – you might see someone walking around in Greta's clothes. It knocked me for six when I saw a woman walk out of the Rising Sun wearing Angela's favourite beige-and-black trimmed trench coat. Also don't be rash and throw everything away. Save a handful of items. You might regret getting rid of the lot.' He stared past Dolly's shoulder. 'You two would have got on, you know. I talked about our life in the seventies.'

Dolly gaped. 'Angela didn't mind?'

'No. She talked about her husband. It was obvious to me that Reg was her true love. I think she guessed you'd been mine.'

What could Dolly say? That she'd had to block thoughts of Fred out for so long because every memory took her back to the overwhelming sense of loss of 1975? That no other man had ever come close? That often, over the years, she'd hated his guts?

'It didn't detract from what Angela and I had. She was a wonderful woman. But it was always you, Dolly,' he said quietly. 'I'm sorry you didn't meet anyone else.'

'How do you know?' she snapped. 'Don't flatter yourself.'

He promptly left and Dolly hurried into her sister's room. Face first, she lay on the bed and punched the stripped pillows, body shuddering with the ache at what could have been. Eventually she sat up and sniffed loudly. Fred was wrong. There was no reason to keep anything of Greta's.

32

Dolly and Phoebe headed into the Trafford Centre; it had been a forty-minute drive north from Lymhall. Dolly had picked her up on the way, nodding at Fred who looked out of the front window. The two women walked into the grand food court, made to look as if it had been built as part of a huge steam ship that even had an on-deck swimming pool. They navigated the seating area and headed into the hustle and bustle of the shops on the ground floor, the knots across Dolly's shoulders becoming tighter. Yes, she'd been eating healthier, preparing salads, steaming vegetables, but apart from the recent sessions with Phoebe and Flo, and the apple crumble, she'd not baked for so long. A cake might sink in the middle, biscuits might fall apart, a pie's crust might turn out rock hard. She didn't care what others thought, she cared that she might have lost her skills. Until finding the notebook, her life was at ground zero, as if she'd lost so many other things along with her sister. Slowly she was picking up old social habits, chatting with strangers, making jokes, and doing her laundry, keeping the bungalow clean, things she'd taken for granted before Greta died, all important but dressed up as insignificant. Dolly wiped her clammy hands on her jacket.

'Greta and I came to the Trafford Centre first in 1998, as soon as it opened,' she said as they turned left and walked past shiny glass fronts, behind which were clothes and shoes. 'The design bowled us over, the paintings, sculptures, the rococo and baroque interior – Greta read up on it when we got home. We agreed the marble throughout is beautiful with its shades of ivory, jade and pink. As for all the gold decor – it's real gold leaf, you know?'

'Gran loved it here too – the authentic artefacts, the three domes. She'd bring me for a girls' day out; we'd see a film and eat out.'

Children scurried past carrying helium balloon animals and crowds gathered around pop-up perfume and cake stalls in the centre of the walkway. Dolly and Phoebe finally reached the far end and a glass front framed with cartoon drawings of cakes and pastries. The neon sign at the top said *Bake-off*, with a chef's hat sitting on the B. After leaving their coats and bags in lockers, they walked into a spacious kitchen, wearing the navy aprons the receptionist had given them. The room smelt of cleaning fluid, was rectangular and had whitewashed walls. Phoebe bit her thumbnail and Dolly hesitated before linking arms. They'd been told to stand by workstation number five. The four other pairs of bakers were already in position. The workstation was made up of a long unit, with an oven underneath, and various utensils lined up in a regimented fashion on top, clean and impatient to start.

Dolly took her arm away to adjust her apron and Phoebe raised a hand, touching the pearl and diamond ring hanging around her neck. Two pairs at the back, young women, sported pink hen party sashes, hazy eyes and vodka breath. There was another younger woman with someone who could have been her mother. The other participants were middle-aged and looked like a couple. Phoebe wore her usual hoodie and joggers – today's were dark marine with cream trim that showed off her green eyes. Greta always said tan and chocolate shades brought out the best in Dolly's. Her brown eyes were the only clue she had to her father's appearance. Greta's were blue like their mother's.

As a teenager Dolly had gone through a phase of wanting to know more about her father. Classmates at school had started to ask questions. Egged on by a friend she'd marched around to her mum's flat one day after school. Dolly had been living with her sister for a number of years by then and had been saying to her sister, for days, that she was sick of being treated like a child when it came to her dad. To her surprise Greta's car had been outside. Dolly had a key and let herself in. She heard them talking in the small lounge.

'She can't ever know,' said her mum, in between sobs. 'I'm so ashamed of what happened. That bastard ruined everything. We have to protect her, Greta, whatever it takes. I love that girl to bits and wish I found it easier to say that to her face.'

That was the only time she'd ever heard her mother say she loved her. Then and there, Dolly decided it was a waste of energy looking for a man who'd treated her mum so badly. As she got older his importance dwindled further. Boyfriends came into her life and despite her sister and mother's reservations, these men gave her more faith in the opposite sex and a future of her own that might include getting married. She'd left school at sixteen and her sister was there to help when she opened a bank account, applied for her driving licence, filled in paperwork for her first job. You didn't need a birth certificate for everything back then and in any case, Greta was always there handling the documents, simply pointing out where Dolly had to sign. Dolly had been grateful. The certificate might have revealed her father's name, though perhaps that was unlikely, and after witnessing her mother's upset that afternoon, after school, Dolly decided it didn't matter.

However, Greta's help could have been orchestrated, she could have acted on purpose to hide the certificate and the truth about Dolly's dad.

'Welcome, everyone!' cut in a breezy voice belonging to a man in a white chef's jacket and chequered trousers. The party people at the back stopped passing around the bottle Dolly had spotted. 'My name's Dan and I've run my own bakery since I was thirty. The last few years the business fell on hard times and I came up with the idea of running these bake-off sessions. Countless inexperienced participants have contacted me afterwards saying an afternoon here inspired them to carry on baking.' He gestured to the room in a welcoming fashion. 'Food is about fun. Eating's not only about feeding your body. It's about taking time out of life, during your day, to leave stress behind and savour delicious flavours and textures. It's about cooking for loved ones, nourishing your soul by creating a dish from scratch.' He smiled. 'Of course, we all enjoy convenience food or takeout now and again, but what I'm trying to say is... I hope today helps any of you who, for whatever reason, are fearful of cooking.'

Dolly stole a glance at Phoebe who was hanging on every word.

'Right!' Dan clapped his hands. 'Those keen amongst you might have given it some thought and suspected we'd go with an Easter theme today.'

The middle-aged couple nodded at each other.

'Remove the tea towel covering the basket in front of you.'

Dolly and Phoebe stared at the ingredients – sugar, eggs, bread flour, yeast...

'Hot cross buns!' he announced.

'I didn't think of that as being special to Easter,' whispered

Dolly. 'I eat them all year round.' This was going to be a disaster. Proof that not only had Dolly never had a long-term relationship, a family of her own, never travelled much, but that her baking skills weren't a real achievement either and Greta had only pretended to love her cakes and biscuits.

She shook herself. *Get it together.*

'On the bench, at the back, you'll find an array of ingredients,' said Dan, striding past the workstations. 'Fresh and dried fruit, icing sugar, colouring, sprinkles, custard powder, spices... You must make six basic buns, according to the recipe I've given you. Then use your imaginations. They can be filled or iced or both. All I ask is that they are round and risen.' He looked at the clock. 'You've got two hours. You must leave the dough to rise for forty minutes, thinking time for how to add a little magic.' He looked the clock. 'Right, go for it...'

Almost three hours later Dolly groaned with pleasure, sitting at a large circular table in a room adjacent to the big kitchen. Coffee cups littered the table along with plates of buns, and sugary, spiced smells hovered temptingly in the air. Chat filled the room along with drunken laughter. 'This dark chocolate bun made by the couple next to our workstation is so moreish.'

'But not as good as those fancy salted caramel ones – the filling oozed out of them,' said Phoebe. 'They deserved that trophy. I still can't believe Dan said our humble, healthy orange and honey buns were a close second.'

In a celebratory mood, Dolly drained her cup; it was her third. Phoebe had suggested the orange and honey flavour and thought up how to decorate the buns' tops, whilst Dolly made sure the dough was mixed thoroughly and that they didn't over-knead it. The sensation of ingredients between her fingers had reminded Dolly of why she used to enjoy baking: the sense of mindfulness, the physicality, the satisfying sweet homely smells and flavours. Just because Greta had gone, that didn't mean Dolly shouldn't bake; she could freeze bigger batches and take treats around to Leroy and Flo.

'Look at you, Phoebe. The bits you've eaten. How have you found sitting here in front of all this food?'

'That's what I like most about you, Dolly. You talk about the stuff that matters. You don't tiptoe around me. Don't judge. When I was ill at uni, I tried talking to friends but they didn't get it – and I don't blame them, it's hard to understand, and they all had problems of their own... but with you, I know I'm not imposing and I don't have to hide anything.'

A lump formed in Dolly's throat. She wanted to say that was down to Greta, who'd always been forthright, or so Dolly used to think.

'I can't stop going over everything Dan said,' continued Phoebe. 'I might try cooking more. If Granddad allows me.' She smiled. 'He loves busying himself in the kitchen.'

'Back in the day it was meals out or sandwiches. He never learnt any cooking skills in the children's homes.'

'He makes a great Thai chicken curry and even better pancakes than Gran's.' Phoebe fingered the ring hanging from her neck. 'If I chose and prepared ingredients myself, I might have a different outlook on food.'

Phoebe gazed around the table and smiled at the young woman who'd come with her mother. She and Phoebe had talked whilst the hot buns were being brought in. Zoe had recently moved back home after losing her job in a bookshop and didn't live far from Lymhall. It had been a great afternoon but the best part for Dolly had been listening to Phoebe laugh.

'I couldn't have done this without you, Dolly.' She sighed. 'I wish my friend Maisie had got in touch. She'd love to hear how this went.'

'There's really no way you can find her?'

'Not that I can think of. I reckon she's gone abroad. Maisie would talk about her trips and ask how my counselling was going. We didn't dwell on it but she made me feel... seen. As if she got why I was struggling; she could see behind the facade.'

'I'm sure she, and your gran, would be very proud.'

Dolly had never seen those green eyes shine quite so brightly.

'How's it going sorting through Greta's room? Have you found anything? Granddad mentioned the portable box file.'

'No – nothing but bank statements, council tax statements, receipts for big purchases. I can't find my birth certificate, nor Greta's. It's weird.'

'Granddad's been in a weird mood since he came back from yours last week, especially after meeting up with his old boss a couple of days ago. He also grew up in care.' She sighed. 'It makes me sad that he still thinks about that awful time. Gran used to encourage him to talk about it, but she isn't around any more.'

'I know bits but Fred used to prefer to focus on the present, when I knew him.' Occasionally he'd talk about the children's homes he'd lived in, when they curled up together, after an early night, saying how happy it made him to have finally found someone like Dolly.

'Granddad said he never really made many friends until the last home, when he was a teenager. He hated that place when he first moved in. A staff member told him it would either make or break him. Those first nights he cried into his pillow, trying to shut out the shouting and arguments. But eventually he made good friends and things got better. He tried to track them down when he came out of prison.'

'Did he succeed?'

'He found a few. His best friend had been in and out of rehab and periodically homeless. Another went to prison. One had long-term depression. I said once that, actually, he'd done well, considering. It was a stupid thing to say. He got quite cross and snapped at me.'

'Why?'

'He said no one could ever understand how hard it is to be thrown out of the care system at eighteen with no support, no money, no family. No one had a right to judge those who struggled.' Phoebe's cheeks flushed. 'He was right, of course.'

Dolly thought back to how excited Fred used to get furnishing his own flat and a smile crept over her face. And how she could never understand why he kept wanting to meet Greta and her mum. He'd take them flowers, brush off disapproving looks. He must have been hoping to finally create a family of his own. A crack appeared in the shell, in her head, that she'd locked thoughts of Fred into, over the years. A chink of light cut through the hard, black crust. Fred had made mistakes but he hadn't had it easy.

'Your birth certificate...' said Phoebe. 'Would a fresh pair of eyes help? Greta might have left a clue in the dining room or lounge.'

Dolly brushed a crumb off her striped jumper. She'd bought it on Sunday when she and Leroy had gone shopping. He'd wanted a new pair of shoes for work and couldn't stop talking about the Rising Sun. He'd done his first shift on the Saturday and was already compiling a list of ideas he had, to bring in new staff and keep them.

Leroy had his sparkle back.

'Easter Monday, do you fancy coming around for lunch? Leroy is coming, I invited him Sunday but he's working. I've invited Flo as well; her parents have a big deep clean job on, a large office in Salford – they often do jobs like that on public holidays when people aren't at their desks. I said she could bring

Anushka. They can spend the day at mine and work on their skills builders badge. Ask Fred if he wants to join us – he could bring dessert.'

Phoebe's eyes lit up and she touched Dolly's arm. 'Are you sure?'

'The more pairs of eyes, the better,' she said, briskly.

'We've got to find your birth certificate before next month's challenge. You might need to pay extra to fast-track a passport application, but it's not an impossible feat to get one in a few weeks – an old friend of mine did it. April, the bake-off, that was my year of firsts' last challenge. But I never got to do the first one properly, the May one, because I lost my luggage and came home early. That needs remedying. So bring it on.' The young woman with her mother, Zoe, stood up to go and gestured to Phoebe, who went over. They took out their phones, exchanging numbers.

What did Phoebe mean? Passport application? Dolly put down her last bite of bun and sat up straight. Of course. Her stomach fluttered.

Could Dorothy Bell finally be going to Paris?

33

With 'Boogie Wonderland' playing in the background, Dolly walked out of the kitchen, surprised she'd heard the doorbell. Flo and Anushka were helping Leroy peel parsnips and singing along at the tops of their voices, having admired the huge chocolate egg Leroy had brought with him – a gift from Steve for putting in extra hours, despite being so new to the job. Reluctant to leave the caramelised smell of the beef joint sneaking out of the oven, Dolly went along the hallway. Why had she invited Fred? She looked in the mirror and brushed a strand of hair out of her face.

Fred held a round Tupperware box and took off the lid. 'Pineapple upside-down cake. You made it often enough for me.'

He hadn't forgotten.

'It looks delicious.'

The strained look left his face. The first time she'd baked him a cake he'd not been able to speak for a few moments. No one had ever made him one before – not with love, not with his favourite ingredients. Fred always thought pineapple sounded exotic.

She glanced over his shoulder. 'Where's Phoebe?'

'She came with me in the car because she wanted to jog back to Lymhall. She's had a... difficult couple of days.'

Dolly moved on to the outdoor step and spotted Phoebe outside Leroy's bungalow doing stretches.

'Go straight in, I won't be a moment.' She brushed straight past him and hurried down her drive and turned right. Phoebe stood up and went to put on her earphones.

'Wait!' called Dolly.

Phoebe turned around. She stared at Dolly's feet. 'You've still got your slippers on.'

'What's the matter? Why aren't you coming in?'

She shrugged.

Dolly shook Phoebe's arm gently. 'It's me. A woman who ate out of food tins for a year, forgot how to wash, almost killed her goldfish...'

Not looking up, Phoebe exhaled long and hard. 'I've binged for three days straight. Granddad meant well but he gave me a chocolate bunny on Good Friday and it triggered me. I was stressed as it was, and in any case, Easter and Christmas are always tricky.' She kicked a pebble. 'I look hideous and bloated. I don't want anyone to see me and I don't want to eat anything.'

Dolly placed her hand under Phoebe's chin and lifted her head until their eyes met.

'Do you trust me?' she asked.

'Apart from the luggage theft, prying and stalking? One hundred per cent.'

'You look no different than when we were at the Trafford Centre last week.'

'You're just being nice.'

'But you and I, we don't do that, Phoebe, layer what we say

with unnecessary decoration. Our conversations are like a plain sponge cake without the butter icing and sprinkles. I speak the simple truth. Surely you'll feel even worse on your own? Also, didn't Susan say you mustn't over exercise? What did she say to do after a binge day?'

'Carry on eating as normal,' she mumbled, 'that if I starved myself, the bingeing would come back.' Her voice wavered. 'I can't believe this has happened. I've been doing so well.'

'What have you had for breakfast?' Dolly raised an eyebrow.

Her eyes welled up. 'I've gone and undone all my hard work. It's been weeks since my last binge.'

Dolly tucked her arm around Phoebe's waist. 'How about a small roast? I'll knock up a fruit salad as an alternative to your Granddad's dessert? That will keep us both on track.'

'You're sure I don't look puffy?' she asked, in a whisper.

'Do I look okay?'

Her eyebrows knitted together. 'Of course.'

Dolly pulled her close and squeezed. 'See? People aren't too bothered about the detail of how others look.'

As they walked back to Dolly's bungalow, and stopped outside the front door, she told Phoebe about a packer at Hackshaw Haulage. He'd lost his previous job, took to drinking, ended up losing his home and partner. He got into rehab and was three years sober when he joined the trucking company. Six months in and he had a relapse. It lasted a week. Dolly's boss gave him another chance, he was a good worker usually. They chatted over lunch once, and he told her how much AA helped. His friends there insisted relapses weren't the end of a journey, they were part of it. That he had to play the long game and the main thing was to get back up and carry on, one day at a time.

Dolly went to push open the door. 'So the last couple of days, love – it's just a blip and goodness knows we all have those.' She hesitated. 'What was stressing you? Anything I can help with?'

'Granddad was under the weather, he must have had a bug, but it got me thinking... how would I ever manage without him?'

'Oh, love.'

'I know it's silly. I'm grown up now.'

'Not silly at all, although I can't see Fred going anywhere soon and for what it's worth, you've always got me. I mean...' Dolly pulled at the sleeve of Phoebe's top. 'We're friends, right?'

Phoebe slipped her arms around Dolly's neck and gave her a tight hug, before hurriedly pushing open the door. 'I Will Survive' by Gloria Gaynor welcomed her inside. She slipped off her rose-gold-heeled trainers and disappeared along the hallway. Dolly ran her fingers over her neck. It felt good to be useful; to have someone to care for, apart from Maurice. She went into the lounge and crouched by the tank. He swam over and bobbed in front of Dolly, whilst Fanny carried on pecking at gravel.

'Look at us,' murmured Dolly. 'With new friends. A new life.' A memory shot through her, like a fast-forwarded film in her mind, about her days last year in front of the television eating takeout in clothes that hadn't been laundered, speaking only to Maurice, keeping the curtains closed. She and Maurice stared at each other, water in both their eyes, but in a good way, this time.

That was the difference between her and Phoebe – or, rather, Phoebe's illness. Dolly assumed all people were like Maurice, in that her appearance didn't register with them – unless they were losers like the men at that speed-dating evening. Whereas the voice in Phoebe's head told Phoebe that she was the centre of their attention; that every aspect of how she looked mattered to strangers.

For a person who was so down-to-earth and no-nonsense, it was odd that Greta had obviously wanted to make a good impression too. Her sister didn't care what people thought of her opinions and was unwavering in an argument. So why had she cared so much about looking smart and respectable? Dolly understood Phoebe's concern about being left without Fred; Dolly used to wonder what life would be like without Greta. She'd always imagined her sister's death would be like the ending of a movie about two sisters who'd led unremarkable lives. She hadn't expected a sequel full of intrigue.

'Come and get it,' Flo called in a grown-up voice.

Dolly hurried into the kitchen and grabbed an orange, banana and two apples. She rifled in one of her cupboards and found a tin of peaches in the back. She chopped the fresh fruit and squeezed a lemon over the chunks. Phoebe and Fred were in the conservatory, Flo had insisted they wait there, once Leroy had served drinks, being that it was sunny and important guests deserved the best seats.

'Cheers everyone,' said Leroy when everyone sat around the dining-room table.

'Happy Easter,' said Fred.

'They... weren't all happy.' Dolly shot Fred a look. 'Easter can get rather messy.'

A tentative smile formed on Fred's lips as he caught her eye. 'Ah, yes. Best forgotten.'

'What aren't you telling us?' asked Flo and she put down her fork. Anushka did too.

'Back in the seventies a single mum lived in the room opposite mine,' said Fred. 'She had a small child. That Easter Dolly and I decided to leave them a gift basket. Dolly made chocolate fairy cakes with iced chicks on top. My job was to dye boiled eggs – pretty but practical. Dolly read in a magazine that boiling them with red onion skins did the job. They looked brilliant and you could still eat them.'

'I wanted a closer look when I arrived, so Fred threw one over for me to catch. He'd grabbed one without looking and it was a raw one. It hit the side of my head and smashed.' They looked at each other and a warmth infused her insides; it wasn't coming from the wine. Even Phoebe grinned and took a small bite of beef. The girls chatted about their skills builders badge, Leroy talked about work yesterday and how busy the pub's chef had been with an Easter carvery, Dolly and Phoebe described all the bake-off's hot cross buns. The bungalow had never housed so many voices.

'I might try making them,' said Leroy. 'Steve mentioned they're his favourite but he didn't have time to buy any at the weekend. What's the cross on the top made out of?'

'Shortcrust pasty,' said Dolly.

'I could personalise them. Put an S on top.'

'Wit woo,' whispered Flo to Anushka and they two girls giggled. Phoebe joined in.

Leroy folded his arms. 'Wit woo, nothing. He's been good, taking me on at a drop of a hat, that's all.'

'I thought it was you doing him a favour,' said Fred, with an innocent air.

'I'd love to make them too,' said Flo. 'I could personalise two for Mum and Dad.'

'Why don't you all come around tomorrow evening?' said Dolly. 'I can get the ingredients in.'

'I'm working but am free Wednesday,' said Leroy.

'We're still off school this week, so can stay up late,' said Flo. 'I'd like to make a treat for my parents. The three of us sat down last night. I got out my notebook where I'd written everything Phoebe told me about university costs. I mentioned putting my name down for a paper round and showed them the websites for entomology courses I've researched. Several include a working

year abroad on a research project, and I talked about the student
Phoebe knew who had volunteered in Peru.'

'And?' asked Leroy.

Flo ate her last roast potato and put down her knife and fork.
'They didn't say that much but agreed a paper round was a good
idea, and that a year abroad would look impressive on a CV and
help a student get a good job after graduating. Then this morning, over breakfast, Mum said if I'm still serious in a couple of
years' time I can help out with cleaning jobs and get paid. They
said I had to stop collecting insects in jars but for my next birthday, if I want, I can have wormery. I... I burst into tears. It was *so*
embarrassing, but I've always wanted one of those! And they are
great for composting kitchen waste.'

'Oh, love, well done for speaking up,' said Dolly. 'Well done to
your mum and dad for listening, too.'

'Mum had no idea insects could be useful and she was even
more impressed when I told her honey can be used to fight bacte-
rial and fungal infections.'

Whilst the girls and Phoebe insisted on tidying up, Phoebe
promising to plait their hair later like hers, Leroy took a call from
Steve and Fred and Dolly settled in the lounge.

'Are you okay?' she said. 'Phoebe mentioned you'd been
poorly.'

His face clouded over. 'Is that what's been the matter?'

'She worries. It's natural. But she seems okay now.'

Fred shot her a curious look.

'We've aged, haven't we?' she said and smiled.

'It's not that,' he mumbled and went to speak further but
stopped, instead shuffling in the armchair. 'I've enjoyed coming
around. Thanks for the invite. And, Dolly...?'

'What?'

'You still look great.'

'Right, shall I take a look in here?' asked Phoebe, her face more luminous than when she'd been standing outside under sunrays. 'Are you sure you don't mind us rifling through belongings, Dolly?'

In a daze, Dolly nodded. *Of course I still look great. I never thought I didn't. Who are you to comment?*

Dolly shot Fred a shy smile.

Oh, he'd lost some of his bluster, the fancy clothes, his hair had all but disappeared and his middle had filled out like hers, but he still had those spirited eyes, the kind manner, his caring side – the qualities Greta had never seen were more visible now, without the cocky manner and flash exterior. Grunting as he got up, Fred went over to the record player and leafed through the albums. Phoebe joined him and picked up the photo frame on top that was lying face down. She put it on the floor and asked which LPs belonged to Greta. She stacked them up – The Mamas and The Papas, Frankie Valli, The Beatles and Neil Diamond. One by one she pulled out each vinyl and checked in the sleeves, studying the covers for any handwritten notes. Dolly sat on the sofa going through the box file again. Fred suggested coffee as the hopeful mood in the lounge waned and left to make it. Phoebe put back the records and picked up the frame.

'Shall I search the dining room next?'

Dolly locked up the box file. 'I'll help you. If you give me that I'll put it away in Greta's room.'

Phoebe turned the frame over. The colour drained out of her face. She held it closer.

'We look alike, don't we?' said Dolly. 'Everyone used to say how Greta and I had the same thick lips and snub nose.'

Phoebe's hand shot up, to cover her mouth.

'Sweetheart?' said Dolly.

Tears sprung into Phoebe's eyes and rolled down her cheeks. A sob shuddered through the young woman's body.

'What's the matter?' Dolly passed her a tissue.

'She's really gone. Gone for good.' Phoebe gulped. 'I don't understand.'

Dolly's heart raced. 'You *knew* Greta?'

'No. Yes. This is my library friend. Maisie.'

34

Dolly strode into the kitchen, ran the cold tap and picked a tumbler up from the side of the sink, not caring if it was clean or dirty. The girls were at the dining-room table continuing with their badge work.

'What's up, gal?' asked Leroy after she'd taken several gulps. He put down the dishcloth and listened. 'Nah. No way. Greta may have had secrets, but to carry off a double identity? That's on a whole different level. It must be a misunderstanding. They do say we've all got a doppelgänger out there.'

Dolly wiped her mouth and headed back to the lounge. Fred had his arm around Phoebe. She suggested the two of them go outside to clear their heads. Phoebe grabbed her hoodie. They sat at the loveseat.

Dolly studied the photo frame. 'You're sure she looked like this?'

'The hair, the glasses... She used to...' Her voice caught.

'I know love,' said Dolly quietly. 'The past tense hurts.'

Phoebe took a moment as a robin swooped on to the lawn.

'She used to smell of sandalwood and always looked smart, especially in her favourite tweed coat. Does that ring any bells?'

Dolly's chest tightened. 'Did she wear nail varnish?'

'Yes, clear.'

'Jewellery?'

'A gold cross around her neck.'

'Tell me about the places she said she'd visited,' Dolly asked, numbly.

'I don't get it. I liked Maisie from the off. She didn't need to pretend to have this amazing life. In fact the first few weeks when we got talking she didn't mention travels at all.'

'Did she ever talk about a sister?' asked Dolly quietly.

'Never. Describing all the foreign countries she'd been to, it changed her into someone different, I often thought that. She took on a more animated... younger expression.'

'She introduced herself as Maisie?'

Phoebe pulled up her top's hood. 'Kind of. I was in the queue behind her in the library and saw her card and the name Margaret. The librarian said her cousin was called that and had shortened it to Maggie. I chipped in, said I'd had a lecturer at uni who'd shortened it to Maisie and had backpacked around the world. That's when your sister said that's what she was known as, too.'

Of course, like Maisie and Maggie, Greta was short for Margaret as well, Greta's full name that Mum never used. Dolly had almost forgotten about it.

The back door opened and Leroy's head poked out. 'The girls want to climb the oak tree.'

Dolly checked with Phoebe and then gave a thumbs-up. Fred and Leroy also came outside, nursing mugs of steaming tea; they brought out two for Dolly and Phoebe as well. Flo and Anushka charged outside but Flo stopped, leaving Anushka to climb the branches first.

'Everything okay?'

Dolly pointed to the photo frame. Phoebe explained about Maisie. Red patches formed across Flo's face.

'Greta must have been really sad to pretend to be someone else. When I was little I used to close my eyes and pretend I was the Hungry Caterpillar, eating all my favourite foods and then turning into a beautiful butterfly. Now I pretend I'm David Attenborough, exploring the Amazon rainforest and discovering new insects. Or I'm a pop star, on stage, with Ed Sheeran. I wish I could have helped Greta.'

Anushka called Flo's name and she ran off to join her friend. Fred stood by Phoebe and squeezed her shoulder. Leroy did the same to Dolly. Greta so deeply unhappy that she'd live a fictional life in a library, like a character in the books she'd loved discovering? Dolly thought back to her sister's trips to Stockport and how she always came back glowing. She'd thought that was due to her picking up a new haul of stories.

'Was Paris a place she claimed she'd visited?' Dolly muttered.

'Yes. Also Holland, Italy and Greece – more far-flung destinations too, like India. Maisie...' Phoebe winced. 'Greta even said she'd visited Afghanistan before the Soviet Union invaded in 1979.'

Dolly's brow furrowed. Leroy's hand fell off her shoulder as she got to her feet and paced up and down the lawn, yesterday's rain squelching underneath her slippers and seeping through the toes.

Fred caught her eye. 'You thinking the same as me?'

'Leroy,' she said, 'will you come inside with me a minute? Phoebe, meet me in the dining room.'

The girls came in too and by the time Dolly and Leroy came

back everyone was at the dining-room table. The girls moved their notepads and pens. Leroy and Dolly put down the piles of Greta's notebooks containing the book reviews. Dolly had planned to take them to the tip, but when the moment came couldn't do it; each review had been so carefully crafted in Greta's neatest handwriting. Dolly picked one off the top, opened it and leafed through. Disco music from the lounge had stopped.

'Your granddad and I read these notebooks. Look – *The White Tiger* review in this one focuses on India.' Dolly picked up another. 'In here is a review about Paris, one for a story based in Vietnam, and another for *The Kite Runner* about Afghanistan.'

Phoebe scanned the page. 'Greta's focused on the Afghan landscape, the mountains, the deserts, instead of Kabul and the tough subjects the novel covers.'

'So Greta travelled through her books. Why didn't she in real life?' asked Anushka.

'She didn't like flying,' said Flo, 'must have been scared of heights. Me, I love it. Especially if you get a window seat.'

'But we worked out that probably wasn't true,' said Fred, 'because she loved going in a cable car in Wales.'

'There must have been another reason,' said Dolly. 'This brings us back to the documents that are missing, like her and my birth certificates. Didn't you say that Maisie kept things like that hidden in... what was it... something that looked happy on the outside but was actually sad?'

Phoebe nodded. 'Are there any souvenirs in her room? I thought it must be an object from a trip that didn't work out well.'

'You two visited lots of places in the UK,' said Leroy. 'Did Greta ever buy mementoes of your holidays? The pair of you would always bring me a gift, but it was usually local fudge, chocolate or wine.'

'Not really. Like you say, food items such as preserves. An item of clothing. She considered photos to provide the most important memories. The only holiday I remember as a child was to the beach. She kept a photo of that.' A shiver went down her spine.

'What is it?' asked Fred. He always did used to notice the detail about Dolly.

'Greta had a photo, on her wall, from that holiday. We went to Lytham. A cheerful, sunny photo, but the snap was taken at a difficult time. Greta was only eighteen and had had to leave a job; she'd been very sad about that and if you study her face in it you can tell.'

'What job?' asked Flo.

'I don't know.' Dolly put her hand to her chest, thinking back to previous comments Phoebe had made about Maisie. A spike of excitement, shock, she wasn't sure what, sent blood rushing to her face, immediately quashed by the realisation that Greta might have kept another huge secret from her as well.

'I need to talk to Phoebe alone,' she stuttered.

'How about a game of Cluedo, you girls,' said Leroy in a cheerful tone, 'before I have to head into work? Steve's texted and swears the whole of Manchester has turned up at the Rising Sun for Bank Holiday drinks. Fred, fancy making it a four? I'm ready to open that chocolate egg I brought over.'

Flo and Anushka didn't need telling twice and followed the two men out of the room. Flo closed the door behind her.

Dolly gripped the top of one of the chairs. 'You said this Maisie had children. How is that possible? Am I an aunt?'

35

It couldn't be true. Dolly's sister, a mother? It was as ludicrous as Greta saying she'd visited other continents.

'She only spoke about it once, in depth,' said Phoebe, 'and got quite emotional – most unlike the Maisie I knew.'

Most unlike Greta, too. Underneath the table, Dolly clasped her hands together.

'Greta got pregnant in her teens.'

'What?' Dolly laughed. 'Don't be ridiculous.'

'I'm sorry, Dolly, but I believed Greta. She said she hardly showed and in the last few weeks her mum kept her off school. They didn't tell anyone, not even the doctor. A friend had delivered babies before and helped out when the time came.'

Dolly fixed on the mahogany table, studying the wood grain. If this was true, Greta wasn't cared for in hospital. Anything could have happened. What could their mum have been thinking? However, Phoebe sensed it had been a desperate situation, the two women not wanting neighbours or anyone else to know. Their mum had a hard enough time as it was, in the fifties, a single woman with a string of boyfriends and if word got out that such a young girl was *in the family way* – the words Maisie had used...

'I think your sister felt she'd let your mum down. She'd always mentioned having had kids, but it turned out she gave the baby up. Greta said it was as if she'd given away her identity as well, as the mum she so wanted to be.'

Dolly walked over to the conservatory and stood with her back to Phoebe, looking out of the glass at the borders her sister used to love tending.

'The father came into her place of work a few years after. It was a travel agency and—'

Dolly pressed her arms closer to her body. Could this be why she worked at Hackshaw Haulage – hearing the truckers' stories from abroad was the closest she got to following her dreams? But why, then, did she leave shortly after Dolly and Fred split? And why would having a secret baby mean Greta could never travel? Phoebe explained that the father was a new customer for the agency, having set up a successful hotel business. Greta couldn't control her temper when she saw him and shouted how their child would never know where it came from and that was his fault. Unsurprisingly he denied everything and walked out. Her boss fired her immediately, saying she was hysterical and lucky not to be sectioned.

'The framed photo of my sister looking miserable, in Lytham. It's all adding up.'

'She actually cried, you know? We sat by the computers; no one else had come into the library yet. She spoke in a whisper about the one possession she'd kept from when the baby was just hers – a pair of yellow booties with orange bows. She used to kiss the baby's feet before putting them on.'

Dolly jolted before striding out of the room. She rushed into Greta's bedroom to fetch the small wooden chest. She almost broke the lid as she yanked it open and took the booties to the dining room. Dolly ran a finger over the knitting. Instinctively she smelt it, disappointed with the mustiness. 'She didn't say whether it was a boy or girl? You couldn't work it out?'

'No, and Greta never spoke about it again. That photo frame might hold the answer – holidays are supposed to be happy. The back of it might be hiding a clue.'

Oh, to have had a nephew or niece, and one that would have been roughly Dolly's age, the fun they would have had playing together, and going to the Victoria Baths – and side by side they could have fended off the stupid school bullies. Greta must have had such feelings of missing out, magnified by a thousand. Dolly tucked the booties into her trouser pocket. She'd taken Fred's advice after all and kept a small bag of mementoes, telling herself she could always throw them away at a later date if she wanted. She went into Greta's room again, confronted by the wardrobe, full of the memories of Greta's clothes. Was the shame of a teenage pregnancy the reason she always strived to look so smart and respectable? Dolly held the booties to her face once more, imagining Greta's despair when the baby smell eventually wore off. It cut through Dolly that she'd not been trusted with the truth, her sister, her mum, neither had confided in her, but giving up her own flesh and blood must have sliced through Greta's heart.

She tipped the bag upside down, over the bed. An array of items fell on to the mattress – Greta's silver hair and hand mirror set, her gold cross necklace, a man-sized Roman numeral watch, her sister ever practical, and a drawing Dolly had done as a little girl, of the three of them eating ice creams, Mum, Greta, Dolly, with sticks for arms and legs. Heart racing, she looked in the bottom of the bag. She searched under the bed. On top of the wardrobe. Pulled open every drawer.

'What's the matter?' asked Phoebe as Dolly walked back in, biting on her fist.

'The photo frame. The last time I saw it, it was lying on top of Greta's tweed coat. I think I must have put it in the bag for the charity shop, changed my mind about getting rid of it but got distracted and not taken it back out.' She threw her hands in the air. 'How could I have been so stupid?'

36

After making an urgent phone call, Dolly took the train into Stockport first thing the next morning. She couldn't face driving and needed fresh air. Despite the pinch of April, she'd kept her window open all night. Away from the tannoy announcements and squeaking of train brakes, she sat by a window and turned away from the spitting rain to stare at a Coke can rolling on the carriage floor, as the train pulled away. The revelation that Greta had a child formed a clamp around her chest leaving her struggling to breathe, as if she were a squashed drinks can.

As if she'd lost her sister all over again.

Dolly rubbed her forehead as the train pulled into Stockport station, hoping to rub away her headache. Fred hovered at her side as she stood by the doors and tilted his flat cap, letting her off first. Leroy had offered to accompany her to the charity shop – he'd tell Steve he couldn't go in early, as planned, to discuss his ideas on staff management. But Dolly hadn't wanted to disrupt his plans. Phoebe was meeting Zoe, the young woman from the bake-off. They'd been texting since last week and were meeting in Manchester to visit bookshops.

'Hope you didn't mind me butting in when Phoebs offered to cancel her plans,' said Fred. 'It's so good to see her making friends.'

'I could have come on my own,' she said in a flat voice. 'But I'm glad you did – Leroy and Phoebe would have insisted. It's partly your fault, anyway, that I've had to come this far, taking your advice not to donate the clothes locally.'

Fred smiled to himself as they headed out to the road that swept downwards past a McDonalds. A homeless woman sat by the doorway. Greta's child might have fallen on hard times. Did they look like her? Have her red-tinted hair? Maybe they'd grown up down south, lived the London life, saw the north as alien. As Dolly and Fred walked down Wellington Road, towards Merseyway Shopping Centre, she studied everyone her age who passed. She, Greta and Mum were of average height and had the usual twang of the Mancunian accent.

Dolly's niece or nephew could have been anyone.

'...and remember how we always went to Stockport's indoor market?' asked Fred and he pulled down his cap as a gust blew rain on to his cheeks. 'The knife stall that sold cutlery, scissors and kitchenware. The rails of clothing; you could buy a tracksuit for less than four quid. We used to choose a selection of cheeses. Eating them back at the flat, with crackers and a bottle of Blue Nun, would leave us feeling rather grand.'

'What?' Dolly glanced at Fred as they passed a queue of buses. Her nose wrinkled at the smell of diesel. They entered the precinct.

'Nothing. Come on, let's get to Prince's Street and that charity shop.'

Dolly drew to a halt and pulled the sides of her coat more tightly across her chest. She peered up from under her hood. 'What if they've sold the frame?' she whispered.

Fred held the tops of both of her arms. 'You and me, we never used to do what ifs. Why start now?'

That had been a quality she'd loved about Fred – he very much lived for the moment, a possible consequence of growing up in care. If she ever said the words 'what if', he'd challenge her immediately – 'What if I don't get on with my new flat mate? What if the dentist can't fix this toothache?' – he'd raise an eyebrow and distract her, often with a kiss. She forced her gaze away from his face. His lips. Kissing Fred would trigger a cocktail of emotions, an intoxicating blend that no other man had ever replicated.

Ten minutes later they stood outside the shop. Dolly glanced in the window, at the orphaned belongings. Fred pushed open the wet door and they went up to the till. She explained about the frame and the man fetched the manager. A sturdy woman with large, purple-rimmed glasses on a chain around her neck, appeared from the staircase at the back.

'It was with a bag of good quality clothes and shoes – a tweed coat, cashmere jumpers.' Greta wasn't extravagant as buying the best meant her clothes lasted for years.

The woman put on her glasses and pushed them firmly up the bridge of her nose. 'A black-and-white photo of a mother and two children, you say?'

Yes.

No.

More like a child and two mothers.

'I dropped the bag off a couple of weeks ago.'

'We keep personal items we find for three months before throwing them out. I'll be back in a jiffy.'

Dolly and Fred searched the shop, scanning the shelves of books, CDs, DVDs. A couple of frames stood amongst a collection of ornaments but were the wrong size and colour. The woman didn't take long.

'Sorry love, it's as I thought, we've hardly got any personal items, only a pair of fancy prescription reading glasses and a handkerchief embroidered with a name. At the moment upstairs is practically empty. Times are hard and donations have really dropped off the last year or two. Most bags are sorted and on the shelves within a couple of days.'

'You're sure?'

The woman's face softened. 'I hope you find it elsewhere.'

Dolly and Fred went out into the rain again, and made their way back to the shopping centre. Her hair became soaked. Dolly didn't care as much as Fred, who put his umbrella up and held it over her.

'It doesn't make sense,' he said. 'If it's not in Greta's room or in that shop, where can it be? We'll check the car boot again when we get back.'

Dolly dug her hands deep into her coat pockets. 'One of the bags had a hole in the bottom, I've been telling myself it didn't matter – I laid the tweed coat over the bottom first. But I had to lug the bag across a couple of streets. It dragged at one point. The hole must have torn more and if the frame was inside and slipped down the side...'

They stood opposite Primark and Fred pointed up to the left. He suggested they go to Costa for a drink. Dolly hadn't eaten breakfast, couldn't face it, but now she ordered a croissant and large Latte. She also bought a sandwich and juice carton; Fred didn't ask why. They sat in silence by the front window as, now and again, shoppers outside passed by. Since Marks and Debenhams had closed down, Stockport was never as busy.

'You always did love hot chocolate,' said Dolly. 'Said it was the drink of angels.'

'More the drink of the devil, these days; it plays havoc with my indigestion.' When he'd drained the cup and she'd finished her croissant, he reached across the small table and squeezed her hand. 'Did I do the wrong thing? Telling you the truth about Greta, the private detective, her threats?'

'The truth can never be wrong, can it? Otherwise, what's the point? How many people must pass from this world to the next without realising their whole existence here was based on lies? How could Greta have passed from one decade to another carrying such secrets?'

Fred wondered aloud if Greta had ever offloaded to a stranger as sometimes that was easier, in the way she had as Maisie, to Phoebe. It happened a lot in prison. Fred was out of his depth when he first went in, the other lads who been in trouble many times could see that. He kept out of the way of a lot of them but a few were decent enough. Fred picked up his teaspoon, turning it from side to side, drops of hot chocolate falling on to the saucer.

'I talked about you in a way I couldn't have to any of my friends on the outside. The plans I'd made for us. We'd have a villa in France, a flat in London, and a family home in the suburbs with our two children. I confided in one lad, Mick, about what Greta had done.' Fred looked up. 'He said she sounded like one hell of a woman. Mick meant it in a good way. Over time I came to think that too. She always had your back, Dolly.'

Fred had made plans? Dolly had too. When they were together she'd dreamed of a short, glittery wedding dress with the Bee Gees playing as she'd walked up the aisle; they'd have a disco afterwards to celebrate, with party food like cheese-and-pineapple hedgehogs. She and Fred would rent a flat within walking distance of their favourite Manchester haunts and would eventually own a cottage in Glossop and enjoy two weeks a year on the Costa del Sol.

They finished their coffee and on the way out Dolly gave the juice and sandwich to a homeless man outside. She and Fred walked around the shops, not buying anything, just talking comfortably.

'Remember that time I thought I was pregnant?' she asked as they eventually stopped for soup and a roll, out of the showers, in a café up a backstreet.

'I've thought about it often – broken my own rule about "what ifs" and imagined how things might have been different if you'd tested positive.'

The two of them had talked of nothing else at the time, both daunted by the responsibility and practical aspects of becoming a three. In her teens and all alone, pregnancy must have filled Greta with such fear.

When the rain stopped, they headed back up Wellington Road to the train station. It was late afternoon. Fred held her arm as she climbed into the carriage. She didn't pull away and they sat next to each other, arms through each other's – arms that stayed that way until they walked past his car and stopped at the end of her driveway. His body went rigid as he stared at the For Sale sign.

'I have to, Fred. I can't live here. Not any more. I rang the estate agent before going out this morning.'

Phoebe appeared in the distance, waving, and bounded over. She'd styled her hair on top of her head, applied eye shadow and lip gloss, small touches that indicated a change that making a new friend might bring, not in appearance but self-confidence. She wore a wide smile on her face, news about her day pouring out.

'Zoe and I found an amazing brunch place in the Northern Quarter. I had mashed avocado on toast, so did she. Then we shared a cake afterwards. We went to WHSmith and Waterstones.

She got talking to one of the managers and he said to drop her CV in. Then she took me to Forbidden Planet on Oldham Street. I've seen it before but never been in. Zoe loves reading manga – they're Japanese graphic novels – and showed me her favourite series called *Fullmetal Alchemist*. I bought the first one to try and...' She caught her breath. 'I decided not to get off the train at Lymhall but to come here and...' Her mouth fell open. 'You aren't moving, are you?'

Dolly nodded.

'But this is such a lovely loop,' said Phoebe. 'You've got friends either side and... you and me, we aren't far from each other...'

'I don't want to,' said Dolly, in a dull tone. 'I can't imagine not being within shouting distance of Leroy and Flo.' She met Phoebe's disbelieving gaze. 'It means a lot having other friends close. But my life in Manchester has been based on lies.'

'Did you find the frame, then?' Phoebe's voice had flatlined.

'No,' muttered Fred, still staring at the sign.

Dolly gave a big sigh. 'I need a coffee and there's a wedge of pineapple cake left.'

Phoebe sat in the lounge, staring out of the front window, whilst Fred and Dolly sipped their hot drinks. Maurice and Fanny were eating the peas Dolly had dropped into the tank – their afternoon tea. Phoebe went over to the record player and picked up the octopus plushie, turning it inside out, again and again, from the orange happy side and then to the sad blue.

'I still can't believe I'll never see Maisie... Greta again,' she said.

'Are you angry that she deceived you about her true identity?' asked Dolly.

Phoebe took a moment. 'Perhaps I should be, but no. The friendship we had, that was honest; I could tell she really cared, the way she talked, asked me questions, listened. I've put up a facade in recent years, not let people see the real me. I can't judge anyone else for doing the same. Greta must have had her reasons.'

Dolly wished she could be so generous.

Phoebe gazed at the opposite wall and the shelves of Greta's books all colour coordinated. 'What if Greta hadn't been talking about the framed photo?' She walked over and ran a finger over the novels. 'I've been thinking about that manga I bought today. The last time Greta and I met, it was in the November before she stopped going to the library. I remember because she was cross how people were still letting off fireworks even though Bonfire Night had passed. We got talking about our most loved book ever.' Phoebe nodded to herself, acknowledging the memory coming back. 'We both chose *The Alchemist* by Paulo Coelho and...' Her voice wavered. 'We laughed at how that confirmed our friendship was meant to be, even though it's probably the favourite read of many people around the world.' Her eyes glistened.

'It's a great story,' said Fred gently, and he wiped his mouth.

'What's it about?' The only Alchemist Dolly knew was the bar in Spinningfields that Leroy had talked about.

'An Andalusian shepherd boy dreams of treasure and goes on a journey to find it, across Spain to Tangiers, on to the Egyptian desert... he follows his heart. Thinks big. That's the message of the story,' said Fred.

'Agreed,' said Phoebe, 'but it's stuck in my memory because Greta took another view. The treasure, in the end, turns out to be back home, where the shepherd boy first dreamt of it. The book summed up for Greta that however far she travelled, whatever sights she'd seen, what she really cared about was right back in England; that however happy globetrotting made her, there'd always be an underlying sadness until she was back where she belonged.' Phoebe turned to the bookcase and scanned the shelves. 'That would fit, wouldn't it? With everything she said about where she'd hidden important things.' She pulled out a slim, tangerine-coloured book with an image of the pyramids on the cover, and opened it. The three of them looked at each other as two documents fell on to the carpet. She gasped and scooped them up, gave them to Dolly and sat on the floor in front of her. Fred moved away a little so that Dolly could open the documents with privacy.

37

She unfolded one of the documents. The white paper had curdled to yellow.

Greta's birth certificate.

Born in 1934 and the father, as Dolly already knew, had been their mother's one and only husband. It was the Great Depression and he lost his job soon after Greta was born; they ended up queuing at soup kitchens and their marriage never recovered from the shame he'd felt. Dolly's mother tried to be understanding but couldn't ignore the temper he'd developed. She said it was a relief when he got called up at the beginning of the Second World War. He survived but never came back and she eventually got a divorce on the grounds of desertion.

Dolly folded the certificate and placed it on the sofa. She picked up the other; this had to be hers. She'd never even known her dad's family name, her mother having given Dolly the marital name she'd never stopped using. Dolly unfolded it. She looked straight at the father's details and... the box was blank.

No. This couldn't be.

There'd been no internet back then; she couldn't scroll back through social media, see if her mum had left any hints on private posts or messages. Fighting the temptation to screw the certificate into a tight ball, she folded it up, but not before her eye caught sight of her mother's details. The room spun as if she'd drunk whisky, not coffee. The words loomed large as if the truth sinking in was enlarging the font. A spasm tore through her and, clutching the certificate, she ran into the hallway. Almost tripping, she reached the toilet moments before vomiting. Footsteps sounded and Phoebe appeared at the bathroom door. Dolly wiped her mouth and eyes with toilet paper and a second spasm sent her reeling, another attempt to rid her body of a sense of betrayal and lack of belonging.

'I need to be alone. Please, Phoebe. I'll text you both later. I promise.'

Dolly sat on the side of the bath, waiting until she heard the front door close. Leaving the certificate on the bathroom floor, she went into the kitchen, made herself a strong cup of tea and sat in the conservatory. She took the turquoise tea flask with her. When they went on holiday it accompanied Greta to every stately home, every beach, every botanical garden. Her sister felt the cold increasingly with age. A warm brew, on tap, kept her mobile.

Darkness fell but Dolly didn't move. A bat swooped outside as moonlight streamed through the windows, on to the tea flask, on to Dolly's mug full of undrunk tea. She finally moved into the lounge and in the shadows, knelt in front of the tank. Maurice and Fanny gently flapped their fins and the tension across her shoulders disappeared. Dolly pulled on a coat and went around to Leroy's. She rang the doorbell. No reply. She tried again. She jumped as a hand shook her shoulder from behind.

'First things first.' Leroy pointed to the For Sale sign. 'What's all this?'

'Can we not talk about it? Not tonight. Fancy eating together?'

The line of his jaw looked hard and tense. She reached up and touched his cheek. He breathed out, squeezed her hand and took out his key. 'Tell me all about the charity shop.'

Whilst Leroy turned on the heating, she went into the kitchen and sat huddled at the table, in the dark until he came in and switched the lights on.

'I'm in the mood for stir fry,' he said. 'It won't take long; I've got chicken and vegetables. You peel, I'll chop.' Leroy poured wine; it almost flowed over the rim as he studied his friend. As they washed their hands and picked up knives, Leroy chatted about how Steve had approved his ideas for better employee engagement, including a well-being programme for staff and a rewards system. Dolly ate her meal in silence and when she'd swallowed the last mouthful, Leroy went around to her side and held her in his arms. He'd done that many times last year, when he'd entered her bungalow and waded through the litter. Her body shuddered and tears streamed down her cheeks. Leroy tightened his embrace.

'I need a tissue,' she croaked.

Leroy grabbed the roll of kitchen towel. She tore off a square and blew her nose loudly. She told him about the birth certificates. How her father's details weren't on hers.

'Oh, flower, I'm sorry. It must be so disappointing.'

'That's not it.' Her face crumpled again. 'My mum wasn't my mum. It explains so much. Why we were never close.'

'*What?*'

'It was Greta.' Dolly twisted the damp square of tissue.

'Greta? No.'

She nodded vigorously.

'Honey, are you *sure*? Christ...' He let out one of his low whistles.

'Crazy, isn't it?' Her voice choked up. 'But, then, it isn't. I now know completely why Greta looked so unhappy in that photo by the beach. The last couple of years of her life had been turned upside down by giving birth.'

'This explains why she didn't want you to go to Paris. It wasn't about France; it was to do with the paperwork – you'd have needed to see your birth certificate to get a passport. Where was it?'

Dolly told Leroy about *The Alchemist*. Everything Phoebe had said.

'Greta said her treasure was right at home?' He rubbed her arm. 'That means you. She was so proud of you, Dolly. Remember when you adapted the bungalow, to make it easier for her, with the arthritis? You had the conservatory built to raise her spirits? You stayed put to oversee the builders, but because of the dust and noise she'd spend the days at my place, whilst I was at work.'

'What of it?'

'I came home once and she was in low spirits. On her own, she'd been dwelling, I guess. She said you were the best sister anyone could have. That you'd never once complained about looking after her, never saw her as a burden. She worried that your life would have been so much better without her around.'

'I wouldn't be here without her, as it turns out,' she said, stiffly.

'But isn't that the point? She could have... taken a different path, dangerous as that would have been back then. Or after the birth, had you adopted, that would have been understandable, especially in the 1950s, but she and your mu— grandmother worked it out. Despite all the hardships, they kept you as close as they could.'

'Why not tell me? I don't know who I am any more. Suddenly

I haven't got a sister, I'm an only child – and I never knew a grand-parent, yet it turns out I did.'

Fred's words about confiding in strangers stoked her memory. Dolly looked at her watch. Nine o'clock. Was that too late? Not if she hurried.

38

Dolly knocked on the rustic wooden door of the one-storey farm cottage. The narrow road was a fifteen-minute walk from the church and the only reminder of the village's agricultural history. Ivy grew either side, clinging on like a small child. By an empty milk bottle, on the ground, stood a flowerpot in the shape of a boot, filled with daffodils. The voluminous lounge curtains were split in two by a crack of light determined to compete with the moon. Yet no one answered. Dolly rapped again and was about to leave when the door creaked open. Its entrance framed pinned up hair, a long floral dressing gown and velvet slippers.

'Dorothy Bell? What do you want at this time of night?'

'I'm sorry if it's late. Can we talk? It's about Greta.'

Edith switched on the porch light and squinted. 'You've been crying?'

Dolly shivered and with a tut Edith jerked her head. Dolly slipped off her shoes and waited for Edith to bolt the door again, before following the old woman along the hallway. An automatic air freshener puffed as she walked past, and the smell of cedarwood escorted Dolly into the lounge. Unlike Edith, the room had no sharp edges with its curved sofa, spherical lampshade and circular decorative plates.

'Nice wallpaper,' muttered Dolly as she sat on the sofa. Edith clicked off the television, moving to and fro in a padded rocking chair.

'I'm sure you haven't interrupted my programme to admire my furnishings.'

Dolly placed her palms together, fingers intertwined. 'I know about Greta.'

The chair stopped rocking.

'She wasn't my sister.'

Edith glanced sideways at the fireplace's flames.

'What did she say to you, that morning back in the seventies after my boyfriend, Fred, proposed? You mentioned that she was upset; Greta told you her worst nightmare had come true, spoke of a holiday that mustn't happen. Now I realise she must have been terrified I'd ask for my birth certificate.'

The flames continued to flicker. Edith didn't take her eyes off them.

'You said she talked about other stuff.'

Edith lifted her chin. 'It's hard to recall.'

'You aren't surprised to hear we aren't siblings. Please. Edith. I need to know.'

She faced Dolly. 'Any secrets have gone with her to the grave. That's as it should be. I'm a woman of my word.'

'But I know she's my mum, it's written down in black-and-white. Why did she hide that? If only she hadn't, I'd have married Fred, and she could have spent her life travelling as I know she wanted.'

Edith pushed herself up. 'An enormous sense of shame overwhelmed Greta – and your... grandmother. Things were different back then.'

'Do you know anything about my father?'

Edith unfolded her arms. 'You're putting me in an impossible position. I may not have liked Greta but a promise is a promise.'

Dolly pressed the balls of her palms against her eyes and took a moment. When her hands fell away, Edith was sitting again. 'I understand. Greta would have admired your loyalty.' Dolly waited. 'Okay, I'd better get back. Thanks anyway.' Her voice faltered. 'An early night is probably wise. The estate agent's already arranged a viewing for the bungalow, tomorrow morning.'

'You're moving?' Edith's eyebrows shot up, over-plucked and barely visible. 'But the two of you created a home. Greta used to boast about the conservatory and I've always envied how close the two of you were to your neighbours. Mine only come around if they want me to sign for their parcels.'

'My whole life there was based on deceit.'

'But was it? Your sis— mother loved you very much. That was clear to everyone.' She pulled out the cushion behind her back and hugged it to her chest. 'Yes, Greta told me about... she got pregnant at sixteen.'

'I've discovered that much.'

'Okay, well, your potential trip to Paris broke her in some way. Your love for Fred was obvious but she insisted the trip must never happen, yet didn't know how she'd live with the guilt of pushing you two apart, if she could. I think that's why she left the job she loved so much, at Hackshaw Haulage, it made it easier for her, in the beginning, not seeing you upset all day.' Edith shook her head. 'Greta thought she'd covered all possibilities of you finding out the truth, up until then, but she must have known that, as you got older, you'd want to travel. She'd been foolish, if you ask me.' Edith hugged the cushion tighter and exhaled. 'Your father...'

Dolly leant forwards.

'He was a fleeting boyfriend of your grandmother's.'

'*What?*'

'He was dapper, charming, showered her with gifts, but eventually your grandmother found out he'd had several affairs. The day after she told him to clear off he... took advantage of Greta in the worst way.'

Lightheaded, Dolly unzipped her anorak.

'He didn't force her,' Edith added quietly. 'At that stage your gran hadn't told Greta what a loser he was, she was too embarrassed to have another failed relationship on her hands. Greta hadn't even known your grandmother and he were dating; she'd only been told he was a good friend. He called around to collect his things, your gran was out at work. He told Greta he was leaving to travel the world, that he'd send postcards and call for them both when he finally settled somewhere exotic. Of course, she was impressed that he was about to do what she'd always dreamed of. Then... well, you know how men can be. He told this naive sixteen-year-old that she was more beautiful than Elizabeth II, who'd just become Queen. One thing led to another and before she knew it... Greta was young. Scared. Didn't think she could say no. So she tried to act grown up about it. Pretended it was okay.'

Dolly's eyes filled.

Greta always had kept her distance from men. Dolly couldn't see for tears as she recalled the holiday in York. It had been a coach trip, a mix of couples and singles, Greta would have been in her early sixties. One night there had been a dance in the hotel bar. Greta had been chatting to a man who'd eaten dinner with them, a friendly, polite sort with a great sense of humour. He asked Greta to dance and shortly after they got up, the record switched to slower music. He put his arms around her waist, all very proper, but Greta froze. The man looked confused as she pulled away, grabbed her bag and left. She told Dolly she hadn't wanted to lead him on, as she didn't feel the same.

'Your gran blamed herself. Greta didn't even know she was pregnant until she was far gone. She honestly believed this man would stand by her – he was back in town by then, setting up in the hotel business – but he dismissed her as if she were a delusional child. She didn't have it out with him until he came into her place of work, a couple of years later. He laughed at Greta. Told her she would never amount to anything.'

'Bastard.'

'Quite. But there was never any question of you not remaining part of the family.' She sucked in her cheeks. 'It may sound odd but I felt jealous of Greta.'

'How so?'

Edith put the cushion behind her back once more and sat upright. 'Because I've never known a love like Greta's for you. As soon as she clapped eyes on you her heart was lost – her words.' Edith raised her hands. 'No doubt about it, she wanted you to know the truth, but your gran had made her promise never to tell you. Then, over the years, I think the secret loomed bigger and bigger. She knew how much you loved Fred and didn't know how she was going to face seeing you day in, day out, at work, at home, knowing that she was the one who had sent him running.'

'She really told you all of this?'

Edith explained how it had all spilled out, jumbled, in between sobs; she'd had to force Greta to slow down. Afterwards Edith made them cups of tea. As it so often did, Greta's favourite drink restored her spirits – and resolve. She apologised for the fuss and asked Edith never to speak of her secret to anyone. During the weeks that followed Greta pretended their chat hadn't happened and would ignore Edith at church meetings. Their relationship gradually returned to its former frostiness.

'But, in the end, you were the best sort of friend,' Dolly whispered.

'Greta chose to call you Dorothy,' said Edith as they both got to their feet, her voice sounding scratchy, 'because she liked the nickname, the idea of looking after a *dolly* for real. It shows what a child she was when you were born. That man deserved to be flogged.'

Dolly leant against the hallway wall for a moment, whilst Edith unbolted the door.

'Right, be off with you, now,' she said in her familiar brisk tone. 'I need my sleep, even if you don't.'

As Dolly walked down the driveway, Edith called after her.

'Greta may have wanted to travel the world, but you were her whole universe.'

39

The hot cross bun dough was left to rise.

'Sorry we were late,' said Fred, as they all settled in the lounge, smelling as if they'd shared a bottle of cinnamon perfume. Leroy had suggested playing cards and half-heartedly Flo was choosing a game, no doubt missing Anushka who couldn't come as her family had planned a visit to relatives in Birmingham.

Phoebe squeezed his arm, sitting at his feet by the armchair. 'It's the anniversary of Gran's death today. Five years. We came straight from the crematorium.'

'Sympathies,' said Leroy. 'I still can't believe Mum's gone after nine years.'

'I'm so sorry,' said Dolly. 'I hope you didn't feel obliged to bake tonight.'

'Angela wasn't one for moping,' said Fred. 'She'd be looking down crossly if I'd stayed at home.'

Was Greta looking down too? Willing Dolly to understand? The young couple who'd viewed the house today loved the conservatory, said it would make the perfect playroom for their imminent baby. The estate agent said Pingate Loop was highly *desirable*. Greta would have said that word was far too sexy to describe their cosy home. Yet sex sells and a couple of hours later the couple put in an offer.

Dolly sat on the sofa, next to Leroy, Flo kneeling on the floor, mechanically shuffling the cards. She caught Dolly's eye and let them fall on to the carpet. 'Dad said I mustn't be nosy, you'd tell us in your own time, but why are you moving? You're one of my best friends.' Her voice caught. 'I don't want you to go.'

'Why don't we talk about that later,' said Leroy swiftly. 'I haven't played Pontoon for ages. How about I deal?'

'It's okay,' said Dolly and she held out her hand. Leroy moved up and Flo slouched next to her on the sofa. This little girl wasn't so little any more, making practical plans regarding university funds and being keen to earn.

'I found out, love... Greta wasn't my sister. She was my mum.'

Flo didn't say a word. A lawn mower sounded from outside. 'That can't be right,' she said eventually. 'How? When? Why did she need to pretend?'

'She had me very young. Back then people wouldn't have approved. It's... been a shock, as if my life here, with her, was a charade.'

Flo wrapped her arm around Dolly's waist and squeezed. 'Greta loved you, whatever,' she mumbled.

Dolly buried her face in Flo's hair, breathing in the coconut scent whilst she gathered herself. 'There's something else. I went to Edith's last night.' Flo sat up again. 'My dad was much older than Greta and... let her down on so many levels.' Her middle clenched even though Flo had stopped squeezing. 'What does it say for my family, that we couldn't be honest with one another over something so significant?'

Fred ran a hand over his head. 'They were honest with their

feelings though. The way Greta cared, how protective she was, the gifts she bought you, the advice she gave you at work. Seeing you both together gave me my first real inkling of the relationships I'd missed out on. No one had been by my side since the year dot whereas you had two people who never left.' He fiddled with his watchstrap. 'Not that I want to paint my past as a black canvas. There were streaks of colour. Other unwanted children became my people and over the years new friends filled the gap. Eventually I met Angela and Phoebe, and for the first time since you and I parted, I was blessed with a sense of belonging. We weren't – aren't – blood-related but that's never mattered.'

Phoebe scooched over the carpet, to Dolly. 'My parents didn't bring me up,' she said. 'Gran did and then Granddad. Families can be messed up; I learnt that at high school – I had friends with parents who hardly spoke or made things difficult after a divorce. A girl in my class lived with her older sister and her sister's fiancé. Another was fostered. One lived with her gran and a Labrador; she spoke about that dog as if he were a brother.'

Maurice had become family. He was always there. He made Dolly want to care for him in the same way that she'd never begrudged looking after Greta.

'Once my mum was gone, relationships framed my life,' said Leroy. 'Along with work, we'd built a strong team at the restaurant and supported each other through deaths and illness. And I think I'm going to be right at home at the Rising Sun. Then there's Jamaica, the family over there I never knew about all these years. Winston and I talk regularly online.'

'Mum and Dad are always talking about labels and how we shouldn't use them,' said Flo, taking Dolly's hands. 'That could apply to families as well.' She looked away. 'My secret has taught me that, anyhow.'

The silence that fell was interrupted by the kitchen timer.

Leroy got to his feet and Phoebe followed him. Fred gave Dolly a hug. She took his hand. Skin on skin, it felt so intimate. He tickled her palm with his thumb like he always used to and for the first time all day her breathing eased. And a sensation she hadn't experienced for so long flickered in the pit of her stomach.

'Flo, can you help me for a minute?' she asked.

Flo followed Dolly into her bedroom and threw herself on to the bed, moving her arms and legs as if making snow angels, the kind of spontaneous happiness Dolly hoped her young neighbour would never lose. Flo hadn't seen the new lamp before, in the shape of a flamingo standing on one leg, nor this duvet set – she loved the purple colours. It matched the dark purple bedside table that was actually a small vintage suitcase permanently open and attached to the wall. Attracted by how neat and compact it was, Dolly hadn't been able to resist bidding on it in 1987, thrilled with the contents that included a colourful batwing jumper and a pair of red pixie boots with shiny buckles.

However, an increasingly uncomfortable sensation ran through Dolly, when she came across an upcycled case in the bungalow, the table in the conservatory, the cupboard in the kitchen, the aluminium flowerpot in the garden. Since seeing Phoebe's upset at losing the trunk, since finding out about Greta's true longing to travel abroad, she couldn't help feeling even more sad that the belongings were parted from their owners and hadn't reached their true destination. Yet the sisters had given each case a new purpose and made use of the contents where possible.

Dolly lay down next to Flo. 'I want you to help me pull something through to Phoebe and Fred – I've had a twinge in my back today – but first... your secret. You've been such a good friend, listening to all my problems, being there for me these last months. How about you let me in?'

Flo bit on a fingernail. 'Okay. But only because I think it will help you.' She shuffled into the mattress. 'I'm pretty sure I'm adopted.'

Dolly turned her head away for a second. What? She hadn't expected that. So it wasn't that Mark wasn't her real dad – Flo didn't believe either of her parents were blood-related. She looked back to scan the nose shaped just like Mark's, the hands that danced in the air when she became enthusiastic, like Kaz when she spoke about a new contract the business had landed. Dolly would never have guessed. With Flo approaching her teens, they might have thought now was the right time to drop hints.

'What exactly have your parents said?'

'Nothing. I've been very cross about that.'

Dolly lay on her side. She reached out and pushed away a lock of hair from Flo's face. 'What's made you think this, then?'

'It's been more obvious since year six. They've understood me less and less. We always argue and never agree about important stuff. I used to think that was normal until I heard a girl talking in the toilets at school. The evening before she'd found out she was adopted and told her friend it made sense. She'd always felt on the outside, like I do.'

'A lot of children feel like that, especially as they approach the teenage years.'

But Flo had proof. A boy at school said you can't have ginger hair unless one of your parents has. Georgie in her class had red hair, like her mum. Callum did too and his dad's was ginger. Flo's mum was blonde and her dad was mouse, whatever that meant. The only mice Flo had seen were white and furry or plugged into a computer.

Flo sighed. 'At first it took away the trust – if they didn't tell me the truth about such a big thing what else were they hiding? So I get why you might be angry with Greta. But in a year or two that anger might disappear. I've decided, now, it doesn't matter so much. You see... Mum and Dad have made a real effort lately, with all the insect stuff. They *do* care. And since I've met Fred who grew up in children's homes... Greta loved you, isn't that the most important thing? Mum knows the exact tickle spot, above my hip, that always gets me laughing. If I'm fed up at school, Dad makes me waffles with chocolate spread, my favourite.'

Greta knew exactly how to cheer Dolly up – a game of Scrabble with a shandy and a packet of cheese and onion crisps.

'I don't like doing lots of different activities or social stuff like they do,' continued Flo, 'with their golf and Zumba, and evenings out with friends, and I think cleaning's boring. But... they want me. Even when I'm in a mood. That's enough, isn't it?' Her face puckered for a second and she turned away, lying with her back to Dolly. 'I was very angry last year and got really fed up when they suggested Guides, thinking they were trying to change me again, that' – she buried her face in the duvet – 'that they were disappointed with the baby they chose, if I wasn't biologically theirs.' Her voice sounded muffled. 'But with your help, Guides has turned out all right.'

Dolly moved closer and placed an arm around Flo. 'Of course, you might be wrong.'

The two of them just lay there for a while.

'What did you want me for?' Flo asked in a full voice, and stood up, wiping her eyes.

Dolly pointed in the corner of her bedroom. 'Help me with that, love.'

'Okay. First I need the loo.' She disappeared out of the room, bumping into the door frame as she did so.

Lying awake all last night, Dolly had begun to understand why Greta had kept such a secret, but that didn't mean she believed big things should be kept hidden. She slid her phone out of her back pocket and scrolled until she came to Mark's number.

Quickly she texted, asking him to pop around after Flo was in bed tonight. A jewellery box, on her dressing table, caught her attention. It was white leather, a little battered now. Greta had bought it for Dolly's sixteenth birthday. When you lifted the lid a ballerina spun around on a disc and music played. Dolly had said she was the best sister ever.

She thought about Phoebe being brought up by grandparents, Fred by strangers but later finding his own family unit. Then there was Leroy who found a sort of family at work, and more recently with relatives afar online. And now Flo who'd decided that, if her suspicions were proved, there were worse truths to find.

Worse truths aplenty there could be, than finding out a mum did everything she could to keep her daughter close, after a man had treated her so ruthlessly; that she had made sacrifices to put her child first, believing she was doing the right thing. The toilet flushed and Dolly put away her phone. She went over to the jewellery box and lifted the lid; the ballerina spun around and around.

'Look at your buns!' said Leroy to Flo, as she and Dolly appeared by the kitchen door. 'Perfectly rounded. Mine didn't rise as well but at least the pastry on top looks like an S. The M and D letters look great on yours; your parents will love them. Now we need to ice them.'

Dolly and Flo pulled Fred's steamer trunk into the kitchen. Dolly patted the top of it and smiled.

'This is where it all started,' she said. 'The lost luggage. The notebook. The challenges Greta helped create. I don't know why I haven't given this back yet.' She pushed it over to Phoebe. 'You'll need it for our trip to Paris.'

40

Funny, how an item of lost luggage had led Dolly to packing her own, and for the same destination. She sat on the bed and gazed at the copy of *Matilda* next to the flamingo lamp. The first challenge of Phoebe's that Dolly had completed had involved going up in a fictional balloon. All these months later she was flying again, but this time for real. She turned her attention to the wheeled pink duffel lying next to her. It was from the auction she and Greta had attended in 2013. It had contained a hardly worn sparkly plum jumper perfect for Christmas Day, along with suspenders and open hole crotch panties. Dolly hadn't liked to laugh at Greta's icy expression that could have snuffed out the flame on top of any plum pudding. It was the last week of May and cheaper to go midweek, so they were flying out tomorrow, Tuesday, and coming back Friday. She picked up the notebook where Greta had always listed the items they landed from each auction, overtaken by an urge to add an inventory of what she'd packed for Paris.

One striped jumper I bought on a shopping trip with Leroy who'd wanted to buy a new outfit for a party that Steve has invited him to. Wit woo.
A practical shirt to go under a new woollen tank top that Phoebe says is all the rage now.
Floral blouse with fancy cuffs and lowish neckline in case we treat ourselves to dinner out – worn on a night in Manchester with Fred, last week. He called it a date.
One pair of jeans that didn't fit a few months ago.
Four pairs of socks – an extra pair for emergencies.
Pants and bra.
Toothbrush. Talcum powder. Deodorant. Hand cream. Vaseline. Paracetamol. Ibuprofen. Anti-allergy pills. Plasters. Mosquito repellent. Sun cream. Aftersun lotion.

Dolly hoped she hadn't forgotten anything.

Small make-up bag containing mascara, lipgloss, concealer and blusher – modern brands purchased after experimenting during a girls' night with Flo and Phoebe over the early May Bank Holiday weekend.
My best silk scarf in case my luggage gets lost – a nice surprise for the winning bidder.

Dolly had already packed her rucksack, having thoroughly examined her passport, gripping the dark blue and gold cover tightly. Phoebe was right, they'd been able to fast-track it. She'd bought a French handbook and had been practising over the last month. Dolly had never needed to learn foreign words before. Or bought foreign currency – she went through the colourful Euro banknotes again, physical proof that she was really about to leave the UK. Flo had checked everything and suggested a packet of boiled sweets to suck as her ears always popped on an aeroplane.

Determined to get an early night – their flight left before sunrise – as a last check Dolly took out one particular item from her case. No one knew she was taking it. She held it to her cheek for a moment before putting it back.

41

Dolly peered out at the sky, on a high that wasn't due to their altitude. As the aeroplane lifted its nose in the air, she recalled Greta's supposed fears about engines failing or turbulence.

However Dolly agreed with Phoebe that flying was fucking fantastic.

It reminded Dolly of the first time she'd had sex. With Fred. Greta had always drilled into her to wait until she was married, that you could catch an STD or get pregnant, and no man would hang around after that. Back then, more than once, Fred had held off, sensing Dolly had reservations. But like the plane's take-off, when it finally happened, sex with him had made her feel like the best version of herself, a woman with adventures on the horizon, and apparently a bottom to die for.

The announcements over the tannoy were in French as well as English; Dolly swelled with pride at recognising the words *s'il vous plaît*. She wore a new blazer with gold buttons. It didn't suit her baggy trousers or comfortable walking shoes, and she'd got a roll-up anorak in her rucksack. But this was Paris! Phoebe had insisted Dolly take the window seat. Last year the television screen had provided Dolly's only view of life outside the bunga-low. Now, she couldn't take her eyes off the floss of cloud, and billowing sea far below. Maurice would have been equally capti-vated, no doubt preferring the reassuring hum of the engines to the sound of soap actors arguing.

'Flo was right about ears popping during take-off.'

'I'm not sure we'll manage to get the photo she wanted, of that stink bug species that has recently invaded Paris.' Phoebe pulled the top of her hoodie off her head. Over the sweatshirt she was wearing the dusty-pink Zadorin gilet with the maroon collar that Dolly had found in Phoebe's luggage all those months ago – an extravagant present from Fred, it turned out, to lift Phoebe's spirits during an especially rough patch.

'Oh, she'll be too excited to think about that anyway,' said Dolly. 'Summer half-term starts this weekend. Mark and Kaz are taking her to the bug displays at the Manchester Museum that they were due to visit at the beginning of April.'

'Has she forgiven you yet?'

'If the strength of her goodbye hug yesterday was anything to go by, I'd say yes.'

According to Mark, Flo had been very angry at first. She'd run to her room and slammed the door when they'd mentioned the word 'adoption'. But the smell of waffles tempted her out, to face a tearstained Kaz. Flo had told Dolly afterwards how she hated seeing her parents cry, like when her granny died or the news channel showed harrowing war scenes. Waffles getting cold and Flo kicking her feet under the kitchen table, she'd eventually listened. Firstly, the red hair: it was perfectly possible not to have parents with the same colour. Something to do with recessive genes. Flo googled it afterwards. As for all the activities, pushing Flo to make friends... her parents finally opened up to Flo about them being shy at school years ago, and wanting their daughter to have an easier experience. Mark and Kaz admitted they'd never considered that Flo could be genuinely content with her few friends, her insects, her reading. As for those insects, Kaz said that as cleaners, Flo's interest was hard to comprehend; bugs were an inconvenience at best and an expensive problem at worst. Yet she and Mark admitted Flo had provided an alternative view and that, on closer inspection, even cockroaches had handsome features, with their fine antennae and cherrywood shells.

Strange how, going against the logic of there being billions of people on earth, and billions of job or relationship possibilities, parents assumed life would treat their offspring exactly the same as it had them. Dolly's mother and grandmother never once considered that she would find a decent man. Dolly had assumed Maurice was happy leading the life she did – until he'd jumped out of his tank. She should have taken drastic action years ago – jumped out of her life in Knutsmere and moved away from the domesticity she shared with Greta baking, doing charity work, gardening; she should have shown green-fingered Greta that she had roots of her own that sprouted from a different seed altogether, that she wasn't simply a cutting from their family.

'Fasten your seatbelts.'

They were approaching Charles de Gaulle airport. Dolly offered Phoebe a boiled sweet. Yesterday Fred had come around for lunch. He'd talked about how tourist aviation had changed. Back in the day, passengers all watched a big screen at the front, then personal screens came in, one for each seat. Now in-flight entertainment was changing again as everyone brought their own devices. Back in the 1970s the departure lounge was like a fancy hotel and there was more freedom to walk up and down the plane, even during slight turbulence. Until the 1990s smoking was allowed on flights.

Fred had apologised for rambling and moved around the kitchen table for a kiss.

All these years later, the prospect of sleeping with Fred wasn't scary, but he didn't seem as keen. The hole in her heart regarding Fred's disappearance had almost closed up now, almost mended. On a couple of occasions he'd stayed late, but when she'd suggested they go to her bedroom he'd tried to tell her something and ended up making excuses. It looked like he wasn't quite over Angela yet.

'Granddad said we must take lots of photos,' said Phoebe, as the aeroplane descended.

'You don't mind that... me and Fred have been getting closer? Is that with okay with you, love? I don't want to cause upset. I know how much you loved your gran.'

'Gran would have been the first to tell Fred to get out dating. In fact she said as much, towards the end. Told him he wasn't to use her death as an excuse to stay in the house in front of *Only Fools and Horses* reruns.' She held Dolly's nearest hand. 'I'm genuinely pleased to see him looking so happy. Who knows what's around the corner? I think he *should* make the most of every day he's got left.'

Dolly squeezed her arm. Phoebe worried so much about her granddad not being around.

Glad it hadn't been lost, they collected their luggage. Dolly would get to wear that fancy scarf after all. More importantly, the special item was safe. She took a moment whilst Phoebe headed to the Ladies, stood quite still, by their luggage, and listened to tourists chatting. She stared at the luxury gilt-fronted shops selling perfume and handbags, trinkets and clothes. What an eye-catching kiosk, selling macarons in every colour.

For a fleeting moment a deep sense of loss flushed through

her veins, loss on behalf of Greta who'd never got to cross the English Channel.

'I checked out the train service,' said Phoebe when she came back. 'It's not much more expensive to get a taxi straight into the centre and share the fare.'

'Great idea and my treat,' said Dolly. 'No arguments.'

Phoebe tucked her arm through Dolly's and they made their way to the taxi rank. It took them to their hotel in Saint-Germain-des-Prés, *on the left bank* – Dolly had always thought that sounded so glam. Yet the room was affordable with a shared bathroom. The receptionist let them leave their luggage in her office as check-in wasn't until later. How exciting to wake up within a short distance of the Louvre or Notre-Dame.

'But the main reason I like this hotel,' said Phoebe, as they strolled through the welcoming spring sunshine, 'is that Les Deux Magots café is only a street away. It's the perfect place for breakfast.'

'According to your notebook entry, you wanted to go because of the literary greats who'd frequented it like Hemingway, Sartre and de…'

'De Beauvoir. That's right. Zoe's really jealous I get to visit it. Here we are.' She pointed to the corner of a boulevard, a sandy-coloured building with several floors, each with a black balcony outside. The café had a green canopy and shiny glass front, a contrast to the old church, opposite. The tables outside were already full, despite the fumes and hoots of passing traffic. They joined a queue at the front door. Dolly was happy to wait, observing Parisians drinking coffee out of dainty cups, in their tailored clothes and shaded frames, picking at omelettes or ham, fruit salad or pastries. Back in the 1970s she and Fred wouldn't have wanted to go back to England.

Seated inside, layers removed, French handbook on the table,

Dolly bit into a chocolate croissant, looking up at two Chinese figurines, each either side of a corner of one of the far walls. The building used to be a novelty shop and the café's name referred to them. How disappointed Flo would be – she thought *magot* might mean maggot. She'd explained that over the centuries maggots had saved countless limbs from amputation, thanks to their ability to eat infected tissue.

Dolly gagged slightly as she finished her pastry, instantly restored by the burnt-caramel smell of coffee as she took a sip.

'So we'll go to Notre-Dame after here,' said Phoebe, and she wiped her mouth with a white napkin.

Dolly moved the turquoise flask to one side, in her rucksack, and took out a map of Paris. They'd spent several enjoyable afternoons planning their itinerary.

'Then after a snack lunch we'll check in,' continued Phoebe. 'I can't wait to see the Eiffel Tower later. It's supposed to look fantastic at night.'

An evening trip to the tower fitted in well with Dolly's own plans. Yes, she'd wanted to challenge herself to travel, and to come to Paris with a person who had turned out to be rather special. However, there was another important reason she'd needed to come here, to do with the book review notebooks Greta had filled. She'd flicked through them, most nights, since her visit to Edith.

'Sounds great,' Dolly said. 'You're sure you don't mind me going off for an hour on my own?'

'No. I've got that ticket booked to go to the tower's summit.'

'I would tell you why, but...'

Phoebe put down her napkin. 'Being good friends doesn't mean we can't keep some stuff private. If you're missing a panoramic night view, I know it must be important.'

42

Using the black ink of a Parisian night, Dolly wrote a goodbye wave to Phoebe in the air; her young friend was queuing outside the Eiffel Tower's lift. At eight, its hourly light show that lasted five minutes had dazzled them. It was now just before nine. Earlier, they'd stumbled across a tiny pizzeria that had been minding its own business in a narrow backstreet. Dolly must have taken a hundred photos of her pizza topped with pansies. As long as Phoebe felt happy eating more, she'd wanted to treat them to Cointreau coffees and dessert; the sticky tarte Tatin kept winking at her, across the restaurant. However, her budget-conscious young friend wouldn't hear of it after the expense of the taxi from the airport, but said she'd love to look for a crêpe truck later.

Amongst the chatting crowds enjoying the mild evening, Dolly stared at the illuminated tower. A cheer went up as it started to sparkle from top to bottom again, like a million fireflies. She took a video for Flo before taking out her Paris map. Pont Alexandre III was twenty minutes away on foot. Dolly hoiked up her rucksack as she made her way along the bank of the Seine, the upper promenade separated from the busy road by a row of trees. A bloodhound approached, walking its owner, a stout man wearing a fur hat with ear flaps. A flash of neon cycled past, followed by strolling lovers with their hands in the backs of each other's denim pockets. Dolly upped her pace and looked ahead at Pont Alexandre III, magically lit up. It was a gilded, ornate bridge, with pillars at each corner bearing golden statues. Out of breath, Dolly reached one end and almost running, aimed for the bridge's middle.

Chest heaving, she leant against the concrete, decorative railing, before turning to look down at the river's intertwining ripples of street lamp and moonlight. Dolly reached into her rucksack and took out the turquoise tea flask. She unscrewed the lid, remnants of a silicone seal still visible on the rim. She'd had to break the seal back in England, to remove the bag of contents and mix part of them with the talcum powder in her case, a mix that she'd tipped back into the flask once unpacked, at the hotel.

'Sorry about that, Greta,' she said to the flask. 'French regulations made things difficult but, on the plus side, you always did like to smell nice.' She placed the flask on top of the bridge and held it with both hands. 'Last year I needed you close, in the house and whenever I went out. I was lonely, you see, even though I had Maurice. I lost my confidence, lost my energy.' She ran a finger around the black rim. The staff at the crematorium had been very good about sealing Greta in there; her mother always had enjoyed a good cup of tea. 'When I found out about you sending Fred away, about leading a double-life as Maisie and then about being my mother, I stashed you in a cupboard, out of sight. I'm sorry if it was dark. Sorry the food tins in there were stacked messily.' She paused as a group of young women bundled past, cameras for necklaces. 'I went to the lost luggage auction as usual, last December, and I've discovered the list of firsts that was your idea. The balloon debate, speed-dating, swimming, the bake-off, and now this trip to Paris... All these have helped me find me again. They've given me a good friend, brought me back to Fred and have provided Maurice with a companion.'

How Greta would have rolled her eyes at that last comment.

'Remember how you believed those cases with a colourful ribbon tied around the handle must have contained especially loved items, as the owners made that extra effort to make their cases identifiable? So every year we'd bid on those with a ribbon attached. Yellow was your favourite as it's symbolic and represents support for absent loved ones. You suggested to Phoebe that she tie that yellow ribbon to the steamer trunk.

'Somehow, I think you sensed that your list of firsts would find its way to me.'

Dolly reached into her pocket, pulled out the ribbon and for several seconds held it to her lips.

'The weekend after next, Phoebe, Fred, Leroy, Flo and I are throwing a party, to celebrate the Queen's Platinum Jubilee. Takes me back to the silver one in 1977. The homemade bunting, the long trestles at sunny street parties with salmon paste sandwiches and bowls of iced gems – and the Sex Pistols sailing down the River Thames playing their risqué version of 'God Save the Queen'; you were disgusted. The Queen has now served seventy years, around as long as I've been living, not knowing you gave birth to me. Like her, you witnessed the Welsh mountain disaster, the first man on the moon, the creation of the internet, the Berlin Wall coming down, the Twin Towers attack.

'All that time you held your own life-changing event close. Like the Queen, you followed a sense of duty.

'I wish you hadn't.' Her voice croaked. 'But I understand why. Phoebe, Flo and Fred, they've shown me that family, it's not about labels, it's about caring and kindness.' She held the flask tightly to her chest. 'Your book reviews show a particular fondness for stories set in Paris, such as *Me Before You*, *The Hunchback of Notre-Dame*, *The Lollipop Shoes* and *The Little Paris Bookshop*. As Maisie, it was your suggestion that out of all the places in the world, Phoebe came to this capital first.' Dolly wiped her eyes, the new Maybelline concealer smudging across her hand. 'I reckon this is the perfect resting place.' She leant over the bridge's railing, tilted the flask and carefully shook it. 'I love you, Greta.'

A gentle breeze carried away the sobbed whisper, 'Bye, Mum,' along with white ashes that smelt of sandalwood as they floated down on to the Seine.

43

As the sign lit up to unfasten seatbelts, a different Dolly got to her feet, one who'd been abroad. She'd eaten freshly baked baguette, visited Montmartre, the majestic Sacré-Cœur; she'd tried a Moroccan tagine and drunk Pernod. Whilst Phoebe went to the Père Lachaise Cemetery, Dolly navigated the Métro and found the Pompidou Centre. She'd done her research before leaving England and discovered one of its new art exhibitions displayed a series of insect paintings. Dolly purchased several postcards for Flo. The Gothic hawk moth one was her favourite. But most importantly, *Greta* had gone abroad. Dolly pictured her mother cruising down the Seine, calm and serene, alongside gliding bateaux-mouches.

They pulled their cases into the arrivals lounge, Mancunian accents replacing French ones. It was almost lunch time. Phoebe switched on her phone. Her breath hitched.

Dolly steered her to one side, away from embarking passengers. 'What is it?'

'It's from our next-door neighbour. I insisted she had my number after... in case...' She read it again. 'I *knew* this would happen. Granddad fell ill early this morning. He's gone to Stepping Hill Hospital.' She gripped the phone tighter. 'In an ambulance.'

Why did she think Fred might become unwell? Dolly directed Phoebe over to nearby chairs. They sat down and read the text again. Heart thumping loudly in her ears, she put her arm around her young friend. Dolly stared at the tan steamer trunk.

'Deep breaths,' she said, briskly. 'Fred is as tough as old boots. How about we get a taxi to mine and drop off our bags, then I'll drive us straight to the hospital?' Dolly led the way past hordes of passengers and security staff, cleaners with mops and stewards dressed in coordinating colours, and out of the terminal. The last time she'd been to Stepping Hill was when Greta had the heart attack. In the ambulance, on the way, she could tell from the paramedics faces it was too late. But despite Greta's cold hand, Dolly chatted, telling her how loud the siren was and about the roast she'd make for their dinner later.

* * *

They parked up and clambered out into a chilly breeze – the temperate Parisian air hadn't followed them over the Channel. Dolly consulted the sign with lists of the different departments, linked arms with Phoebe and headed right, to the Accident and Emergency entrance. The receptionist took their names and they found two seats, next to a man with a bandage on his hand. A toddler cried in the row behind and opposite a woman slumped against the wall, half asleep. Plastic coffee cups littered tables alongside curled magazines.

'Do you think he could be really ill, and that's why we have to wait?' asked Phoebe, moving her legs out the way for a teenager on crutches. 'He hasn't answered any of my texts. I hope it's not his—' Cries of the toddler behind turned to screeches and Phoebe put her headphones on again. Dolly tried to read a magazine but could only look at the pictures. Finally, they were called and headed through automatic swing doors to the sound of machines bleeping and squeaking trolley wheels. The smell of hand sanitiser reminded Dolly of tequila. The nurse apologised for the wait. They'd been running tests. She directed them to a cubicle and swept across the medical blue curtain. Dolly focused on the tiled floor, gathered herself for a moment, then looked up at the bed. In paisley pyjamas, with his hair dishevelled, Fred sat propped up, his skin pale, wrinkles emphasised by the florescent lighting. In his hand he held a cardboard sick bowl; screwed-up tissues lay on the sheets next to him. The nurse filled up his glass of water, on the bedside unit. Phoebe almost knocked it over as she gave him a hug. Fred's smile looked as good to Dolly as any view in Paris.

'Sorry for all the fuss,' he said in a hoarse voice. 'I told Sheila not to tell you, she can be a right busybody.'

He was sitting up. Able to talk. Palms clammy, Dolly's fists uncurled. She'd feared a replay of that December day, Greta lying flat in the ambulance.

Eventually Phoebe let go and sat on the bed. Dolly hovered by the curtain. 'Granddad. It's because Sheila cares. Now, what's happened? It's not—'

'It's a stomach upset,' he cut in. 'Never known cramps like it, I could hardly move. They've run tests. It's nothing.' He managed a smile. 'Everything is as it should be.'

Fred had seemed invincible years ago, as if Mother Nature had overdosed him on youthful gusto.

'How has this happened? Gran trained us well; the kitchen's always pristine.'

Finally colour appeared in his cheeks as he broke eye contact with Phoebe. He reached out his hand. Dolly went over and gripped it. She didn't let go as she sat in the chair next to the bed.

'Wilfred decided to eat slimy chicken,' said the nurse in a sharp voice before leaving.

'Granddad! I told you to throw that meat out.'

'I thought it would be okay if I cooked it a bit longer than usual. It didn't smell that bad, Phoebs. I added lots of spices.' He gagged and held the bowl for a second.

Dolly shook her head. 'I've heard of "waste not want not", but even Greta wouldn't have taken things that far.'

He cracked another smile. 'How was Paris?'

'First, coffee,' said Phoebe and she stood up, giving Fred a pointed look. 'You two might want to talk.'

'What about?' asked Dolly as the curtain swished behind Phoebe. 'Fred? There's more to this than you're letting on.'

He let go of her hand and picked up a tissue, smoothing out the creases, then he let it fall on to the bed covers, before taking both her hands. 'Everything's okay, right at this moment. I've found it hard to tell you, I never expected us to...' He rubbed his thumbs over her palms. 'Angela died of bowel cancer. She'd been suffering from stomach upsets, bloating, weight loss, tiredness. Last year I had no symptoms but a routine screening test showed I had it too.'

'What?'

'We couldn't believe that fate had stabbed our family twice with the same diagnosis.'

'So... you're ill? Still having treatment? Why didn't you tell me? I'm going to lose you again?'

'I didn't want secrets between us, not any more, but after Greta, I didn't want to upset you in case you thought the worst. You see – I really am fine, I meant what I said to Phoebs. This is nothing but a stomach upset due to the stubbornness of a foolish old man. My cancer was caught early. I had surgery but, unlike Angela, didn't need radiotherapy or chemo. The doctors are keeping an eye on me for a few years. That's why Phoebs gets panicky if I'm at all sick. We became closer than ever last year, looking after one other. The shock of my diagnosis... and after her gran... it's still so raw.'

Dolly thought back to Easter weekend, Phoebe's food binge, her worrying over Fred and how she wondered what would happen if she lost him.

'There's a small chance it could still come back. It's best I'm honest.'

'I'm sorry you've been through this Fred.' Her words caught. 'We've only just found each other again.'

'That's why I've held back from taking things further. I'd understand completely if you didn't want to risk getting hurt once more. What if things continue to go well for us but then the cancer comes back? You looked after Greta all those years. What if I hold you back? This is your moment, Dolly – look at you flying, literally, all the way to Paris.'

She gazed at the lips that used to make her laugh, make her tingle. Still did. The eyes that could never hide jokes nor passion. Dolly raised one eyebrow. 'I thought we didn't do "what ifs". What happened to living in the moment?' She reached out a hand and combed his hair to the side, with her fingers. 'Your prognosis is a positive one?'

He nodded.

'Greta going like that, out of the blue, has taught me that the past belongs to nostalgia or regret, the future to hopes or fears... whereas the present belongs to nothing but opportunity, if you've the gumption to grab it. Your granddaughter has set a great example. She's finished her twelve months of challenges and those I've done have given me a taste for more.' Dolly straightened his pyjama lapel. 'It's time you and I shook off the comforts of suburbia, the routine and familiarity we've fallen into, and created our very own list of firsts for the next year. Starting this June.'

'Next month?' His eyes brightened. 'You're serious?'

'Get your thinking cap on, Wilfred Taylor. Tomorrow I'm coming over to yours with a pen and notebook.'

44

Dolly's front window was decked with purple and platinum bunting, and a matching flag had been stuck in the artificial succulent's plant pot on the windowsill. She and Flo had spent the morning decorating. Pingate Loop was so small it would have been a tiny street party. Dolly had suggested one inside her bungalow instead, on Saturday the fourth of June – the day of the Queen's Party at the Palace. She and Flo had eaten pancakes when her young friend came over at ten, fuel for dressing the lounge, hallway, dining room and kitchen. Phoebe arrived a couple of hours later to set up the buffet with Leroy.

It had been half-term week and Flo and Anushka had helped Dolly with baking, along with Phoebe when she wasn't working. Full Tupperware boxes were stacked in the fridge. They'd made scones, shortbread and fairy cakes, deciding the party food should have a thoroughly British theme. Leroy had brought a large Victoria sponge, with the number seventy iced on top, and a bottle of champagne. Phoebe's friend Zoe, from the bake-off experience, would provide homemade sausage rolls. For old time's sake, Fred insisted on a cheese-and-pineapple stick hedgehog; he'd buy pork pies and was still in Lymhall putting the last touches to a trifle, a lemon one similar to the official Platinum Jubilee one. Dolly also made a fruit salad and vegetable sticks with dips. Flo and Dolly had already set up a Union Jack paper tablecloth in the dining room and a centrepiece with three mini flags in. Bunting in the shape of crowns hung in the conservatory which was filled with red, white and blue balloons. Flo had loved sprinkling platinum glitter across the table and was excited at the prospect of her and Phoebe setting up a mocktail bar.

'Mum and Dad don't think we should have a royal family,' said Flo. 'But they admire the Queen for all her years of service and are looking forward to the party. They say she has a stiff upper lip. It sounds painful. You might have had that last year, Dolly, when you found it more difficult to talk.'

'Let's change that Carly Simon record for a funkier one,' Leroy said, as he and Phoebe came into the room having made sandwiches and cut them into triangles. Flo had insisted everyone should wear Union Jack colours. Phoebe wore red track-suit bottoms with blue socks and a white top. Leroy navy trousers with a polo neck shirt covered in white and red flowers.

'What time is Steve coming over?' asked Dolly as he put on 'Native New Yorker'.

Leroy couldn't control his hips that were now swaying. 'Around four. The new assistant manager is working out well, he's happy to leave him for the evening.'

The doorbell rang. Flo ran to answer it. Anushka was due any minute. The two girls were still full of the Guides camping trip they'd been on last weekend, to celebrate the Jubilee. Dolly heard excited comments about a trifle and moments later Fred appeared in the lounge.

Leroy clapped him on the back. 'How's planning your year of firsts going, Freddy?'

Fred side-stepped in time with the beat and Flo joined in. 'I always thought this tune was one of the catchiest of the 1970s. As for the list? Great, thanks. We're fine-tuning it at the moment. Travel's going to be a big part of the next twelve months.'

'I thought it might be,' said Leroy. 'I've talked to Steve about going back to the Caribbean in August and him coming with me. I fancy Puerto Rico' He coloured up. 'We're... seeing each other. Nothing official. He's good company.'

'He must be. You've spent all your weekends with him since I got back from Paris,' said Dolly.

Flo and Phoebe exchanged grins.

'He hasn't had a holiday for years either,' continued Leroy, ignoring her. 'August is a bit cheaper there, hot but still comfortable. I can see it now, us dancing in clubs to Ricky Martin music. What I'm trying to say is... why don't you two add it to your list and come along too?'

'Wow!' said Flo. 'The Caribbean has the most amazing sand fleas and mosquitoes.'

'And you can help us research exactly how to deal with them, Flo," said Leroy quickly, seeing Fred's face.

'That's so cool,' said Phoebe. 'I'd be jealous if I wasn't focusing on an exciting project of my own. Being friends with Zoe, and the trip to Paris, have reminded me of how very much I love books. Zoe's told me all about her bookselling career and I've enjoyed working in retail. Uni isn't for me, not at the moment – who knows, I might go back one day, but my dream, right now, what my gut's telling me, is to find a job in a bookshop and try to work my way up.'

'Oh sweetheart, that's perfect,' said Dolly.

'Phoebs, that sounds like a plan, lass.' Fred beamed from ear to ear.

'If it wasn't for insects, that would be my ideal job too,' said

Flo. Phoebe explained to her about the writing and reading clubs Zoe had set up in previous jobs, whilst Leroy put on another tune.

Dolly's foot tapped to the music. Puerto Rico? She and Fred had talked about visiting other European countries, trying to come up with a place that he hadn't visited yet. The Caribbean would be a first for both of them. With the heat and the bugs at that time of year, it would certainly push them out of their comfort zones. Because that's what their list of firsts was all about... not just doing enjoyable things like seeing the Northern Lights or eating at a Michelin-starred restaurant. Punting in Cambridge might not sound reckless but both of them had lost their sense of balance as the decades passed. Then there was a ghost-hunting trip at night, in York – neither Dolly nor Fred had ever been able to sit through horror movies. Seeing the Golden Pavilion in Kyoto was a big one, the culture of that city, the food, navigating their way around a place where very few people spoke English. They'd collated a long list of challenges together and were in the process of narrowing them down. Going up in a hot air balloon for real might be the first one for June.

The song 'More, More, More' came on and Leroy put his arms around Phoebe's and Fred's shoulders. Flo pulled Dolly away from the goldfish tank and they joined the circle, the five of them dancing in time to the music and singing the chorus.

As another verse began, Dolly glanced at Leroy. The lost luggage and everything that had happened since finding it, everything they'd achieved since last Christmas, had unbroken both their shattered hearts. He gave a barely perceptible smile, just for her. Eyes pricking, she gave a nod back. Unable to resist any longer, her hands clapped in time to the music. Everyone else joined in, forgetting it might be too loud for the fish.

Dolly didn't think they would mind, Maurice and Fanny were

probably too busy celebrating. Once the fishes' news was out her friends' cheers would no doubt shake the bungalow's foundations. With all the jubilee arrangements, the yellow dots on the bottom of the tank hadn't registered, not until a few moments ago, when Dolly had taken a proper look at the cluster of something very special.

A brand new future was about to hatch.

ACKNOWLEDGMENTS

After finishing writing this novel, Dolly, Leroy, Flo and Phoebe felt like real friends. What a journey I felt I'd been on, with them. I'm so proud of Dolly. After the last couple of years I think many of us can relate to the experience of coming back out to real life, after a period locked away. It's not always easy when everything seems to have changed, but that doesn't mean there aren't new joys ahead.

I send huge, heartfelt hugs to all those readers who struggle with eating issues like Phoebe – and like me. I drew on personal experience when creating her and from time to time I still hear the voice in my head that tells me I'm lacking in some way, and that food will provide the answer. Whilst it doesn't mean difficulties with eating won't strike again, over time you *can* learn the tools to cope, if you do the most important thing – open up and talk to family, friends and professionals who can listen and help. I've learned to be kinder to myself, to not let that inner voice talk to me in a way I would never let anyone else – and to stick with people who accept me completely for who I am.

Before all else, *you do you*. It's enough. As Leroy found out.

Nerves always strike when I hand my work over to my agent, and then editor, and I'm grateful to perceptive Clare Wallace from Darley Anderson Agency, and to hardworking Tara Loder at Boldwood, for handling my characters and their stories with such love and care.

Of course, I wouldn't be writing if it weren't for you readers and the reviews you give my published books that inspire me to write the next one. Every little ounce of feedback, every purchase, is very much appreciated in a book world where there are so many amazing authors.

I must thank Jessica Redland author, former Brown Owl, for her advice about the Guiding storyline. You couldn't meet a more generous, friendly writer and I consider myself very lucky to be alongside her at Boldwood Books.

Huge thanks to The Friendly Book Community on Facebook, you have been so welcoming and supportive, and are such a lovely bunch of readers.

Thanks, as always, to the amazing bloggers who take part in blog tours and review my books, and to super-efficient Rachel Gilbey. Also huge thanks to Claire Fenby, Jenna Houston, Nia Beynon, Amanda Ridout, and the rest of the Boldwood staff.

I must mention Martin, Immy and Jay, aka Team Tonge, who are always there to brainstorm a plotline and encourage me along the way. Professionally, and personally, I'd be lost without you three.

The last word has to go to Maurice who, alongside Fanny, is still waiting for his life to change completely. Flo reckons being a parent is a challenge, and has told him the two of them need practice. Therefore each day, after school, she sits by their tank and pretends to be a different kind of baby goldfish. Maurice is very fond of Flo and would like to say to her, and all his human friends, that the things that matter most aren't to do with looks or image – even if his ornamental bridge and especially Fanny are rather appealing. No, they're to do with the simple things in life that we often take for granted – like sun rays on water, a friendly face nearby... and frozen peas.

MORE FROM SAMANTHA TONGE

We hope you enjoyed reading *Lost Luggage*. If you did, please leave a review.

If you'd like to gift a copy, this book is also available as an ebook, large print, hardback, digital audio download and audiobook CD.

Sign up to Samantha Tonge's mailing list for news, competitions and updates on future books.

https://bit.ly/SamanthaTongeNews

Explore more gorgeously uplifting stories from Samantha Tonge...

ABOUT THE AUTHOR

Samantha Tonge is the bestselling and award-winning author of multi-generational women's fiction. She lives in Manchester with her family.

Visit Samantha's Website: http://samanthatonge.co.uk/

 twitter.com/SamTongeWriter
facebook.com/SamanthaTongeAuthor
instagram.com/samanthatongeauthor

Boldwood

Boldwood Books is an award-winning fiction publishing company seeking out the best stories from around the world.

Find out more at www.boldwoodbooks.com

Join our reader community for brilliant books, competitions and offers!

Follow us
@BoldwoodBooks
@BookandTonic

Sign up to our weekly deals newsletter

https://bit.ly/BoldwoodBNewsletter

Printed in Great Britain
by Amazon

38246553R00170